NOW
YOU KNOW
IT ALL

DRUE HEINZ LITERATURE PRIZE

NOW
YOU KNOW
IT ALL

JOANNA
PEARSON

University of Pittsburgh Press

This book is a work of fiction. Names, characters, businesses, organizations, places, events, and incidents are either the product of the author's imagination or are used fictitiously. This work is not meant to, nor should it be interpreted to, portray any specific persons living or dead.

Published by the University of Pittsburgh Press, Pittsburgh, Pa., 15260
Copyright © 2021, Joanna Pearson
All rights reserved
Manufactured in the United States of America
Printed on acid-free paper
10 9 8 7 6 5 4 3 2 1

Cataloging-in-Publication data is availabel from the Library of Congress

ISBN 13: 978-0-8229-4699-1
ISBN 10: 0-8229-4699-8

Cover design: Henry Sene Yee

For my dad, Larry Pearson, the Gusto King,
and all the Gustovians (you know who you are!),
and, in loving memory of my Nana, Josephine "Jo" Lingerfelt Whisenant

Dear shadows, now you know it all,
All the folly of a fight
With a common wrong or right.
The innocent and the beautiful
Have no enemy but time;
Arise and bid me strike a match
And strike another till time catch.

—W. B. YEATS, "IN MEMORY OF EVA GORE
BOOTH AND CON MARKIEVICZ"

CONTENTS

NOW
YOU KNOW
IT ALL

ROME

THERE WERE RUINS AND FOUNTAINS AND A FURY OF
beeping horns. Naked putti lounging fatly in marble. Gorgeous, long-armed
women in skirts and strappy sandals, and young men leaning out of their cars
in mirrored sunglasses. Old men in storefronts arranged cheeses and sau-
sages tenderly, as if tucking in sleeping infants, while chattering tour groups
trailed guides holding red umbrellas, and honeymooners licked perfect gela-
tos. There were long, hushed halls filled with onlookers crowding around
famous paintings: Jesus flanked by apostles, emperors crowned with laurel,
mythical women in half-dress being chased by centaurs. There were church-
es in which frescoes glowed in dim magnificence above altars. Gold coffered
ceilings. Pietàs. Aqueducts. Domes.

In the catacombs, we followed a man with a bowtie and a stutter who
told us of the city, its slaves and rulers, while the bones around us listened in
untroubled silence. We'd seen so much beauty by then we'd been rendered
insensate to it, like gorging on sweets to the point of sickness, or until one

tastes nothing at all. Our eyes could not absorb one more basilica. We were tired and dust-covered, our shoulders sunburned. We were sick of each other and sick of washing our underwear in sinks. We were finally seeing all the things—beautiful, famous things we'd waited all our young lives to see—but we couldn't appreciate any of it any longer.

"Please don't talk to me," I said to Paul in the hostel's small kitchen while a troop of merry Australians cracked open beers nearby. Friendships formed quickly here, and yet somehow Paul and I had managed to remain alone. We were pinched and irritable-looking, clutching our respective *Lonely Planets* like shields. We must have resembled a couple even though we hated each other. Maybe this even made our coupledom appear more authentic.

"Believe me, I have no desire to," Paul said, slapping two thickly slathered pieces of bread together into a peanut butter sandwich, like he did every night, no matter where we were. Who ate peanut butter sandwiches in Europe?

The trip had seemed a good idea at first, but now even the sight of Paul—his socks, the sound of his breathing, the way he chewed—repulsed me. It was like a horrible stranger had assumed Paul's shape, donning his body like a cheap suit. Everything about him I'd once found pleasant or appealing had been twisted into cruel caricature.

And yet here we were, with a coveted semiprivate room in the middle of July, the height of tourist season. Travelers from all over the world crowded outside the gates of the hostel each evening, waiting to see if one of the dorm beds might open up. Every hostel in the city was full to capacity, and late-arriving backpackers found themselves having to pay for low-end hotels, or, more bravely, sleeping in parks with new friends made on nights out. We had reserved in advance, following a travel itinerary plotted by Paul, who preferred to leave nothing to chance. It was just the two of us, and one silent girl from Japan who rolled her nightshirt neatly, tucking it under her pillow in the morning. How could we give this up? Rome, of all places. City of Seven Hills. We were bound together, Paul and I, by our good luck, by our reticence with others.

Our first night there, while the other backpackers were still out exploring the nightlife, sharing wine at little outdoor tables in the piazzas, falling in love, Paul and I read silently in our room. Even the quiet Japanese girl did not return before the curfew. I listened to Paul whispering to himself before he went to sleep, and I knew he was reciting words to stave off disaster, a godless prayer. When I'd first met him, I'd found this ritual endearing. It had given him a certain pathos. Now, of course, it was but one of the many things about him I hated—almost as much as he made me hate myself.

So I went on a day trip without him.

That morning, while the rest of the hostel slept off their Chianti and Paul lay in the half-light with his mouth hanging open, I rose and dressed quietly. In the relative calm of the early hour, I made my way to the tour company's designated meetup spot. The tour company was family-owned and specialized in intimate walking tours, guided day trips with no more than eight other people. I'd chosen Tivoli almost at random. I'd seen photos on the brochure—grand fountains set against statuary of ancient gods, lush hillsides, Hadrian's Villa. My eyes would blur at yet more ruins, more beauty. But I wanted the rush of water falling, crumbling walls, a place where I might pretend to be a Roman emperor, a plebe, anyone but myself.

When I got to the location, I saw two middle-aged parents and their five blonde daughters, the girls arranged from tallest to smallest like a line of nesting dolls. They all wore the long blue skirts of pioneer women. Although her face looked ancient, the mother had the round, taut belly and loose-hipped gait of a woman in late pregnancy. Her skin was the deep golden bronze of an aging sun-worshipper; the rest of her family was fair.

The father stepped forward, formal, almost bowing as he spoke.

"We're the Gooleys," he said with a sweep of his hand to indicate his brood. He retreated to the spot beside his wife before I could offer my own greeting.

"Hullo," the oldest girl said then, moving out from the line of her sisters.

Her voice was warmer than her father's. She wore a braid that fell down her back to her waist, Laura Ingalls Wilder–style. "You're our eighth!"

She thrust her hand toward me, unnaturally self-possessed for a child her age. A preteen? An early teenager? It was hard to tell with her prairie-settler clothes.

"I'm Lindsay," I said, accepting her handshake.

She beamed at me like someone emerging from a cave, from hibernation.

"Welcome," said our tour guide, a bearded Irishman. "It'll be you and the Gooley family today. Not how these things typically go. But it'll be grand."

"I'm Martha," the oldest Gooley girl said, squeezing my hand as if I were her new best friend. "I'm so happy you're joining us." She introduced me to the rest of her sisters as we all piled into a van. Connor, our guide, turned from the driver's seat to smile at us, and Martha took the seat next to mine, leaning into me as if we'd known each other for ages.

We wended our way toward Tivoli while Connor told us little facts about Hadrian's Villa, the Villa d'Este, and the town of Tivoli, where we would have lunch. I studied passing Vespas, squinting out at the hills to which we were headed.

"Where do you live?" I whispered to Martha, and she bowed her head slightly.

"Japan," she said, answering with polite formality. "We're there on mission."

I nodded, careful to keep my face neutral. It hung there unspoken: an understanding she somehow confirmed with the steadiness of her gaze. I had intuited a fundamentalist religiosity about this family from the moment I'd sighted them. Now the only question was of which variety.

"Mother teaches us," Martha said, "She used to, when she felt well. But we also go on trips like this as part of our education."

She spoke to me in a way I'd come to recognize in the handful of home-schooled children I'd encountered: with a strange, otherworldly adultness, a lack of self-consciousness I found unsettling. Martha was fifteen, an age at which awkwardness was not just to be expected but mandatory in my experience.

I explained to Martha that I was in college, about to enter my final year at the big state school back home. A wonderful education, I told her when she asked. A funny little wistful look passed over her face. I found myself delivering a brochure-ready vision, which she absorbed with rapt attention: heavy textbooks and students gathered in glossy quads before bearded professors with elbow patches, football games and friends on the weekends. All this was pure fantasy. The whole reason I'd ended up in Italy with Paul in the first place was because of our shared sense of alienation. Both of us had fancied ourselves special eggs, the type that ought to have been coddled in boutique classes at a tiny liberal arts college with an expensive price tag. That hadn't happened; we'd ended up lonely at a gigantic university, consoling ourselves with our own perceived intellectualism—a shared sense of grievance that had proven an excellent homing device. We'd met in class, connecting over the fact that we felt awkward and overlooked, the kind of people who signed up willingly for honors seminars on restoration drama and then complained to each other when the professor seemed not to notice us.

"I bet you have a million friends," Martha said, her heart-shaped face wide open with sincerity. "You seem so nice." She sighed and clasped her hands like a schoolgirl, laying them in her lap.

I flushed and didn't respond.

A bump in the road jolted us. Two of Martha's sisters had begun to sing a round up front—it was a song I recognized from a church camp I'd attended as a young girl. So maybe Protestant, not Catholic? Then again, maybe everyone sang that song.

I wondered what Paul would think when he woke and found me gone. I must have sighed unconsciously.

"What's wrong?" Martha asked, leaning toward me, all pale blondeness like a Northern Renaissance angel.

"Nothing," I said. "I'm happy to be here."

"Me too," she said, pressing my hand again. Her touch was warm; my hands were cold no matter the season, but once again she didn't flinch. "Cold hands, warm heart," she added, giving me a little smile.

We parked in a large lot with several other vans and tour buses. Martha's sisters spilled out into the sunny morning, their braids and long skirts and white ankle socks catching the light with too much brightness. Their laughter was wholesome, like a stream of fresh milk from a pail.

Or seemingly wholesome. Wholesomeness was a slippery quality. The first time I'd met Paul, I told him I'd been struck by this very quality of his. He was unfashionable, almost prim with manners. He'd been offended when I remarked upon it. He told me he'd grown up on a small hog farm in eastern North Carolina.

"See?" I'd said. "Exactly."

"*Wholesome* isn't the word for it," Paul answered.

His parents' farm had been bought up by one of the big industrial farming operations when he was finishing high school. They'd been one of the last holdouts in their county. The air smelled like shit there, Paul told me. If you called that wholesome, then there you have it. In school, he'd been shy and lonely, made odd by his habits; he was unable to stop himself from counting ceiling tiles, touching light switches again and again. He'd hated school but preferred it to home—his father, the gummy-eyed piglets slick in their afterbirth, the stench of the full-grown hogs. He'd been scared of them, the way they grunted, their snouts and tails, the horrible human quality of their squeals.

I followed Martha and the line of Gooleys through the ruins of Hadrian's Villa. I was already thirsty and tired, eager to hurry through the sprawling complex. But I could feel Martha pausing behind me, taking the measure of the place. We came to a large, open area: the Serapeum. The water of the Canopus gleamed, reflecting back trees and sky. Martha exhaled, holding up one hand as if to snap a photo. I touched her elbow gently. She smiled at me. For a moment, it felt like we'd stumbled onto some other ruined world, the stripes of trees painted onto the still, dark water and the silent columns rising above. It really did snatch your breath—I almost said this to her, but I figured she, too, must be thinking it.

"The rot of decadence," Martha whispered.

"What?"

"Papa said he'd show us where it all started."

She drew one finger down the line of the column.

"The Romans were a culture of decadence," she said. "Immodesty. That's why their empire collapsed." She raised an eyebrow at me. Or just raised her eyebrow. And I felt conscious of my bare legs, my uncovered shoulders, multiple piercings in my ears—although in no way did I look avant-garde or rebellious. Then she locked eyes with me, and her gaze was serene and without judgment. I had the sense that she was parroting something she'd heard many times and didn't wholly believe, testing out the sound of it.

Ahead of us, Connor made polite conversation with Mr. and Mrs. Gooley. Mr. Gooley was broad-shouldered with the serious shuffle and stoop of a clergyman. He wore fat white tennis shoes that looked like they'd come straight from the box. His wife was squat as a saltshaker, her gray hair pulled into a stringy ponytail and her heavy belly a hindrance to which she seemed to subjugate herself unquestioningly, like a cow or a mare. I watched her listening, absorbed, grave. From a distance, her face looked like Martha's.

"They're so serious," I said finally, because I did not know what else to say. "Like Roman senators."

Martha laughed generously.

"My father would appreciate that he's given that impression."

We trailed her sisters and parents past statues and the remnants of friezes, making our way to the Maritime Theatre. Even when we weren't talking, Martha didn't leave my side, careful to match her pace to mine.

"Do you like having such a big family?" I asked her. My only brother still lived at home with my parents. He worked for the same towing company as my father. They had the same gestures, the same long nose and humorless mouth. It was almost like they were a single blank-faced person split in two, leaving my mother and me completely to ourselves whenever I was home.

Martha laughed again.

"Oh, my family's not all that big," she said. "My grandfather, on the other hand, had twenty-five brothers and sisters. And my father is one of eighteen."

"You're Catholic?" I asked her finally.

She shook her head.

"No," she answered. "But we're suckers for Catholic saints. My mom really likes them. She's into miracles. That's why we came to Italy."

"For the miracles?"

She nodded, looking even younger, more childlike, in that moment.

"We could use some. For my mother," she said, and then her voice dropped several decibels. "And for the baby. The baby needs a miracle."

I looked at her, awaiting further explanation, but she turned away. Her mother seemed so old—Biblically old, like the fact of any pregnancy for her at this point was in and of itself a miracle. No wonder there was something wrong with the baby. Martha appeared distracted now, gazing upward at a broken hunk of wall looming above us. By then we'd caught up with the rest of the family. One of Martha's younger sisters, who was sucking on a red lollipop, tugged at her arm with a sticky hand. We both turned to our tour guide, who was describing the architecture of the Maritime Theatre. The remaining columns seemed to huddle together above the murky water.

We formed our own semicircle, listening to Connor as he spoke. The air was hot and still. Clusters of other tourists moved around us. I thought of Paul, wandering the streets of Rome alone.

Paul and I had gotten along well at the beginning of our trip. Bright-eyed, fresh, we ticked off cities. First Paris, with its cafés and wide boulevards, the Parisians so elegant and dismissive; then Geneva, placid and pretty and a little dull; then Interlaken, blue-green picturesque and mountainous, the night air so clean and cool it made breathing seem like sucking a peppermint. We'd quickly assumed the attitudes of backpackers, joining that temporary, rootless world wherein tips are easily traded and breezy acquaintanceships made and forgotten. Paul took little notes in a notebook he carried. We both were there on travel grants, theoretically doing research.

Before we'd left the States, our friends had made little jokes about this being the culmination of our secret romance. But I knew otherwise. Paul had confessed to me his crush on Lulu Robinson, a gloomily poised poet who'd already published a chapbook and would graduate a semester ahead of us. I'd always hated Lulu, with her dark hair and big eyes, her raw talent, but I softened for Paul's sake, for the melancholy that crept into his voice when he spoke of her. I knew better than to mock him for the way he dissected their paltry exchanges. She might as well have lived on a different planet—perfect and untouched, not yet spoiled by humankind—for all her awareness of him. I confessed a similar crush on Rhett Williamson, just to even things out. Rhett had had the same on-and-off-again girlfriend since sophomore year. We were friends, of sorts, and Rhett did leave me tongue-tied and pitiful, but I knew it wasn't quite the same.

"You're better than that," I told Paul once when he described an encounter he'd had with Lulu at a party. "You just haven't figured it out yet."

He smiled wanly at me.

"Of course you'd say that," he said. "You're the only one who gets me."

This had pleased me so much, so painfully, that I'd had to leave him in the library abruptly, telling him I must be sick from something I'd eaten.

I understood the pleasing, problem-solving symmetry of Paul falling for me. I had, of course, considered it. I knew the shape of his mouth, the way his lips moved silently in class. I could read the tension in his jaw, could gauge, by his expression, when he was arguing with himself internally. No one else would notice, though, unless he told them. He'd had a lifetime of practice concealing his compulsions, starting back when his father used to smack his knuckles with a hanger anytime he caught Paul touching the furniture, or made him sit with his hands in hog shit whenever he washed them until they bled.

Things were fine until Milan. We'd missed the train we meant to catch and so had ended up on a slow train with no seats left. We stood there, gripping the poles and swaying, while the train swung along the track. It was dark when we finally reached the station, and we were tired, our legs wobbly.

Paul got an email from his father just after we arrived: his mother was in the hospital again. Her white count had dropped precipitously. I'd met Paul's mother once when she'd come to visit: a tiny woman, elven almost, shrunken down to the bone, with big brown eyes and shoulders like the handles of a child's scooter. She'd been in treatment for breast cancer on and off since Paul was fifteen. I knew all of Paul's stories of her; she loomed like a demigod in Paul's private mythology. A self-described Southern Baptist housewife, Paul's mother loved him, in her way. He loved his mother back, ferociously, inexplicably, despite her sharpness.

Paul blinked furiously when he told me. I looked away to let him collect himself. A crowd of adolescent Milanese boys passed us then, speaking loudly. One of them knocked against Paul's pack so hard he stumbled. He flushed, and I watched him tighten his hands into fists.

"Please," I said. "We just got to Italy. It's only a few more weeks."

We continued down a series of increasingly narrow streets looking for our hostel. By the time we found it, we were ravenous. A group from Sweden happened to be standing in the entryway, having predinner drinks and discussing where they could find a late dinner. They invited us to join them.

Maybe it was the shots the Swedes had offered us before we left, which we'd accepted despite our empty stomachs, but there was something loose now about Paul, jolly and volatile. Normally, he was slow to warm up in a crowd, but now he strode ahead of me, exchanging banter with the tallest of the group, a dimpled blond guy with a big laugh. It worried me. I thought of Paul's mother, back in her room at the community hospital in the eastern part of the state. They were considering moving her into hospice, Paul had said, but his father was very clear that his mother didn't want him to feel he needed to come home yet, didn't want him to cut his trip off early. "Once in a lifetime," his mother had said to Paul, squeezing his wrist before he'd left. She'd only ever gone as far as the Maryland state line.

"But I feel like I have to go home now, right?" Paul asked me. "No matter what he says."

I didn't answer him.

He seemed to interpret my thoughts correctly, though, and his mouth hardened.

Then he hurried to catch up with the two Swedes leading the way. Paul fizzed and crackled with energy, jabbering with our new acquaintances. It unsettled me to see him so lively.

As we entered the small, dark restaurant, I pulled Paul aside.

"It's okay if you're not up to this," I said. "We can find a slice of pizza somewhere low-key. They have that here, right?" I meant to make my voice light. I didn't want to mention his mother again. He shrugged, already seeming a little drunk, which wasn't impossible given the strength of the shots, his low tolerance, our hunger and fatigue.

"I could use a night out," he said, and I saw him do a counting gesture with his fingers. It was quick—a pressing of each finger onto his thumb.

"Okay," I told him. I touched his arm gently. He was my friend, truly, and so when I chose to touch him—rarely, platonically—it was meant as emphasis. *I'm here if you need me,* I tried to make my touch say.

He brushed me off, maneuvering to the bar and ordering his drink beside two of the Swedes. I sat down with one of the women, Karolina. The restaurant was dark and cramped, built to look like the inside of a cavern, and filled with the loud chatter not of Italians but of other backpackers like ourselves. Ordinarily, I would have hated such a place on principle, avoiding it at all costs in search of an "authentic" trattoria, but tonight there was an energy carrying us, and I was prepared to submit to it.

When Paul and Karolina's friend Erik brought back drinks, we all cheered. Eventually, there was pizza. We tore into it brutally, laughing and calling one another by new nicknames, citing inside jokes created only an hour beforehand. We had the air of old friends, friends who went back years. Paul outtalked everyone, and I watched the strange glitter in his eyes, the reckless way his hands swirled. There was a new edge to him.

I went with it, emulating the volume of his speech, the way his hands moved. I laughed louder. We ate and drank like animals, laughing with pizza sauce smeared on the sides of our mouths. When I felt Erik's body shift beside me, moving a bit closer, I let myself lean into him, his carnal warmth and smell of sweat. I found him loud and unfunny, a little bucktoothed, which was maybe unfair, but for tonight, I decided that wouldn't matter. I saw the way Paul was openly flirting with Karolina, something he would never have been able to do unless he was very drunk. He was funny, charming even—I could see this reflected back in the way Karolina beheld him.

By the time we walked out of the restaurant into the surprisingly cool night, it was like we were engaged in open competition. Karolina had slung her arms over Paul, pretending she was unable to walk. Maybe she couldn't quite walk—we'd had a lot of sour-tasting wine, stuff they surely only doled out to tourists. I let Erik hold my hand. It would all end quietly at the hostel, I figured. Paul and I had our own room, and the Swedes shared one of the large coed rooms lined with bunk beds.

"Wait here," Erik said when we got back. "Sit with me awhile and watch the stars." He gestured to the open courtyard in the center of the hostel, a small atrium with plastic chairs and potted plants, cigarette butts and empty wine bottles and abandoned novels.

I looked up. There were no stars, the sky choked with clouds and city light.

Ordinarily I would've said no. I looked to Paul, wanting some signal, perhaps, but his eyes were dark and inscrutable.

"Sure," I finally said. Erik flung himself onto one of the chairs, and I settled onto his lap.

Karolina made a clicking sound with her mouth, waiting, it appeared, for Paul to say something, to invite her up to his room. But when he said nothing, she made the clicking sound again, and then she and the rest of the group headed off to bed. Paul waited a beat longer, watching me. I saw him touch the pad of each finger to his thumb five times quickly. His mouth moved like he was going to tell me something, but instead, he walked away.

I kissed Erik for a while, letting him fumble at my bra until his motions slowed and his head lolled back like a flower too heavy for its stem. He began to snore softly, his breath smelling like cured meat. I said his name, but he didn't respond. I rose and padded off to find my room.

It was dark when I entered, well after 3:00 a.m. I closed the door quietly, careful not to wake Paul, but then I heard the creak of his bed. I could make out his shape, alone in the darkness.

"You're awake," I whispered. I no longer felt tipsy, only dehydrated and wired.

"Couldn't sleep," he said, and his voice sounded like it came from the bottom of a well. I thought of his tiny mother, feverish now, praying in her hospital room. She was hateful, too; I knew that. Whole lists of unfamiliar people and ways of being scared her, and so she hated them.

"Oh, Paul," I said, and I climbed into his narrow bed with him. He let me take his head and pull it against my chest. I felt sorry now—for my selfishness, for not correctly reading the evening. Paul moved his hands to my back. I could feel him breathing, the thud of his heart.

"Lindsay?"

I knew what he was asking, and I let him. He was nervous, as if engaged in an elaborate act of contrition. He whimpered at the end, then collapsed to my side. I felt the urge to brush his hair back from his forehead—it was a maternal gesture, which was maybe the wrong sort of expression in that moment. I felt a giddy sadness that I distrusted—it was too much like nostalgia. We pulled apart. It was dawn.

We slept late into the day. I woke sweating in a hot stripe of midday sun. I was parched, my mouth bitter. I had a terrible headache. I felt Paul's familiar-yet-unfamiliar body against mine. I decided I would not say a word. It would ruin what had happened.

But when Paul woke up, I saw the way he looked at me. His repulsion was so powerful I could have believed I'd transformed into one of the bristled sows on his father's farm.

"Oh, God," Paul said. I could see his mouth working in silent, anxious recitation. "Oh, God," he said in disgust, in anguish, in regret. "That shouldn't have happened. I'm sorry. Are you—should we?" He made a kind of raking gesture then that I somehow understood.

Relax, I told him. I'm on the pill. I had been for years, to help regulate my cycles.

Of course, I should have known Paul well enough to have predicted what might happen: he kept at it. He muttered to himself. He teared up. He worried aloud. While we wandered the Duomo, he calculated due dates, his brow furrowed. Of course, he said morosely, his parents would want him to marry me. As if there were a baby definitely happening. As if that baby were a monster. As if I were a monster who'd entrapped him. He paced like a prisoner. He did not let up in the days that followed.

"You'll tell me when your period comes?" he asked, not once, but many times, contagious in his misery. "You'll let me know?"

I scoffed.

"I can't go home now," he said, shaking his head like a scolded child. "Not now, not with this."

"There's nothing keeping you," I said, but it wounded me to say it.

"You don't know for sure."

"It's your mother you're worried about," I said, but it wounded me again, and deeper, the way he went on. "This is about her. Your mother. We're fine. The same. Like nothing ever happened."

I explained to him the unlikelihood, the almost-impossible odds. Eventually, when no logic would prevail, I gave up. I laughed bitterly in his face while he fretted. I called him an idiot in the lovely, uneven streets of Florence. Finally, on a train from Venice, I brought him into the swaying bathroom stall and showed him what he wanted: blood.

I was wicked about it. Disgusting, like a hog on his daddy's farm, wallowing in filth.

"Here," I said. "Touch it."

He blanched, but he did what I said.

"You know your mother's dying."

I said it plainly, watching his face contort. He already knew, but saying it out loud was cruelty. "She's dying, and there is no baby. Go home to her if you want. Just go home."

The train swung on a curve, and he fell back, catching himself against the foul little sink. I could see it in his eyes, the frantic way they flickered: fear, relief, fear. I shoved him out of the way so that he couldn't even wash the blood from his fingers.

And then we arrived in Rome.

To see the full majesty of Hadrian's Villa, of much of the grandeur of ancient Rome, we had to imagine it in its unruined state. The complex had been set up as a sort of retreat, an imperial enclave from which Hadrian could govern outside the city. By the time of the decline of the empire, the Villa fell into disuse, and people stole the most valuable statues. Marble was burned to extract lime to use for building material. The Villa, we learned, was eventually used as a warehouse during the Gothic Wars.

"It had to be trashed before anyone bothered to protect it," Martha observed.

"Isn't that always the way?"

Two of Martha's little sisters were chasing each other near one of the shallow pools.

"Stop!" Mr. Gooley yelled, his voice sharp enough that several other passing tourists paused to stare. He grabbed the arm of one of his daughters and yanked. The little girls went silent, chastened, but it was Martha's reaction that I noticed. She'd flinched. The angles of her face had hardened. I saw the way she'd stiffened all over.

"You okay?" I asked her.

She nodded, but her jaw didn't unclench.

As we followed Connor out of the Villa, Martha touched my arm to stop me. Mr. Gooley had an announcement for us. He cleared his throat and spoke. Instead of going for lunch as planned in our tour package, the Gooleys would be heading back to Rome early. Mrs. Gooley wasn't feeling well.

"We don't want to spoil your fun, though," Mr. Gooley added, knitting his shaggy brows. He and Mrs. Gooley both had mirthless, Old World faces, so it was improbable to think of them in any proximity to the word *fun*: laughing at a little table with a white tablecloth, passing bread and olive oil, drinking aperitivos. I couldn't even imagine it.

I shook my head.

"It's okay, really. I'm not so hungry. We can all head back together."

I dreaded the thought of the forced conversation with Connor if we had to ride in the van alone. A wild and inexplicable panic was also rising in me at the thought of Paul, whom I'd left without a clue to my whereabouts. But he hated me, I reminded myself. He would be fine.

"Please," I said. "It's okay." I smiled at both the Gooley parents in a way I imagined to be earnest and appealing. "Martha and I have had such a nice time. It'd be lovely to have the drive to chat more."

I smiled weakly at them, realizing the truth of my own words: I *did* like Martha. It felt simple and reassuring to talk to her. To take a brief reprieve from Rome, with its constant horns and sirens, the frenzy of traffic and majesty. I was not yet ready to take leave of Martha, but there was something else I felt—a sense of protectiveness. Mrs. Gooley rested one hand on the curve of her abdomen, where I could envision the baby floating peacefully. She had to be fifty at least, I thought, the good Mrs. Gooley. I wondered about the magnitude of the miracle this baby required.

I looked to Martha, thinking I might see gratitude in her face. I believed that I offered her something fresh, a vision of life outside the stultifying duty and discipline of life as a Gooley daughter.

Martha wouldn't look at me. She held a bit of her long skirt in one hand and twisted it. She bit her lip, glancing at her father.

Mr. Gooley shook his head.

"No," he said. "You're very kind, but we must be getting back. You've paid for the tour. You should get your money's worth. I've already hired another van."

I laughed a nervous laugh. The whites of Mrs. Gooley's eyes looked yellowish, her face almost gray in the strong sunlight.

"Please," I said. "I don't mind at all. It's okay, isn't it, Connor?"

Our tour guide lifted his hands in a helpless gesture.

"I'm sure Martha agrees. Don't you, Martha?"

I was uncertain why this direct appeal felt so important, why I was making myself such a fool.

"No," Martha said softly.

She still wouldn't meet my eyes. Mrs. Gooley knelt then, slow, like a hot-air balloon on its descent. She vomited quietly, and the dirt darkened and ran sour with bile.

I hurried over and knelt beside her. Everyone else seemed paralyzed, unsure what to do.

"Are you okay?"

"I'm fine."

"Let me help you up."

She touched the back of her hand to her mouth and then wiped her lips. Our backs were to the others, offering us some semblance of privacy. Mrs. Gooley stood up carefully, refusing the arm I offered her, then turned to face her husband and daughters again.

"I'm so sorry," I said to Mrs. Gooley. "About the baby."

Her face jerked up then, the cords in her neck tightening hideously. Her hair was dry and sparse, thinning at the center part. When she looked at me, her lips peeled back into a grimace.

"I know what it looks like," she said, shaking her head, still cradling the heft of her belly. "But there is no baby."

I turned to Connor now, trying to meet his eyes, to find someone who would witness and affirm my bewilderment.

The Gooley girls lined up like doleful ducklings, Martha included. I watched the way their expressions shuttered and went blank. They wore now, down to the tiniest girl, perfectly unperturbed masks of docile stoicism.

Mr. Gooley heaved out a great sigh, leaning down and offering his wife an arm. His knees clicked as he helped her to her feet, handing her a white handkerchief to dab at her mouth.

"Mrs. Gooley has liver cancer," he said to me, his voice flat. "It causes fluid in the abdomen."

He wheeled around with more grace than I expected from a large man, and the rest of the Gooleys followed him. I watched them go with a swishing of skirts, Martha at the end. She turned to me for a quick moment and her face briefly opened before closing again, completely. Her eyes flashed a warning to me, and I thought I understood then what she'd meant about a baby. A hideous prickling sensation ran down my spine. I almost called out for her to wait, to come with me, to run away from her poor, sour mother, great with tumor, and her father, the patriarch. But I couldn't have been sure. I feared being wrong. I watched Martha recede, and said nothing. The Gooleys filed neatly behind a line of parked vans and buses, then disappeared.

Connor and I got sandwiches and sodas from a little tourist stand on our way out of town instead of lingering. We both ate while he drove, and then I fell asleep. When he shook me awake, I thought I saw relief on his face. Perhaps I really was the unbearable one. I'd behaved awfully with Paul. I had to make amends.

It was late enough in the day that small clusters of weary backpackers were leaning against the walls near the reception desk inside, waiting to check in. One of them, a sunburnt boy with blond hair and a sprinkling of acne on his chin, nodded at me. I hurried past him, up the stairs and down the hallway, to our room. My hand was shaking as I worked the key into the door. I was breathless when I entered, ready to face Paul. To apologize.

His bed was neatly made, the sheets pulled tight and crisp under a shaft of afternoon sun. My pack slumped against the bed, next to the Japanese girl's. Paul's belongings were gone.

There was a torn bit of paper on my pillow with a hastily scrawled note: he had changed his flight.

I sank onto my bed, the golden yellow light of the Roman late afternoon washing over me. I closed my eyes.

What I'd shown Paul, in my cruelty, in my desperation to calm and absolve him, had really just been sleight of hand. I'd cut myself—the dumb, soft meat of my inner thigh. I'd transferred the blood.

The truth was that my little plastic clamshell of pills sat on my dresser back home, along with the floss I'd also meant to bring but had forgotten.

Rising, I opened the window and looked out onto the street below. A man was pushing his bicycle up the sidewalk and a group of girls in tank tops coaxed along a nervous little dog on its leash. Bells were ringing from a campanile in the distance. Martha and her family were somewhere in the city, maybe saying grace before a quiet supper. Elsewhere, across an ocean, lay Paul's mother in her hospital bed. Two pigeons landed on the windowsill, heads bobbing as if to better appraise me. Brushing them away, I stuck my own head out a bit farther. At the end of the block, a small crowd had gathered to watch a fire-eater. She tipped back and opened her mouth wide to extinguish the flame, making it look effortless—an everyday sort of miracle.

BOY IN THE BARN

WE ALWAYS KNEW THE BOY WAS THERE, SOMEWHERE ON
the other side of the woods that lay behind the house where we spent our
childhood summers. It was my grandmother's house, a low-slung red-and-
white ranch perched way back on a slope in Burke County that felt remote,
accessible only after driving a series of nauseating mountain curves, though
a mere twenty minutes from town. Our grandmother presided, hands big and
warm and busy, always splotched with soil or flour. She favored floral house-
dresses, worn soft with the years, smelling of sweat, and she was strangely
beautiful for a woman so old, a woman who refused to pluck the one long
whisker that corkscrewed from her chin. "To keep me humble," she said to
us when we dared to point it out. Now that curling whisker seems like either
a lapse or an affectation, but at the time, everything about my grandmother
seemed authoritative, intentional—the butter left on the windowsill, the
blackened sponge she used on everything, from dishes to the grout behind

the sink, the sickly sweet–smelling syrup she poured us whenever we had a tickle in our throat. Her actions held weight, were inarguable.

She and her daughter, our mother, did not speak to one another but had reached a kind of détente when it came to us girls. Those stays with my grandmother served a purpose. Our father, remote and cerebral, could not handle my sister and me for a whole summer. He had his research to attend to and required time uninterrupted by the voices of his children. Our mother needed to travel for her teaching engagements at summer conferences. Her *workshops*, my grandmother said with a sniff, as if the word itself were mockable. When she was not a disaster, our mother was brilliant, and she fluctuated like this, between accolades and opprobrium, throughout our childhood. To our grandmother, my mother's entire livelihood as a poet was silly and offensive, a hobby run amok. We learned early on the art of neutrality, poised between two such formidable powers.

My sister and I slept on foldout cots on the screened-in porch those summers at our grandmother's house. My grandmother referred to this as camping, and she had the old-fashioned habit of giving us each a hot-water bottle to take to bed because it was cool at night there, even in July. We ate butter beans and corn bread and stews flavored with the fatty bits of ham. Like farmers, we rose with the sun.

Our mother had told us that the man who owned the parcel of land behind my grandmother's place had a boy locked up in his barn. At night, the man let the boy out but kept him tied to a stake. The boy ate table scraps and drank rainwater from a bucket, pacing the yard on the radius of his tether like a dog. Our mother claimed she'd seen the boy when she was a child. Maybe the boy was the old man's son or nephew; maybe he was not even a blood relation. Whatever the case, our mother said, the boy was hardly human anymore. He'd turned wild, learning to communicate not through speech but by a series of low growls and high-pitched yelps.

Our grandmother scoffed when she heard this, then clapped her hands as if to dismiss this idea, yet another of our mother's falsehoods.

"Nonsense," our grandmother said. "But there are chiggers and copperheads back there. And Hugh Shuffler is one mean sonova, so y'all stay off his land, hear?"

My sister, overburdened with empathy as a child, soft as a crescent roll, started crying, convinced of the wild boy's existence.

"Stop your boohooing," my grandmother said, giving my sister a rap on the hand. "Children are starving. Cry over that if you need something to cry about."

My sister sniffled and quieted. But it didn't change the sounds we'd heard from my grandmother's sleeping porch at night: whistling snorts, weird subhuman hollering filtering through the foliage.

"Y'all want badness, there's plenty out there without your mother's fool stories," my grandmother said with a jerk of her chin. She crisscrossed and tied string across the doorframe every night when she put us to bed, pulling it taut and then placing a series of teacups filled with water on it so that we'd have difficulty opening the screen door without upsetting her arrangement. A redneck security system, she called it, for the nights she had her Bible studies. She wanted us to stay put while she was out. It was only years later, deep into our own adulthood, that we ever questioned these so-called evening Bible studies of our grandmother.

"She was a good-time girl," my sister said. "She had friends. Drinking buddies."

And I could see it, our grandmother coasting down the long gravel drive with her headlights off, waiting until she'd hit the main road before she'd turn them on and cruise into town, or more likely, out to one of the bleak roadside joints miles from anything else.

I could also see that wild boy in the barn, his skin raw with bites and scratches. The man in the house would finish up his supper and throw out scraps, greasy crusts and chicken bones, for the boy to scrabble over, hungry, his mouth dripping like an old sore. Our mother swore up and down she'd witnessed all this. We believed her.

"Your mother'd tell you the sky's green and y'all'd go running out to look," our grandmother said.

"Doesn't make it not true," my sister whispered the moment our grandmother was out of earshot. "I've seen the sky turn green sometimes."

My sister and I were meeting up in a spot I hadn't been to in years. She'd suggested one of the newer restaurants in town—charming little places with fairy lights strung over outdoor patios and food served on rustic blue earthenware. Fresh flowers in mason jars, locally sourced produce, lavender-infused cocktails. That sort of thing. People were venturing over from Charlotte, Winston-Salem, even Atlanta, tourists looking for off-the-beaten-path, small-town mountain charm. I'd insisted, however, that we go elsewhere, so we were meeting at a dim, sticky hole-in-the-wall called Brown's Village Pub, which offered french fries, chicken fingers, and beer. Brown's had been there since we were children, and it remained the haunt of shift workers, long-haul truckers, and grim-faced retirees. The lighting favored those with thinning hair and bad complexions. The music playing was always from at least three decades ago.

I watched the door for my sister to walk in.

I'd ordered a lite beer, served to me lukewarm in its bottle, as a kind of punishment. There were three old-timers there already when I'd arrived, and I could feel their gaze on me, scrutinizing rather than complimentary.

The door jingled and I looked up. My sister.

She tipped her head to the barkeep, the old-timers, and then to me, easing her way through the dim booths and small tables like a regular. My sister still wore her work clothes: a collared shirt and stiff, unflattering pants. We're both tall, but my sister is physically imposing, with broad shoulders and hips, the functional muscularity and heft of a landscaper. I have, unsurprisingly, the build and pallor of a medical coding specialist. My sister keeps her hair clipped short and goes to the same barbershop our Uncle Ronnie did. She's not one for makeup, my sister. Her appearance makes people read her a certain way.

"Well, they're not wrong, are they?" I've said to her. My sister lives with her companion, Jenny, in a little cottage on the east side of town. *Companion* is the word selected by our grandmother, and we've stuck with it. Jenny is kind, solemn, and still, like a little girl struck dumb by the sight of a full moon. She loves my sister. They are, unlike any of my own companions and I have ever proven to be, well suited for each other.

"Doesn't matter," my sister's always answered, prickly when it comes to the subject of her Jenny. "People ought not assume."

"Assuming makes an ass out of you and me."

One of our mother's favorite expressions. Now that our mother's ashes are spread over Linville Gorge, we say it for her.

"Rachel," my sister said to me, like it was a greeting.

"Marie," I answered.

"Where's your wedding ring?" she asked, scraping a chair up to the end of my booth. She eased herself down with a sigh.

I retracted my left hand, tucking it in at my side, naked and vulnerable, clammy as a fish. This was not our designated topic.

We were meeting to discuss my grandmother's estate. Our grandmother had finally died at age 103, having outlived her younger siblings as well as her own daughter. I knew we'd argue, my sister and I, over what to do with my grandmother's house and land. I wanted to sell it; my sister, keep it in the family.

"How's Caleb?" my sister asked when I failed to answer her first question.

"He was going to call, but I haven't heard from him."

I let my eyes fall on a young, slim-hipped man across the room. He wore cowboy boots and jeans that sagged a little on his skinny butt. He couldn't have been that much older than my son, Caleb, and when he turned to me and caught my gaze, I thought I read sadness in his face. But then again, I was reading sadness everywhere: in birdsong and tree light, harmless pop songs on the radio and the doleful way the grocery store checkout clerk handed me my receipt.

"We should head on up to the house," I said to my sister. "Start clearing stuff out tonight. I've only got tomorrow off."

The young man was walking over to our booth now, two sloshing glasses of beer in his hands. He clunked them onto our table without any gentleness, letting foam spill out.

"Ladies," he said, giving a nod to my sister and then looking me deep in the eyes, slow and meaningful. There was a sprinkling of acne that fell across his forehead, blondish scruff on his chin. He and Caleb might have overlapped in high school, even. *You've got the wrong idea*, I wanted to tell him, but my throat was burning, seeping heat upward to my cheeks.

"Thank you," I said, pushing both beers toward my sister. "I'm all set, but my girlfriend here is parched." I put one hand on my sister's shoulder a little possessively, grinning up at him. Anyone who looked at us for more than a second could see from our faces we share blood.

The boy looked at me and then my sister, his eyes running back and forth, making an apology of sorts. He hitched up his jeans and turned back to the bar with a little sniff.

My sister laughed a little and shook her head.

"You can't help yourself, can you," she said, like it's my fault this boy came over in the first place, like I'm sending out signals to boys and men, radiating a kind of broken-winged-bird helplessness that pulled them over like foxes. It's a vulgar, deeply ordinary heterosexuality she accuses me of, a feeble ploy, a beacon I cannot turn off. I've always coaxed that same boring trouble, old as sin.

"I didn't ask that kid to bother us."

"No," she said. "I mean, don't bring me into it. You have no right."

I flushed, turning to watch the boy in his cowboy boots instead. He was already across the room, and I wondered if he was the type to make a fuss. Brown's was okay, though. The modern age was moving stealthily into mountain towns, at least with the young people, and the older folks were mostly understanding, if you didn't put on a big show about it. Things were easier for my sister now than they'd been when we were growing up, or so she told me. Even here.

"Enjoy your free beer," I said.

She took a sip calmly. The skinny boy at the bar was gesticulating a little wildly, like he was telling a hilarious anecdote. I didn't want to look at him for fear of egging him on. One of the old-timers moved really slowly to the jukebox, turning on a Hank Williams song like he was on our side and wanted to muffle this young buck.

"You and your trouble," my sister said, rubbing a little divot near her jaw. I could tell from her voice, though, that she wasn't holding it against me. "That's where Caleb gets it from."

Sure, blame the mother, I thought, but that wasn't what I said.

"Caleb's doing fine," I said. "He's in a good place. Where they specialize." I waved my hand, thinking about the things they'd told my husband and me when we'd brought Caleb in. Tom and I were barely speaking at that point but had come together for his sake, for the sake of our boy. We'd signed the forms together in silence—a six-week stay, minimum, a mighty chunk of change, but there was financing, and better not to think of it now. We'd each shaken the hand of the bosomy social worker and let her lead our boy away. I hadn't looked at Caleb when we left him there. I hadn't cried.

My sister nodded, her eyes locked on mine like she was imbuing me with some special power while that skinny blond cowboy sidled up to some new guys who'd just walked up to the bar.

"I truly hope so," she said.

"Let's focus. The house."

"Listen," my sister said. "There's something I found in Mamaw's papers. You'll want to see."

We began sneaking out of my grandmother's house the summer I turned twelve. My sister, already fourteen by then, was a tender, soft-jawed girl who babied the chicks my grandmother raised and gave names to the toads we caught, who bawled for days when a kitten we adopted got run over. A late bloomer, my grandmother said of her, whereas I was advanced. Already I'd slipped down the hill to Enola Gardens, an enclave of motor homes and double-wides, a place our grandmother forbade our going. She referred to the children down there as ragamuffins. "Bless their wormy hearts," she said. And yet that motor court was where I'd found my first boyfriend, charismatic, rat-tailed Dylan. We'd sat together with our feet in the creek, kissing and trying to smoke his stepdad's cigarettes while my sister caught crawdads. She never said anything, but I could tell by her silence that she disapproved.

It was my idea to sneak out that first time.

"Wanna come?" I asked my sister.

She was lying on her back, staring at the ceiling. We'd listened for my grandmother coasting her Lincoln down the gravel drive that night, knowing she wouldn't be back for hours. Already, I'd practiced unrigging her security contraption several nights in a row. It wasn't too hard, requiring only a little patience, small fingers, and dexterity. Upon our return, we'd just rig it right back up as it was.

"You just want to make out with your new boyfriend," my sister said.

I climbed over to her bed and sat with my knees at her shoulders. I began to rub her head like our mother sometimes did when my sister came home from school crying.

"I want to find that wild boy. Let's see if he's still there."

My sister looked up at me, her eyes reflecting the light left burning by the back door.

"And rescue him?"

I thought of the wild boy, growling and wordless. It reminded me of a distant memory. A visitor. Someone our mother had brought to meet us when we were little. A big boy, oversize and off, with a problem of the brain that made us all very respectful, able to talk only in serious whispers.

"Sure," I said to my sister with her terrible nobility, her righteous sense of justice. "We'll bring him home to live with us."

She tilted her chin, satisfied by this response. I waited while she put on her boots, slow and deliberate, tying the laces carefully. When she was ready, I held the string on my grandmother's contraption for her to step over.

"You're barefoot," she said.

I shrugged and grabbed a pair of rubber flip-flops. I was at the age of small, pointless rebellions, little acts of defying weather and circumstance that only ended up hurting myself.

"I'm good," I said.

My sister made her gesture for "whatever" but clasped my hand.

We set off across my grandmother's property. In winter, you could see the little curl of smoke rising above the trees from where the old man's house sat. Once, we'd walked there with my grandmother to deliver a bottle of medicine when the old man had hurt his leg. "But you don't even like him," I'd said, and my grandmother had shushed me, grabbing my shoulder like she was trying to straighten my spine. "Neighbors help one another," my grandmother said. "Liking ain't got a thing to do with it." I remembered the old man's face peering out from the wedge revealed by his partially open door. We hadn't seen any sign of a wild boy or anyone else on the premises that day.

My sister and I clambered over rotting logs, pine straw, and broken branches. We slowed as we got closer, the thick night closing in around us. I took a breath, thinking of the stories our grandmother had told us about mountain lions snatching babies in their teeth, hapless hikers falling into Linville Falls, the time our late grandfather got bitten by a rattler and came back with his ankle swollen up the size of a melon.

It had cooled off. The moon hung like a pane of frosted glass in the sky. There was a baying in the distance, and my sister and I froze. Had she asked right then, I would have turned around. The black, rustling woods, the receding light from my grandmother's house, the animal howl we'd just heard—it was all making me lose my nerve.

But when my sister turned to me, I could tell something in her had shifted.

Hard lines of muscles had stiffened in her arms and shoulders. Her face was set. We would execute this thing I'd started.

"What? This was your idea," she whispered.

I nodded, and we continued. It was silent other than the chirring of crickets and the sounds we made: in-and-out of breath, slap of flip-flop, crunch of dead leaves underfoot. Ahead of us now I could see the glow of windows. We'd arrived at the edge of the old man's property.

We paused there, waiting. A jangle of laughter cut through to us, then the sound of several voices. The air held the sharp, familiar smell of fingernail polish remover. There were three trucks parked in the old man's drive, and the shapes of bodies, several large men, standing just to the side. The house was painted a dusky beige, peeling off in strips, and behind it sat a large gray barn. We watched someone enter and then exit the barn, wearing what looked like a surgical mask and booties. When the door of the barn swung open, then shut behind him, it released the smell of smoke and something worse: toxic and dark, the belch from a hellmouth. One of the men carried a flashlight, and the beam of it swung dangerously close to our faces. My sister and I ducked.

She held up one finger, ghostly white in the darkness, indicating a circle of men. They were holding bottles, drinking with their heads tipped back such that we could see the lines of their Adam's apples move in silhouette.

"Bad men."

She whispered it with certainty. I knew she was right. We should leave. One of the men made a punching gesture, half joking, it seemed, clipping another man on the side of his face, and the rest all laughed. The man who'd been hit stumbled, falling forward into a pool of light cast from the porch so that my sister and I could see him. He was moon-faced, fleshy, with hair so blond it was luminescent. He appeared simultaneously boyish and ancient, a primitive cave creature, his eyes bewildered beneath those white eyebrows.

"Get me back," one of the biggest men said, moving toward the boy-man and throwing an arm around him. "Go on and get me back now."

The boy-man made a funny face. He had the hollowed, hesitant look of someone always afraid. The men standing back watching them laughed again.

I felt my sister stiffen beside me. The air had turned sour now, like fear.

The man moved his arm around the boy-man from what looked like a hug to what looked like a choke hold.

A flashlight shone in our direction.

We turned and ran, tearing through the brush, our bare legs lashed by branches, thorns clawing at us.

We didn't speak until we were back at my grandmother's house, her contraption rerigged, the two of us lying in bed. I had the sense then that our mother had only gotten bits and pieces of the truth, that she'd made up one story to avoid telling another.

My sister reached for my hand and held it in hers.

"Well, I guess she wasn't lying," my sister said.

"There wasn't a boy tied to a stake."

She pulled her hand away from me and made a small, sad sound with her mouth, almost a whistle, the same sound she made when she found me to be a fool. She blew her bangs back from her forehead, letting her shoulders fall, like a runner who has just finished a long run.

"There was," she said. "You didn't see?"

The later it got, the more Brown's began to heat up, literally and figuratively. "The happy hour crowd," my sister observed, taking a sip of her beer. The way she said the word *happy* made me aware of its obvious irony. I'd always liked happy hours. But now I could see the word *happy* for all its overt bleakness, a thing we were willing to pretend at if it got us half-priced wings and two-for-one rail drinks, a way of drowning our sadness in noise and empty calories.

"Look," my sister said, and she shoved a folded piece of paper across the table. "It was in Mamaw's papers."

I unfolded it and read.

"A birth certificate," I said stupidly, looking again at the names, the date. A baby boy, born alive. Eight years before the birth of my sister. Born to my mother, no father listed.

My sister stared at me but said nothing.

A game of pool ended near us, the winners clapping and hooting in celebration—a group of guys, thickly muscled and cologned, in sleeveless T-shirts. *A crew of roughnecks*, my grandmother would have said. I looked over at one of them, one of the winners, and he took a sip of his drink and winked at me. Women were such a scarcity in Brown's that I really felt exotic, like a rare antelope on a plain, something to gawk at or maybe poach.

"I think I remember him," I said finally, and I thought again of that memory, which shifted in my mind, acquiring more color and form: a nice lady arriving in scrub pants holding the hand of a boy with a lopsided gaze, something funny in the shape of his face. "He won't be able to speak to you," our mother whispered, her eyes bright and urgent, pleading. "Please be nice." We'd eaten shortbread cookies from a little platter, the boy eating greedily but daintily, crumbs sifting from his mouth onto his lap in a steady, fine dust. There'd been such a sober feeling in the room that my sister and I had spoken meekly, as if in a church, repentant.

My sister nodded.

"It divided them," she said. "Mom and Mamaw. He needed twenty-four-seven medical care. Mom couldn't do that and live the life she wanted."

"You make it sound like a matter of convenience."

There was a twist to my sister's mouth, like she'd just tasted something bitter. She'd cared for my grandmother up through the end, dropping in every morning and every evening after work.

"I'm sure it wasn't a thing she did lightly," my sister said, her mouth still tight.

If we sold our grandmother's house now, I would have enough money to pay outright for Caleb's program. It was money that I needed. We'd spoken of selling the house before, back when it was all hypothetical, and my sister had disagreed, using phrases like *our history* and *ties to the land* and *what Mamaw would have wanted.*

I nodded slowly, sipping my drink, thinking of Caleb. There are parents who give up their lives for their child, who submit themselves unconditionally. What Caleb needed was structure, support, a place where he couldn't get his hands on pain pills and vodka. I'd often thought that my grandmother might have been able to handle Caleb. But there are limits for everyone. I love my son, although, like all love, it is knotted and strained.

"He died at twenty-two. No one told us."

I choked on my beer. I almost liked it now, drinking too quickly just to keep my mouth wet, to quiet the whir in my head. My sister did not say *our brother*, but I supplied the word myself, in my mind.

"Who sends off a child with problems to be taken care of by strangers?" I said. I meant it as a sad joke, a knowing deflection. Obviously, the situations were different. My sister missed my intent, though, taking my words at face value. She pressed my hand between hers, giving me a look of such tender pity I wanted to swat her away.

One of the roughnecks across the room was gesturing to his buddy while looking our way. I could feel the heat of their eyes. The skinny guy who'd brought us the beers earlier elbowed one of them and then made a dumb, crude motion with two fingers and his tongue.

"What's that guy's problem?" I said, and took a huge swallow of my beer so I wouldn't cry. "I'm gonna say something."

"I wouldn't," my sister said quietly, unfazed, looking almost bored. "Let's talk about the house." But she dropped my hand so I could stand. Since childhood, she's had this way of disappearing even while remaining physically present. Looking at her then, I could see she was already gone.

I started walking toward the skinny young guy and his dark-haired friend, a bit of a sway to my walk from drinking on an empty stomach. The dark-haired guy gave a little lift of his head, almost a nod, and his eyes sparked with challenge. Like he wanted to spar. It was a familiar tension, an energy that would have to burst. I cannot tell a lie: I've always loved that prelude, the buildup, the point when nothing has actually happened yet but you know it will. The guy gave me a wry smile, an appraising glance, as I approached. I could feel him crafting a witty remark for my benefit.

The skinny blond kid gave me a withering look that reminded me of Caleb. My son and I were onto each other. It was Caleb who set a fire in his bedroom the night after Tom moved out, causing thousands of dollars' worth of smoke damage to our house but, thankfully, no mortal wounds.

My sister and I returned to the old man's house, and more than once. Every night, there were visitors: men in dirty jeans and twill work shirts popping bottles of beer out back. They stood in loose clusters, their harsh laughter rising to us, snippets of their conversations floating to our ears. Always there was a hum of activity, a sense that some vague project was in progress, the men moving casually in a circuit from house to the barn to the porch and back again.

We looked for the boy-man with the white-blond hair we'd seen the first night, but we didn't see him. Maybe we'd been wrong, I suggested to my sister. Maybe the boy-man's eyes hadn't been filled with terror. Maybe everything we'd witnessed was a game, nothing but rough horseplay among friends.

That final night we went, though, we saw him again.

We'd grown bolder at this point, daring to move up just behind a tower of junk the old man kept at the edge of the woods. We crouched there, behind piles of particle board and broken glass, crushed beer cans and singed scraps of T-shirts. There was that same sharp, chemical odor to which we'd grown accustomed. The old man walked from the back of the house out to the barn, his arms full of boxes. His face was smudged, like he'd swiped newsprint or soot across one cheek. He disappeared into the barn, closing the door behind him. A current of energy hung in the air. Somewhere in the distance there was a faint rumble of thunder, and where we stood came little flashes of heat lightning.

A howl rose from the shadows at the other edge of the old man's land, and one of the men who stood leaning against the house let loose a laugh. The window above him glowed soft orange light, rendering his face hideous, leering, jack-o'-lantern-like.

"Look," my sister whispered, pointing.

In a flash of heat lightning, I saw a pale shape hunched against the far side of the barn, toward the back. It looked like a large white dog shivering. I squinted to see more clearly. It was the boy-man with the white hair. He was kneeling, quaking on his knees. He wore a collar attached to a long leather strap that I hadn't observed the first time we'd seen him. The strap ran from his neck down to where it was fastened onto a stake.

A big guy in overalls walked over to one of his buddies, obscuring our view, but I could tell by the way my sister clenched my hand, by the thrum of her pulse in her wrist, that she was poised to do something. *No*, I wanted to whisper, but she beckoned, and I followed.

We crept out from our hiding spot behind the old boards and broken toilet seat, the moldering stack of ancient waterlogged phonebooks, and moved around the periphery of the old man's yard, behind a rickety little shed, over to where the rear of the barn was bathed in darkness. I could see the boy-man better now, crouched on his haunches. He was shirtless, his torso emanating an almost lunar glow. He was weeping softly, forgotten, it seemed, by the other men moving purposefully around him. Up close, I could see the boy-man was older than we'd realized. His face was haggard but soft, like melting vanilla ice cream. He had the pinkish eyes of a rabbit. There were purple bruises splotching his arms.

The man looked up at us without surprise. I could feel my sister trembling beside me. Wordlessly, I went to the leather strap on its stake and undid it, although it was actually only loosely wrapped. It hadn't even been tied. The man could have freed himself with a brisk tug.

I looped the end of the leather strap and gave it to my sister, who walked toward the man. She presented it to him carefully, like it was a jewel or a crystal goblet.

"You're free now," I whispered to the man.

He flinched, pulling back from us as if struck. In another ripple of heat lightning, I could see that his eyes were all pupil, deep black pools. He opened his mouth: a few rotten teeth in a gummy expanse.

"Come on," I said, letting my hand fall lightly on his arm.

But he brushed me off and shuffled over to the stake, carefully reaffixing the end of his strap just as it had been before. When he finished, he let it trail behind him like a leash, lumbering back toward the spot where he'd been crouching. He managed to knock over a metal pail in his path, and it rolled out from the barn to where a trio of men stood.

"Hey," one of the men in overalls said, swinging a lantern in our direction.

The boy-man reared up to his full height and bellowed.

We froze there for a second, too startled to move. The beam of the lantern fell on our bare-torsoed boy-man like a spotlight, and he shrank like a creature dredged up from the depths, unaccustomed to light. The man in the overalls started moving toward us.

"Leave him," I said to my sister. "Run."

And we were running, tearing through the brush and branches, hearts beating into our skulls like mallets, stumbling through those woods, until we finally arrived at our grandmother's.

Not a week later, the place burned.

It was late, a moonless, overcast night. My sister and I heard the explosion from where we lay on the sleeping porch. We crept out barefoot to my grandmother's backyard. Even from a distance, we could see the blooming fire, its howling, hungry petals rising above the canopy. A radiant heat was spreading, and we watched smoke pour up through the trees. The air turned acrid, our eyes watering. Soon enough, we heard the elliptical peal of a siren approaching. There was the sound of shouts carried through the trees, then the thunderous crash of a roof falling in.

We stood there for a long time before we went back to bed.

Our grandmother was still out when the explosion happened, so we didn't talk with her until the next morning. The air still smelled of smoke, and she was out of sorts. She'd seen the fire, she told us, on her drive back. It was a terrible thing, our grandmother acknowledged. Neighbors were neighbors. She'd only ever wished that old man well, never mind what he got up to at night. She was extra harsh with us all day, critical of our every move. She yelled at me for leaving milk out and pinched my sister when my sister sassed her.

"Ow," my sister said. "That hurt." She rubbed the spot on her arm, a whiny little girl again, all her fierce bravery replaced by ordinary adolescence once more.

"You wanna talk pain, I'll show you real pain," my grandmother muttered, swiping hard at the countertops with her dishrag like she had a grievance with one or the other. "I ought to whip the tar out of both of you."

Our grandmother did take us to see the remnants of the man's place once before we left that summer. We took the long way, by road in her Lincoln. Stepping out of the car at the old man's property, we surveyed the aftermath: blackened earth, rubble, everything but the chimney razed to the ground.

Once I'd marched right up to the young blond guy and his friend, I stopped. They were standing by the jukebox, obstructing the hallway that led back to the kitchen and bathrooms, all the way to the bussing stations and the back door.

The blond guy really wasn't much older than Caleb. He smirked at me. The guy beside him, however, let his smile break slowly. None of us spoke for a moment. A current of electricity flickered between us, live and dangerous.

"You look like you like to party," the older guy said. The blond guy laughed, skittish, moving side to side like a crab. I studied his eyes then, wondering not for the first time what kind of high he was on.

"What's your problem," I said, nodding to where my sister still sat, like this might convey my meaning. I hardly looked like a partier. What I looked like was a mother: weary, burdened, brutally capable, with travel-size hand sanitizer and tissues in my purse, and, yes, maybe a few of my son's Adderall, but that was merely a stopgap solution for the postmodern age. Overall, I kept myself together. This was what I'd wanted to emphasize to my sister, to Tom. People dabbled. Sometimes people slipped up. This whole demolition of our life as we'd known it was not my fault.

"Ain't got no problem," the skinny blond guy said. "Different strokes and all. Live and let live." But he was almost snickering to himself as he said it, mocking me with that expression he wouldn't wipe off his young, smug face. It reminded me of Caleb's worst smartassery, the kind you can't call out because it's all tone.

"Hey, hey," the older guy said, and he moved closer to me, putting a hand cautiously to my side. I could smell him, and he smelled good, like spicy deodorant and Ivory soap and bourbon. His voice was soothing, a smooth talker used to getting his way. He had the face of someone who spent his days in the sun, handsome, with crinkling smile lines, but I could see where the collar of his shirt fell open, revealing a bit of his chest where his tan stopped. That sliver of skin untouched by sun was so pale it was intimate to behold.

"Just thought you might like to party. That's all," the man said, and he pulled something from his pocket. He kept his hand low, discreet, as he showed it to me.

There are times when all I want is a cold, clean feeling, like snorting ice water straight into my brain, the whole word sharpening and gaining clarity, my mind turned diamond. And there are times, of course, when all I want is to dissolve into a warm slurry of calm, melting until I'm nothing but a slow, peaceful feeling.

But I haven't, at least not often. That's the part that Tom and my sister misunderstand. My restraint. I thought of this as I let the man's hand fall to my hip. He held out what he was offering, an invitation. No one considers all the invitations I've declined.

"I don't live too far," he said, and there was all this merry mischief in his eyes. It was almost quaint, the warmth of his touch, the subtle way he was trying to guide me to the door like we were dance partners. The blond guy was jittering off to the side, muttering under his breath, no longer even a part of our transaction.

The thing that Caleb fell into was, of course, of a different order of magnitude. When he started failing classes, stealing from us, when I found him trembling, sobbing, wracked with the sweats in his bed—I knew there was a sorrow growing so deep I couldn't possibly reach it. Like my own mother, I recognized what was beyond my capacity.

"Here," the man said, dropping his offering into my cupped palm.

I might have followed him then. I might have forgotten all the paperwork, the business with my grandmother's house, the old, charred bones of the boy in the barn. Because we're all just going along in the best way we can, making whatever choice we can make in any given moment. But there was my sister all of a sudden appearing, a solid, steady presence behind me.

"Rachel," she said to me. "No."

And she took what I'd pressed up against my heart like a pledge and handed it back to the man with a little shake of her head.

"But I'm suffering," I whispered so that she alone could hear, making my voice as plaintive as possible so that she might grant me mercy. I thought of that night of the explosion, flames licking the sky, those gruff, shadowy men, and of our lost brother, licking shortbread dust from his lips, studying us, strangers. I thought of Caleb upstairs after he'd set fire to his room, how he'd wept then, confessing, showing me the small burn marks on his thighs, his hips, the tender parts of his arms—a thing he'd been doing for so long by then, his hurt made legible, a real thing he could point to and feel.

"We're all suffering," my sister said quietly, leading me away.

She walked me all the way outside, the clattering laughter of the men rising behind us, propelling us forward like a leveling force, until the door shut. It was cold outside. We stood there, clutching each other in the sudden quiet.

On the curb there sat an old, squat dog tied to a streetlamp by his owner. He gazed at us with human-seeming eyes but issued only a long, low, doglike sound.

THE WHALER'S WIFE

I STAYED WITH THE WHITWORTHS THE SUMMER I WAS nineteen. I'd gone to Cambridge to volunteer for a youth education program, and the Whitworths were the sort of people who supported this program by letting summer volunteers stay in their basement. The volunteer who had stayed with them the previous summer had been charming and effusive, a go-getter who had overcome a difficult childhood in New Orleans and was headed toward all sorts of success. I knew a lot about him because they spoke of him often, wistfully. I knew I was, and would continue to be, a disappointment by contrast: a white-bread suburban girl, hesitant in all manner of things, mousy and unthrilling.

My mother had flown with me to Boston before the program started because I was still, at that age, nervous about the wider world, and I had a similarly nervous and overattentive mother. She was both my comfort and my humiliation. We decided to make a small vacation of it: the Isabella Stewart Gardner House, the Freedom Trail, Harvard Yard. Before I was due to arrive at my homestay, we wandered through the leafy grandeur of the old Cambridge neighborhoods and located the Whitworths' house, scoping it out like spies. Their house was perfect: handsome yet understated, genteel even in its elements of disrepair. Where I was from in the South, houses were either boxy and unassuming, or overblown monsters of excess looming behind gated subdivision signs with names like Magnolia Club Crest. When I saw this house, I knew at once I would be staying with sophisticated people, people who'd arrived at something of which I had only the vaguest idea. I'd imagined Cambridge as a place filled with people who'd read all the books I hadn't, who watched *films* instead of movies, who engaged in witty repartee and moments of deep thoughtfulness. Intellectuals. Cambridge, I figured, was teeming with intellectuals.

My mother and I studied the house from behind a cluster of bushes. It was slate gray with canted bay windows. There was a modest green yard leading to a small front porch. A child's bicycle lay on its side in the yard, and there were a small pair of yellow rainboots on the front porch. It was late May, and sunlight fell through the trees, landing a splash of light against the side of the house perfectly, as in a painting.

My mother, who was wearing a fanny pack tucked beneath her shirt as a precaution against Boston robbers, suddenly appeared unbelievably embarrassing to me. I was struck by our lack of sophistication, two country mice gawking through the bushes.

"Come on," I said to her. "Please. I don't want them to see us."

"Oh, why not, sweetie? If we happen to meet them, that'll be nice. We'll just explain we were on a walk."

I pulled at her arm rudely, like a child. She looked frumpy, a big touristy goof with her benevolent face and the obvious hump of the fanny pack protruding like a second stomach under her shirt.

"I understand," she said softly. "You're nervous."

Her kindness shamed me.

I was sharp with her the entirety of the time she remained in Boston, prickly and malcontent, until the very day she left me at the Whitworths' house and flew back home. I refused to cry even though my eyes burned.

The Whitworths led me and my suitcase to their basement guest room, applauding my extraordinary generosity of spirit, doing good just like my predecessor from the previous summer. I'd already gleaned I was not like him, not at all. I knew they knew this, too, their words hollow, their voices disappointed from the moment they'd laid eyes on me: a plain old dud. I was not a triumph story—and yet I still thought that perhaps by sheer proximity, I might catch a glimpse of something transformative, erupting large and bright, a splash of light breaking the monotony of the sea.

The good I would be doing was teaching enrichment summer school to rising seventh and eighth graders. The other volunteers and I met in the empty cafeteria of a nearby middle school, where we went through teacher training sessions. We were all college students with little to no past experience teaching but excellent résumés.

A pretty girl from Brown named Prithi sat next to me.

"You've done this before?" she whispered.

I shook my head.

"Second time for me," she said. "I wanted an excuse to spend my summer in Boston again. My boyfriend's interning at a consulting firm."

I nodded as if this meant something to me—boyfriends and consulting firms.

A large woman wearing a silky red top with sleeves like wings was making expansive gestures and talking to us about lesson plans.

"Some of us are meeting up for a drink after training today," Prithi whispered again, tilting her head in the direction of the other volunteers. "Want to join, Gracie?"

I nodded again, as if this whole thing were very natural and ordinary to me—drinks and consulting firms and boyfriends, people throwing these terms around casually. I was one of the few volunteers who was from a public university, a university not in the Northeast. I knew a world of extremes—people who were either teetotaling evangelicals or rowdy frat boys singing drunkenly outside the football game—not this world of reserve and taste, all things held in balance. It seemed essential that I fit in.

When the training ended, Prithi wrote an address down for me on a scrap of paper and nodded in the direction of her housemates, other volunteers. I was jealous of them. I wished that I'd been placed with others my own age.

"Where are you staying?" she asked.

I told her, describing where the Whitworths lived.

"Oh!" she said, her eyes growing large. She stepped back, studying me as if I'd been selected for something. "It's you!"

I frowned.

"The Whitworths are a big deal. Every summer someone stays there. They throw the best parties. And their house is haunted."

"Haunted?" I repeated stupidly. If anyone was haunting the house, it was me. The truth was, I was daunted by the Whitworths—daunted into haunting. I was dazzled by them, so I slunk around the house, only venturing out of the basement when I knew they were gone.

"I'll tell you about it tonight," she said, turning to catch up with her housemates, leaving me to walk back to the Whitworths' haunted house alone.

Now that Prithi had mentioned it, I could acknowledge that the house did feel haunted in a way I'd been trying to ignore. I often sensed someone there in the basement with me. Whirling around, I'd expect to see someone. No one was ever there. I told myself it was nerves. Or simply one of the Whitworths slipping down to grab a spare bulb or battery. It was their basement, after all. The Whitworths were entitled to it. A stack of Disney VHS tapes stood in one corner near a large television. The children's old toys grinned at me from a hamper by the couch. Every now and then, I'd find the youngest

Whitworth child in the basement den, watching a movie, but that wasn't the same thing. I found the warble of her kids' movies reassuring. She wasn't the other presence I felt.

I've avoided describing the Whitworths directly because to face them head-on was to face too much darkness and brightness at once. They were their own sort of eclipse. Here they are, or were:

Margaux, the wife, was beautiful and austere, an ash blonde with a smoker's nervous energy and the lean body of a Pilates instructor. She was in the habit of scraping back her hair and pinning it up haphazardly. She wore mostly black with no jewelry other than a jangling array of bracelets up one arm. On summer Fridays, she liked to sit on their back steps with a glass of wine. She worked as a fundraiser for an arts organization. She was very beautiful, the sort of beauty I'd failed to imagine continuing for women into their forties, or once they became mothers, at least outside of movies.

Bronson, the husband, was handsome and graying, square-jawed like a statesman or news anchor. He was rarely around and worked in something related to finance or development, something lucrative. A former college lacrosse star. I was scared of him, tongue-tied, because he exuded something I wouldn't have been able to label at the time but know now was an unshakable sexual confidence. I call it sexual confidence, but it is also the confidence of wealth. Money, sex—same flavor of ice cream, although I'd only just begun to suspect this.

Ian and Ellis were the twin boys, in early high school. Even though I was five years older than they were, a bona fide adult, they intimidated me. At fourteen, they were so obviously attractive and well liked and confident that I recognized them as a different species from myself, and so I was relieved that they would be at lacrosse camp most of the summer. Early on, there were traces of them everywhere—dirty socks, lacrosse sticks propped against the back door—and then they were gone, off with other beautiful athletes at extended-stay summer sports camps. They were weird hybrid creatures, these golden-haired boy-men, their bodies straight out of Greek mythology.

The youngest was the baby, Adilah, who was two. She was a beautiful child, chubby and blue-eyed with honey-colored curls. Even Adilah, it seemed, knew she was superior to me, issuing commands while shaking her plump toddler fist. "We were traveling through Africa when I was pregnant," Margaux explained. "And we just knew we wanted to name her something that would connect her with the land." Margaux swept an arm across the room, gesturing to that distant continent with a look of wonder on her face. At the time, this struck me as a grand and beautiful sentiment.

They were the most picturesque family I'd ever seen, Bronson and Margaux laughing and beautiful, a married couple like none I'd seen before—nothing like my mother with her fanny pack, my good-natured father with his tired eyes, their long-standing companionship curled at their feet like a loyal, weary dog.

"You must have dinner with us from time to time!" Margaux had exclaimed when she'd first shown me around the house. "Demarque did that last summer, and the children loved talking to him. Demarque was just wonderful. We really bonded. We learned so much from him."

Already, this was at least the twentieth time she'd mentioned my famous predecessor, Demarque. She led me through a well-lit, airy kitchen into the living room.

"You're welcome to spend time in the living room, too," she said. "Or the library. Our home is your home." A doorway to one side of the living room led to a small room filled with books. A sweeping staircase led up to where she and the family lived. She did not, I observed, invite me up there.

The phone rang, and Margaux excused herself to get it, leaving me standing by a large leather couch. I ran my fingers over the edges of a cushion. There was a fireplace that looked unused and a side table with a cut glass lamp. The artwork on the walls looked ugly but important—an oil painting of a gray seascape, a framed print of New Bedford whaling ships. In one corner of the room sat an antique phonograph, above which hung two framed daguerreotypes of venerable, Puritanical-looking people—important ancestors, I presumed. The Whitworths would be a family with a distinct bloodline. I picked up a framed photo of the twins as toddlers, wearing little bow ties. Beside it, in a silver frame, was another photo, a family shot, taken when the twins were school-age. Margaux and Bronson looked the same. There was another girl in the photo as well, much older than Adilah, a teenager. She was smiling so widely that her eyes were crinkled closed.

I placed the frame back down quickly, guiltily, just as Margaux returned to the room.

"Sorry," she said. "One of the people helping me plan the benefit."

She said this as if I would know what she meant, so I nodded, mute.

"We're having some people over three Fridays from now," she said. "Interesting people. People involved in the arts scene. You know the actress and playwright Clara Devoe Jones?"

"Maybe," I said. "Her name sounds familiar." Her name did not sound familiar. I hated myself for my ignorance.

"She's wonderful," Margaux continued. "A real force. She's here doing research for the new one-woman show she's writing. You could bartend at the party we're throwing. Demarque bartended for us when we had gatherings last summer, and everyone just loved him."

I nodded again, helpless.

She smiled and clapped her hands, those silver bracelets clinking on her arm, celebratory.

"Wonderful," she said again, gazing out the window as if her attention had been caught by something—a sudden bird on the grass. "You're going to have such a wonderful summer." But here her voice had gone soft, regretful, like she'd been distracted by a thought too sad to mention. She continued to gaze out the window in such a way that I felt I was witnessing something private, and so I excused myself, retreating downstairs to the basement, where I had my suitcase, a pile of books, and a lonely little room to myself.

I got drunk that first night out with Prithi and the other volunteers. I didn't quite mean to—it was not the joyous drunkenness of youth, but rather a bleak and arduous mission. I wasn't a drinker, really, but when we'd gathered at an Irish bar near Kendall Square and Mo and Shiri and a couple of the other volunteers began ordering drinks, I accepted.

"Summer in Boston!" Mo shouted, ordering a round of shots. He had thick, dark eyebrows and enormous hands and shoulders. He was not handsome but impressively imposing. I wondered if I could develop a crush on him.

Prithi leaned in close to me, her breath sweet-rank from whiskey sours.

"You haven't heard the story of the Whitworths' house yet, have you?" she said, her voice delicious with mystery.

I shook my head, and she leaned in closer, grabbing my arm.

"Upstairs," she said. "There's a bedroom no one goes into. A teenaged cousin or a niece or something lived with them. And then she disappeared. People say she was murdered, but no body was ever found. The husband was suspected, but never charged."

"Mr. Whitworth?"

Prithi nodded, raising her eyebrows.

Another girl, Sara, who'd also volunteered the previous summer, jumped in.

"Mr. Whitworth is hot," she said, taking a sip of her cherry-red drink. "A sexy killer. Hotter than Cole." She gestured to one of the other volunteers, the designated summer heartthrob, surrounded by an entourage of admiring girls.

"He definitely did it," Prithi said again, her eyes gone large and insistent. "I heard there was an affair."

I studied her, my entire face feeling heavy, my eyeballs two fish swimming in the fishbowl of my head. So this was what liquor felt like, I thought. An easy discombobulation. Living with a murderer of teenaged girls—so what?

"That's messed up."

"Um, yeah, it is," Prithi said.

Sara nodded, opting to let the details slide.

"Demarque looked in the room once."

"And?"

"He said he couldn't even make it all the way in. Just started shaking in the doorway. Bad energy."

I laughed. The drinks had made everything hilarious, and also hysterical laughter was my go-to fear response. Sara's and Prithi's faces had a wavery, underwater quality.

"That's crazy," I said. My head felt large and heavy as a melon, and my tongue kept tripping over itself. "They loved Demarque so much," I added, sighing. "It's all they talk about. The Whitworths. They were crazy about him."

Prithi snorted, then burst out laughing.

"He couldn't stand them," she said. "The way they paraded him around. God. Demarque hated it." She shook her head, and I laughed again, because it was funny now, and so obvious: the Whitworths, Demarque.

Mo had come up behind me, one large hand pressing like a bear paw at my waist. I tilted back toward him like a marionette. Prithi raised an eyebrow, her lips curling into a smirk.

She looked pointedly at Mo. "Be good, children," she said.

"Always," he answered, pulling me closer to him.

It was late now, and the bar was crowded, people shouting to one another to be heard over the music. Smoking was still allowed in bars then, and the haze of cigarettes cast the whole place in a sulfurous yellow. The floors were sticky, and I moved through the underworld murk, that tight press of bodies. Mo pulled me to him, and I found myself wanting to be pulled.

We made our way to the hallway that led to the bathrooms, and Mo began kissing me. He pressed against me, all big paws and lapping tongue, like my parents' enormous golden retriever. He pulled at my clothes, and I found myself letting him until something nagged at me—an awareness that the night had gone on for too long and I was not myself. I pushed him off, rubbing my bruised mouth, and stumbled away.

Later, when I wandered back to the Whitworths', I noticed a single light on in an upstairs window. I saw a shape. A face. Someone looking out, pale and forlorn.

I hurried to the basement and thrust my key into the door, closing it hard behind me like a girl in a horror movie. Again, there was the feeling that someone had been there just before me, some scent lingering in the air that I couldn't quite make out.

I vomited, and this cleared my head of any mystery.

The summer volunteer work went forward. I taught my students, passed out granola bars, organized a field day.

I stayed away from Mo. His loud laugh and coarse sense of humor embarrassed me. I'd see him in the hallways and flee—his big ears and goofy grin a reminder of my stupidity.

I told myself I was in love with Cole, my fellow volunteer, with his slender good looks and soft golden-brown hair. He had tortoiseshell glasses and the gentle mannerisms of a folk singer. It was easy to be in love with Cole; everyone was in love with Cole.

In the evenings, I went to my basement room at the Whitworths', careful to avoid them. I began to check my little living space for signs of someone else's presence. There were clues left for me, it seemed. The toilet seat up instead of down, my book pushed from one side of the nightstand to the other, a full cup of water by my bed now emptied. Once, as I was falling asleep, I found a man's tie under my pillow.

I understood then it was Mr. Whitworth who came into the basement. It was his presence I'd noted. Watching me. The murderer.

I cannot say why this thrilled me, why the threat of sharing a house with a possible murderer did not quite seem real. It felt like a subtle sort of game, a game at which someone more sophisticated than I would excel. A grown man, dangling an enticement before me. A man capable of darkness. But not really, I reminded myself. Probably not.

I began undressing with my blinds open. My window faced the backyard, and anyone who happened to be out there, sneaking a cigarette or catching a breath of air, would be able to see me. I left the only pair of lacy panties I owned out on my dresser. I sprayed a tester of perfume into my room before I left in the mornings.

How silly and generic these gestures now seem. As if I were playing at some idea of a daring woman, a crudely drawn character on television. A fool.

On the evening of the party Mrs. Whitworth was hosting for Clara Devoe Jones, the playwright, I felt shy, my hands gone clammy.

"Here's where we keep the wineglasses," Mrs. Whitworth said, gesturing to a cabinet behind the bar. "And we'll have a cooler just for beer. Scotch, whiskey, and bourbon back here—don't worry about doing anything fancy, just ice or no ice. Easy!"

She smiled at me, a tight little smile. I was wearing a low-cut shirt and lipstick, and it occurred to me that I must look to her like a desperate little harlot. I turned away from her, my cheeks burning.

"I'll put the crackers out," I said.

I watched the partygoers that night. Well-dressed people, people of taste, everywhere. You could feel the weight of their collective intelligence in the room. Clara Devoe Jones was beautiful, with large white teeth and cropped hair and elaborate earrings. She was working on a series of historical monologues, the voices of women left at home, their husbands away at war or on long Arctic treks or lost across oceans. Women standing on balconies, watching the horizon, awaiting some word. People clustered around Clara Devoe Jones as if she were a prophet. I could hear her big laugh while the other guests tried to win her affections, courting her like clever suitors. Mrs. Whitworth led her by the arm, proud, the act of playing host granting her this privilege.

As the evening went on, the partygoers talked louder and louder. I could sense Mr. Whitworth on the periphery. I could not help myself but be ever aware of his specific location in any room.

Later, after everyone had left, I helped clean up. I was stacking plates in the sink when I heard laughter outside and walked to the back patio. Mrs. Whitworth sat perched on her husband's lap, holding a glass of wine. She draped his arm over her shoulder, nestling against him.

"A success," she said, raising her wineglass. She leaned down to kiss him. "Don't you think, Gracie? A real success."

She laughed, half sliding off her husband's lap, and I realized she was very drunk.

Mr. Whitworth caught my eye and then brushed a lock of hair from his wife's face with practiced gentleness.

"Come, dear," he said. "Let me put you to bed. Gracie will clean up the rest, won't you, Gracie?"

I nodded stupidly. It was too apparent now: I was their help. A charity case of sorts, the backward girl being introduced to high culture, but only from the sidelines. A cater waiter goggling at the ball. No wonder Demarque had hated the Whitworths, I thought.

I gathered smudged glasses and empty bottles, little napkins flecked with remnants of cheese, and dumped these all in the kitchen. There, I poured myself a large glass of leftover champagne and downed it in a single swig. It wasn't cold anymore, the bubbles going flat. I drank a second glass. Half of a third. My head chimed like a bell.

Closing my eyes, I wondered what my fellow volunteers were doing. Prithi had invited me to a party hosted by Ahmed and Cole at the apartment they shared. I was missing it, having agreed to serve drinks here with the Whitworths. I leaned over and pressed my forehead against the cool granite countertop, dizzy and tired.

Footsteps behind me, and it was Mr. Whitworth. Bronson. He smiled at me.

"Thank you, Gracie," he said. "She passed right out. Another sign the night was a success."

He had two glasses of whiskey in hand, and he handed me one.

"Join me for a nightcap?"

A *nightcap* was something old-fashioned couples drank in black and white. I knew this and was flattered, this dashing stranger so attentive, and to me, no less. Bronson. The *murderer*—it was a sensual word. There was someone giddy and reckless chattering in my brain whom I did not recognize. I took the glass, and he motioned to me, so I followed him. He led me out of the kitchen and to the quiet staircase, where he turned to wink at me, making a shushing gesture with his finger. I followed him up quietly, clutching the rickety banister. We made our way down, past the closed door where Margaux slept her champagne sleep, to the hallway's far end.

Mr. Whitworth turned the knob carefully and pushed a door gently open. I followed him inside.

He closed the door behind us and gestured for me to sit down on the edge of the bed. It was cool in the room and smelled of lemon cleaner. Already, I knew this was the room that Demarque had spoken of, but it was disappointingly plain. There were no obvious signs of struggle, no bloodstains, no stifled energy I could discern. The bed was neatly made, and there was a dresser, above which sat a beveled mirror. The dresser top was still scattered with perfumes and makeup cases, hair bands and a brush—the ephemera of a young woman. Otherwise, the room was bare.

I took a burning sip of my whiskey and saw that my hand was shaking. Mr. Whitworth smiled gently at me, like a surgeon who can sense his patient is nervous, but he did not speak. Setting his own glass down, he put both hands on my shoulders.

I pictured him unbuckling his belt with silent efficiency, shucking his pants to the floor, pressing against me hard as we both sank onto the bed, but these were all abstract thoughts, untinged with any emotion or desire. I watched myself as though from a dream.

"Mr. Whitworth," I whispered, my mouth gone dry and hot.

"Bronson," he corrected. "Call me Bronson."

And then he was tilting my face up toward him by my chin, studying me. Gently, he lifted my arms and pulled my T-shirt off over my head. I shivered, naked in my cotton bra before him. His eyes were on me, but I could not meet his gaze.

He turned to open a dresser drawer, rummaging until he found something. A shirt. It was nothing special—blue-and-white-striped with tiny red florets. A short-sleeved button-up. He handed it to me and nodded, helping as I put it on. The buttons were too small, and my hands shook. He leaned forward to help me, his mouth hovering just above my neck. I could hear him breathing, feel the warmth of it, and smell him, a mixture of cologne and liquor.

He paused, his face hovering mere inches from my own, and instinctively, I closed my eyes for just a second, expecting to feel the pressure of his mouth against mine, for us to collapse into one another, for him to arrange me however it suited him on the bed. But instead, he stepped back. He picked up a pair of earrings from the dresser—dangly and bronze, shaped like feathers. He gestured for me to turn my head, and he inserted an earring into each of my earlobes. His hands encircled my neck, and I inhaled sharply, but he was simply undoing the hair band on my ponytail, shaking my thick hair loose. He picked up a brush, brushing my hair until it crackled and frizzed. As he worked, I could see the nest of someone else's fine blonde hairs still embedded in the bristles.

Then he was touching my face, and his hands were big and dry and surprisingly deft. He swept eye shadow over my eyelids. Wordlessly, he indicated that I pout, and he carefully drew a bright lipstick over my lips. Long minutes passed. I had the feeling of being hypnotized by his touch waiting for the moment—*now? now? now?*—when we would proceed to whatever would happen next.

Finally, Bronson stepped back, clasping his hands together the way one might before a finished sculpture. He cocked his head to one side, appraising me, his creation.

I tried to half smile in a way I imagined might be alluring. Like I was being photographed. I posed for him, a stupid schoolgirl seeking approval. He bit his lip as he beheld me, a dampness gathering in the corner of his eyes. He frowned and turned.

I rose from the bed, extending my hand to touch him, hold him there longer, maybe offer some small comfort, but he flinched and drew away. Then he was gone, shutting the door softly behind him and leaving me by myself in that haunted room.

I could feel her now, the chilled ghost of this cousin or niece, whoever she was. Someone bold and laughing, I realized. Someone who knew how to wear makeup and smile at men. Someone who traveled places by herself and made friends easily. A girl at ease with risk and danger. A girl who smirked at her own thoughtlessness, letting moments slip by or seizing them like they were nothing.

My legs were shaking, a trembling that traveled right up into the pith of me, and my right foot had fallen asleep. I was rattled, scooped out and discarded. I stood before the mirror, alone.

A weird, sad little girl in smudged lipstick peered back at me. I did not recognize myself. He'd shaded my eyelids an unflattering green, and the earrings hung tackily, too big from my ears. My dull brown hair was alive with static. I tried smiling, but what swam back to me from that mirror was the image of a doleful clown.

I fled that bedroom then, only able to quiet my breathing when I reached the basement. My sheets were already turned down, the way they might be in a fancy hotel by the maid service. There was the faint imprint of lipstick on my water cup from the night before—a mark that I knew had not previously been there, a mark that I could swear was in the specific color Margaux always wore.

I did not see the Whitworths much during the remaining weeks I was there. They traveled: an impromptu trip to the Cape, I was informed via hastily scrawled note, so that Adilah could splash in the ocean. And then another trip to the Berkshires with friends. A last-minute jaunt to Paris. It was late August. There was a feeling that the town had emptied out, everyone enjoying the dregs of summer.

When the Whitworths were home, I avoided them less scrupulously. Whereas earlier in the summer, I'd been careful to move with stealth, never venturing from the basement when they were awake, I now made myself at home in their library, their living room, reading in my sock feet beneath the glowering faces of their ancestors, daring them to come home and find me so comfortable. I no longer lived on snack food in my room, sneaking up occasionally at night to their kitchen to spoon lumps of peanut butter into my mouth, cutting off careful slices of cheese that I told myself no one would notice, eating furtive bites of leftover pasta and cold green grapes in the glow of their refrigerator. Now I took things openly, mindless of the absences I left behind: whole frozen pizzas for myself, unopened packages of organic cookies, just-bought wedges of uncut Brie. I claimed these things. Luxury food. I cut out huge hunks of a gourmet pie for myself unevenly, leaving the sticky plate in the sink so they would know I'd been there. That I'd been hungry.

Rather than growing more refined, I was turning savage. A brash girl, stubborn and restless.

And on the very last night of the volunteer program, when all the volunteers gathered at what had become our favorite bar, it was no longer a surprise when I found myself sitting in a booth with Cole, pressing my mouth against his. Sweet, stunned Cole. Cole, of the soft, folk singer's voice and sandy-haired good looks. *Why not?* some newly freed part of me thought. Cole's hands were on me, maneuvering with a boyish fervor that made me sad now. I felt sorry for him, and powerful, poor Cole with all his boyish neediness.

Mo bumped against us and hissed at me.

"Slut," he whispered. He whispered it so quietly I thought I might have misheard. "Slut."

He hissed it again, like it was an incantation, or a pledge, and his eyes burned.

I pulled away from Cole and looked at Mo, hard.

Mo tilted his head to the door in a gesture I knew meant for me to follow him. I did so, saying nothing to Cole, his beautiful boy's face melting behind me.

Outside, I followed Mo as he wove behind several parked cars to an alleyway between two buildings. There was a trash can, the cooling scent of urine and rotting food.

"Slut," Mo whispered, and he was jamming me roughly against the brick wall, his hand grinding at my crotch painfully, his mouth hot, too hot against my face.

"Prove it," I whispered, wicked and free, because no one would have ever called me that before.

And then we were doing something like wrestling there against that wall, Mo grunting, shoving himself against me, and my head knocking too hard against brick so that I could feel the wetness of a small gash on my head, a trickle down the back of my neck, and I was pushing him back but also kissing him, hard, too hard, and it was like we hated each other but also wanted to eat each other alive. Then his tongue jammed so hard in my mouth, and his fingers were working swiftly on his zipper, and he was pressing up, up under my skirt, and I felt him urgent and bare. Dazed and electric, I was aware of a hot, ripping feeling, an inward ache, and then I bit him like a wild creature, his tongue bloody in my mouth. He yelped, jerking away. He spat.

Mo stood there for a second, pants unzipped, open to the air, exposed. The whole scene suddenly ridiculous, I laughed, a cackle really. He spat again. And then he moved toward me quickly, his fist landing a hard crack against my jaw. I gasped, doubling over, the pain in the side of my face radiating up and down.

He walked away from me, muttering, subdued.

I caught my breath there in the alley, pulling my clothes back intact, the whole stink and strangeness of the night settling around me. I stood, breathing in the sour air, gulping it like water. I was thirsty, my mouth tasting of cigarette ash and pennies. Finally, I gathered myself, walking back slowly under the long, silent face of the moon.

A single light shone upstairs in the Whitworths' house. I imagined I saw someone standing there. Certainly I must have. A lone figure—Bronson, I assumed. Or maybe Margaux after all. Waiting, watching like a nineteenth-century whaler's wife. I could see clearly then how unhappy they were, Bronson and Margaux, all the sharp little bones of their pretty marriage exposed, like a fish too fleshless to be eaten.

I turned once, twice, pirouetting under the glow of the streetlamp, then curtsied. I stood there, staring back up at that window. Then I waved farewell to whichever one of them might be watching me from that room upstairs.

THE LILY, THE ROSE, THE ROSE

It was deep July, and Cora's son was asking to go to the cemetery again. Her son, Martin, was five and a half and liked to say hello to the tiny lambs carved on top of the smallest gravestones, graves Cora understood to be those of children. They passed this cemetery every day on their walk, and Martin's insistence troubled her. Cora recognized her discomfort as superstition, but it still just seemed like bad luck to walk through the sunlit gravestones with one healthy, skipping child and a belly full of another.

Cora's fiancé, Tom, laughed and said she was just on edge because of her hormones. Maybe that was true. Tom, of course, let Martin wander through the cemetery on their walks and was untroubled, practical about it—the cemetery at least offered a little shade. Or *shades*, he joked, although Cora hadn't laughed.

Maybe Cora's response *was* just another ordinary aspect of her funny pregnancy brain, like when she picked up their take-out meal after work, then found herself weeping as she scraped the entirety of it into the trash.

There was nothing wrong with the food—it was the standard take-out order they always got. She couldn't explain herself to Tom, even after he'd rubbed her forehead patiently, then gone out for a replacement order. "Why?" he'd asked her afterward. "Help me understand." And still she didn't have the right words. Because she was a failure? she thought later. Because certain things she'd once loved and considered integral to her own sense of personhood had dwindled to the point of obsolescence? Whole weekends revolved around finishing a particular streaming television series. She'd abandoned her nascent career as a jewelry maker for consistent work in accounts receivable, and now she couldn't even summon a decent meal for her family without second-guessing. She'd turned, so gradually that it had taken her by surprise, into another woman entirely.

She didn't recall experiencing such emotions during her blissful pregnancy with Martin, which worried her, although Tom reassured her it was completely normal. As one of the few male teachers at the middle school, he worked with lots of women who all said the same thing about their pregnancies: they cried over everything. Cora considered this, wondering if perhaps it was exacerbated by the fact that she was also now Old.

She hadn't initially thought of herself as Old, even though on all her medical forms, there was the phrase *advanced maternal age*. She could accept that, compared to the pioneer days, certainly, when rugged women of nineteen squatted to deliver hearty babes with nothing but rags and boiling water and maybe a shot of whiskey, yes, well, she was a good bit older. It wasn't until she received one medical form, however, that listed *supervision of geriatric pregnancy* on her problem list that she felt a little taken aback.

She'd just turned forty, which was young enough these days. She was healthy, besides, and didn't look that bad overall—but, as if the phrase itself had acted as a curse upon her, she now felt weary, creaky, her hips grinding in their sockets like mortar against pestle, the weight of the baby causing her pelvic floor to sag like an old mattress. The pregnancy itself seemed to be aging her. There was not enough space in her elderly abdomen now, either, such that she could no longer govern the workings of her own body, all of its small, embarrassing sounds and emissions. Burps, farts, urine, weird, throaty gurgles—these escaped her in a way reminiscent of her Granny Elaine, who'd motored down the retirement home hallways in her final days to the cheery, oblivious burble of her own flatulence. "She can't help it," Cora's mother had explained to Cora and her siblings, hushing them when they'd giggled. And now, of course, Cora understood. Simply heaving herself upward from a seated position could unleash a host of embarrassing noises or fluid.

Today it was blazing hot, too hot to be on a walk, but Cora was off work and Martin's preschool was closed, and they'd both been stir-crazy. Now she trudged up the sidewalk with the slow, grinding pace of a continent adrift while Martin bounded ahead.

"Wait for Momma," she called, and he would, running several feet ahead and then turning to beam at her. He was a gift, her beautiful boy, with his sturdy limbs and little sticky hands and grubby face. He did a small, wiggling dance for her appreciation, and she laughed.

"I'm going to say hello to the lambs," he called to her, and before she could catch up with him, he was in the cemetery.

Cora sighed, pausing for a moment to clutch her abdomen where it tightened suddenly. Braxton-Hicks. The tightness subsided, and she caught her breath. The light in the cemetery was greeny gold. Though this plot of land was small and unbeautiful, laid out behind an office building and railroad tracks, there was still something quiet to it. She thought of the large cemeteries built as memorial parks, meant to attract picnickers to lush hillsides filled with birdsong and gentle remembrance. By comparison, this cemetery was a cramped afterthought, a moment of hesitation in the midst of regular garbage pickup schedules and dailiness. But there was something peaceful even here. She'd been silly to balk at Martin's wanting to visit. The trees overhead offering their meager shade did make this area something of a reprieve.

Martin had disappeared down a little slope, and she ambled through the flickering shade to find him. She almost ran right into the girl.

"I'm sorry," Cora said, reflexively extending a hand over her belly. Martin was not in her sight line, but she could hear his childlike warble from behind the adjacent gravestones.

The girl frowned, studying her. She was a teenager, Cora thought at first. But closer up, Cora could see the girl was older, maybe twenty-five or so, but on the skinny side and baby-faced, her lank hair dyed a harsh black betrayed by her pale blonde eyebrows, which gave her face a blank look.

"Oh," the girl said. She backed away from Cora, her hand against her heart like a heroine in an old movie.

"Sorry," Cora said again. "I didn't expect anyone here. It's so hot." She added this by way of explanation, as if otherwise she might expect numerous people to convene in this small cemetery, as if this girl were surely a regular.

"Hey," Cora said. "That's *my* necklace."

She pointed now to the long silver chain the girl was wearing with a hunk of polished beryl on the end that spun on a little silver wheel, the wheel mechanism made to look like tiny human femurs. Cora had known only one necklace like this to exist. Her own. She had a sudden faintish feeling, like she was looking now into a distorted mirror, seeing a mistranslated version of herself.

"I had a necklace just like that."

The girl had backed several feet away now and appeared to be bracing herself against a tree. There was a sweet odor to her—pot mixed with patchouli. In the small town where Cora had grown up, teenagers had gathered at night to smoke pot in the local cemetery. Cora had been too shy, too burdened by rule-abidingness back then, to join them. "Ghosts and goths," people always said. "Nothing but ghosts and goths."

"It's you," the girl whispered.

There was, it seemed to Cora, a stark terror on her face.

"I'm sorry," the girl said, backing away further.

Cora was fighting a queasy feeling now, this girl herself like a figment of her imagination, an apparition. She wanted to ask the girl something but couldn't formulate any questions. And then the girl had turned and was fleeing through the back of the cemetery, disappearing into a copse of trees draped with kudzu where the air hummed in the summer heat. She was gone.

Clouds passed over the sun then, leaving all shadow for just a moment, and Cora realized she could no longer hear Martin. A surge of electricity ran through her, and she called to him, shambling as quickly down the slope as she could.

"Martin? Baby?"

He didn't answer, and her heart seized in her chest.

But she found him, his little blond head bent seriously. He was sitting beside a tiny gravestone carved with the image of a rose. She knelt heavily and put her arms around him.

"There you are!"

She was breathing hard, inhaling his scent of baby sweat and dirt.

"Look, Momma," he said, turning to look up at her and displaying a little braided plastic lanyard. "Look at what the lady gave me."

Cora had once owned a necklace like the one the girl was wearing, but she had lost it. Rather, it had been taken from her and never returned.

She had once been a woman of many necklaces—dramatic, architectural statement pieces, one-of-a-kind works made by either Cora or her friends. She'd gone to art school and had achieved early, modest success as a jeweler and metalsmith. She'd loved her array of tools, anvils and pliers and torches, loved soldering, loved the precision and delicacy required. She'd worked in precious metals mostly, coaxing her raw material into strange shapes. She'd exhibited her work in several shows. It had been too strange and impractical ever to be worn, but it was admired always, gushed over. *Whimsical*, people said, or *intriguing, delightful*.

That, Cora thought, was the crux of her old worldview, although she wouldn't have been able to describe it as such at the time: delight superseding practicality. Visual cleverness at the expense of all else. Now, however, she rarely wore any jewelry, not even the most basic hoop earrings or studs. She'd learned this lesson when Martin was still a baby, his little grabby fists going after everything. Motherhood was a lesson in dangers.

The necklace she'd lost had been stored in patient belongings at the hospital. At discharge, they'd handed her a T-shirt and sweatpants that were not hers, but she'd been too relieved to bother saying anything, pulling on the ill-fitting pants gratefully. Only later did she remember and regret her necklace.

It was a strange necklace. She had worn it all the time, a gift that her first husband, Martin's father, also an artist, had picked out for her from a little craft shop they'd visited. A local jeweler with a preoccupation for incorporating anatomical elements into his work, *memento mori*, the owner of the shop had explained to them. They'd been in the mountains, on a babymoon of sorts, before Martin had been born. She'd been in her midthirties then, of course, but looking back on herself, laughing and long-haired with her careless collection of wearable art, she thought of this as the very last stretch of her girlhood.

She'd worn the necklace continually during the months leading up to Martin's birth. She'd been wearing it when her water broke three weeks early and her husband—such a gentle man, despite it all, despite his stormy silences, his quick temper, what he called his sculptor's temperament, and maybe as two artists, they'd been doomed from the start—had rushed with her to the hospital, where they had abandoned a pile of damp towels in the parking deck and maneuvered her to the labor and delivery floor.

All that followed was a blur to Cora. There was something pleasantly soft-focused about it now, none of the pain or terror having stuck in her brain. She'd retained only a vague memory that ended with the raw, soft bundle that was Martin being placed into her arms. She'd been bewildered, weeping at that point, the first indication of what would soon establish itself as a semi-perpetual state. Was she weeping because she was happy? Was she weeping because she was sad? The weeping became a thing in and of itself, setting in and remaining, like a stubborn stormfront over an expedition.

When Cora and her husband had returned home with baby Martin, what followed remained a teary haze, a distant country Cora had once visited and to which she wished never to return. There was no sleep to be had. Something had rewired itself in Cora's brain such that, as ragged tired as she was, every time she tried to lie down, her brain jolted. All the noises of the house seemed louder, to the point that Cora had begged her then-husband to turn off the heater, to unplug all the lights and phones, even though it was mid-January. And then there were the images that popped into Cora's mind unbidden: a pair of scissors jammed up to the handles into the soft spot of Martin's skull; Martin, facedown in the baby bathtub, his cheeks gray; the two of them tumbling down the staircase, Martin's soft-potato body thudding against each step. She asked her husband to hide all the knives. She begged him to store all her metalsmithing tools somewhere safe behind lock and key. She never wanted to see a pair of pliers again. Something in her brain was misfiring— every ordinary implement imbued now with dark significance, every image gruesome with possibility.

She began wearing headphones to drown out the insidious whispers of her house, all that muttering plumbing and refrigerator white noise. She cleaned all hours of the day, whenever she wasn't nursing or tending to Martin, a way of diverting her hands, channeling the thrumming forces inside her. The images in her mind grew like a kind of threat, some other version of herself taunting her, and she started to distrust herself. She dared not hold Martin. She could hardly touch him. The idea that her own milk was poisonous occurred to her—at first it seemed ridiculous, but later so unshakably true that she stopped nursing Martin, growing so engorged that her breasts radiated a toxic heat, which only seemed to confirm her fears. She considered the fact then that bringing a child into the world was the most ludicrous decision anyone could make—all that worry and effort with everyone and everything turning to dust anyway, all of it simply an inevitable slide toward decay—and the hilarious illogic of it provided such relief that she almost laughed.

At some point in the midst of these storm-sodden days, days in which Cora felt herself whittled down to bone and ache, her then-husband took her back to the hospital. She'd still been wearing her necklace. The first thing the nurses did—they were so kind, those nurses, with their soft voices and full but shapeless maternal bosoms—was cajole her out of it and urge her to the shower, where she'd finally washed her sour hair with thin hospital shampoo. The necklace, along with her cell phone and charger, an ink pen that might have been weaponized, and a razor she'd thought to pack in case she ever got around to shaving her legs, was taken away, stored with other patient belongings until the day she would be discharged. She'd felt the necklace's absence at first, the lack of its reassuring weight around her neck, wandering in a blue patterned hospital gown and hospital-issued undergarments.

But she was cooperative. The nurses spoke kindly, and the doctors maintained a quiet hush. She swallowed cups of water and a chalky pill, went to groups with others who wore the stunned faces of passengers stranded at a foreign airport. And something worked. Days passed, then weeks, and Cora began to reemerge into something that resembled her old self. Martin did fine without her—both a personal slight to her own sense of centrality as mother, and a blessing. Her husband was sure-handed throughout the ordeal, indispensable.

Even now, Cora thought of this episode with a kind of shame. It wasn't her fault, they all said, but she could not shake the notion that it was. Her trick brain revealing its worst shenanigans. Though her husband never once cited this incident as a factor leading toward their eventual divorce, Cora knew it must have been one. To see what another person could turn into—raving and lupine, another creature entirely under the right moon—that would be enough. Who could say she wouldn't have felt the same way?

And now, here was a stranger with a haunted face wearing her necklace, the very necklace that marked this intersection when she stepped from one life into another. The very necklace that had, like her old life, disappeared.

That evening, as Tom prepared dinner, the scent of onions and spices rose from the kitchen. She could eat everything again, no longer turned off by strong flavors or smells, and did so. Her friends told her she was lucky to have found someone who could cook. She figured, in her darker moments, that she was lucky to have found anyone at all, being a divorced mother of a certain age with an aptitude for the delusional.

"You two ready?" Tom called.

Martin was lying on his stomach watching a cartoon, an indulgence she justified this far along in her pregnancy.

"Yeah!" Martin shouted, jumping up. He ran to Tom and leapt into his arms. He loved Tom. That was a lucky thing, too. Tom was a natural father. It was why she'd felt so guilty when she'd had her doubts about having a child with him. She had told Martin's father, before their divorce, that she would never put herself through it again, and Martin's father had understood her.

"But lightning doesn't strike twice," Tom had said during one of their whispered conversations after Martin had gone to bed. He was unfailingly optimistic about things. She refused to think of him as naïve, wanting a share of such optimism.

"This type of lightning does," she'd responded, both frustrated and grateful that he'd had no firsthand experience of those postpartum months. He'd known her only as a competent, useful woman, a divorced mother working in accounts receivable, a person of expeditious habits and well-thought-out preparedness. None of that old, luxurious whimsy. "I'm predisposed, apparently. We could always adopt."

He'd sighed and nodded. "If that's what you want to do . . . but there's the cost. We'd have to save." And she'd kissed him, sighing, knowing she would relent, because how could she hold this thing back from him, this man who was so kind to her and to Martin, especially when it was what a part of her wanted, too? And look at her now—she'd responded so well to medicine that she'd eventually tapered off. Her therapist had finally recommended she touch base on an as-needed basis only.

Thinking it might take a while given her age, they'd ultimately started trying well before their wedding was scheduled. Now, of course, the wedding had been pushed back. She was late in her third trimester; the baby could come any day now.

Tom passed around bowls of salad and a stir-fry he'd made.

"Look what I got!" Martin said.

He extended an arm, showing the lanyard to Tom.

"Nice, my man," Tom said. "Who made that for you?"

"The lady," Martin said. "The lady we saw gave it to me."

A crawling heat made its way up Cora's neck. She had the old feeling that something was happening in which she played a crucial role but to which she'd been offered no explanation.

"That's great, little man," Tom said. He was so innocent, oblivious.

Martin rubbed the lanyard between his thumb and forefinger appreciatively.

Something fluttered in Cora's throat, and she knew if she spoke she would stammer, an old and crippling tell.

She looked up at Tom, who simply shrugged.

"Let's eat."

She could tell from his voice, the careful way he maintained a certain cheer, that he was confused, and that he'd registered the stricken look on her face. But he was off to the kitchen then, bringing in a platter of corn muffins.

"Who can eat like this when it's hot?" Cora said, her appetite suddenly diminished. It was less a complaint than a way of saying something, filling the quiet, although she knew it made her sound peevish. The baby was moving inside her, the hard parts of him pressing against her in a squeamish way, like something trapped trying to get out.

"I can!" Martin announced, biting a corn muffin. "Maybe the lady will bring me something else the next time I see her, Momma!" He smiled at her.

"Oh, I doubt you'll see her again," Cora said. "She was just a nice stranger." He shook his head.

"No, she's not," he said. "I've seen her there before. She always says hi to me."

After Martin was in bed that evening, she stalked their house, holding the burden of her belly with one arm so she could walk faster. She could imagine her baby, sloshing gently inside her, but she was so agitated, she flicked the thought away.

"Something's wrong," she said to Tom.

He was sitting on the couch watching her, holding his head in both arms. She'd already explained to him the necklace, how it had been lost, the unlikeliness of its return, the strangeness of seeing someone appear, wearing it. She considered whether she might be the victim of some dark prank.

"It's a coincidence," Tom said quietly, his attempt at being reassuring. "There must have been other necklaces made. Someone had one just like yours."

Cora shook her head. She knew now, with a certainty that was absolute, that it was her necklace. There was only one. The artist had made each as a one-of-a-kind piece. It was her necklace, washing back to her like a message in a bottle.

Tom shrugged.

"I once ran into someone in the airport wearing my old soccer shirt. My last name on the back and everything. He got it from a thrift store. That was pretty weird. I've heard of lost engagement rings getting returned to their owners decades later."

"This is different," she said. "There's some creep wandering the graveyard wearing my necklace. Talking to my son. Giving him things. It's not right."

She paused, leaning against the wall to let a contraction pass.

"I want it back."

She sank to the couch next to him. Tom closed his eyes, sighing.

"I knew this was a bad idea," she added, and he held her while she cried, the new baby fidgeting inside her, ready soon for the rupture of membranes, his passage through her, all the rest that would follow.

During her time in the hospital, Cora hadn't made any friends. She'd existed as a somnambulist, blank-faced and stunned. She watched as the other women buddied up. Macey and Denise always sat together, sharing cups of tea between groups, waiting together by the bank of phones for their turn to call home. The teenagers, Rooney and Sheree, had buddied up as well, the two of them so skinny it seemed impossible either had had a baby recently. A solemn woman around her age named Margaret tried to befriend Cora. Margaret was some kind of high-powered attorney, twenty-seven weeks pregnant still— they were all on a unit that specialized in treating peripartum women—but for some reason, Margaret's visible pregnancy was too distressing for Cora to bear. She avoided Margaret most of all, staying to herself, thumbing through torn magazines or pacing the circle of the unit for exercise. In the lactation/meditation room, she pumped to the same concerto playing over and over through a set of tinny speakers.

Her memory of this time ran together and was filled with lapses. She recalled it the way a blackout drinker might recall a party. She'd still been making jewelry then, or had been prior to Martin's birth, and her hands itched with an awful impatience there in the hospital. She found herself sitting alone, long after the others had left, braiding endless friendship bracelets out of the colored thread brought by the art therapist, passing them out to the other women wordlessly, like a homesick child at camp. Such camp-style crafts were popular on the unit and became a kind of currency, the women making endless rounds of pot holders and keychains and bracelets out of plastic and bits of string, filling in the dead time and bartering their goods like primitive traders. It was through this gratuitous making, a crude approximation of her previous work, that Cora survived.

One day she realized she'd finished a bracelet someone else had started and abandoned. It had been black and red, a simple pattern, and she'd picked it up automatically, knotting it until it was done. She was fast with her hands, working with a mechanized efficiency. She added the finished bracelet to her wrist, along with all the other thread bracelets she now wore, a teenager's crazed hodgepodge of colors, thinking nothing of it until breakfast the next day.

"Hey, that's mine," a big woman said, eyeing the newest bracelet. "You took it." The woman said this with an air of aggrieved disbelief, her small eyes flitting wildly, looking for others to join her in collective outrage.

Cora's mouth fell open stupidly. She looked at the woman, words of apology forming. But she'd grown so unaccustomed to speaking that her mouth had become dusty, unuseful.

"You think you're too good for us? That why you don't say nothing? Think you can take whatever you want?"

This woman was hulking, her upper arms broad and white as fish bellies. She had a neck tattoo, a python curling around her neck in vivid greens and reds. Wanda? Yolanda? Cora could not conjure the woman's name, but she knew she was part of the contingent of women who left daily with nurse chaperones to attend a twelve-step meeting on the third floor of the hospital. "The druggie contingent," Cora's roommate, Barbara, called them. "They're here because they filled their bodies with junk. Their own damn fault, unlike the rest of us," Barbara had said. Barbara was a thin, angry woman with a bipolar diagnosis, locked in a custody battle with an ex who was using her diagnosis against her like a crude cudgel. "I heard one of their babies died. The rest are probably all messed up with crack or fetal alcohol syndrome or whatever."

Cora had simply shaken her head. She was still too bleary and bewildered to have any animus toward anyone, to be pulled into one team or another—teams she hadn't previously realized existed, but there it was. Party lines were drawn: the women who were hospitalized with a dual diagnosis versus the women with primary mood or psychotic disorders. So it was a shock when the large woman had confronted her at the table; she realized then that she'd been read correctly as middle-class, privileged, unused to such mild privations as they all presently endured. The sort of dreamy-eyed dilettante who'd once devoted an entire six months of her life to perfecting a regency-style tiara of tiny fish in platinum with emerald eyes, so lovely and intricate and uncomfortable that no one could actually wear it. What a fool she'd been, sipping red wine with other people in dark, rectangular glasses with their pointless creations.

"Hey," one of the skinny teenagers said. "Wanda's talking to you, Miss Goody-Good. Answer her."

Cora flushed deeply then, her tongue thick and flaccid in her mouth.

"Lay off," Barbara said. "Poor girl's still getting it together."

The other teenager scoffed. A third woman, skinny-armed and with the invisible blonde lashes and red-rimmed eyes of a rabbit, stared at Cora—not menacingly, but with interest.

"I'm sorry," Cora said finally. "I didn't mean . . ."

Wanda raised an eyebrow.

"Fuckin' crazy," Wanda muttered. "Talkin' shit about the rest of us. Like you're any better."

Barbara's chair scraped back abruptly and she stood from the breakfast table, throwing her biscuit down like a threat. They had no knives, of course. A security officer standing in the corner of the room sensed the tension and walked over. Wanda had risen at that point, too, and the two of them stood there glowering at each other.

"Ladies," the security officer said.

And for a second, the two women glared at each other, looming over the rest of them at the table. A hard chunk of biscuit had turned to glue in Cora's throat.

It was over then. Barbara left the room abruptly with a parting huff. Wanda sat back down. And for the rest of her time there, Cora was unbothered. But she saw that a point had been made: lest she be tempted to feel morally superior, lest she be tempted to construe herself as the only victim.

She stayed clear of Wanda after that, the two teenagers, a heavyset woman with dyed black hair, and the rabbity-faced girl. She and the other woman had a separate CBT group while Wanda's contingent went to the NA meeting.

One evening near the end of her stay, she'd been startled to run into the pale girl with the blonde lashes just outside her room.

"I'm sorry," Cora said, her heart speeding up in her chest.

The blonde girl looked away.

"No, it's okay," she whispered. "Just so you know, I don't think you're crazy. At least no more so than anybody else."

Cora nodded. This was a peace offering. She understood.

"I hope your baby's doing well," she said, because this was an accepted nicety, at least among the postpartum women, the one thing guaranteed to elicit smiles and photos and updates.

A look passed over the girl's face, as if she might erupt into laughter, or maybe cry. But this was not unusual, not here.

"Yeah," she said, and hurried away.

Later, Cora found a pack of peanut M&M's and special scented lotion her husband had brought to her missing from her room. But there was no telling who it might have been—even Barbara, her supposed defender. When Cora got ready for bed that night, she could have sworn she smelled chocolate on Barbara's breath. Barbara, who cried herself to sleep every night, so who, in the end, could begrudge her anything?

In the weeks that followed seeing the girl with the necklace, Cora began going to the cemetery daily, sitting on the bench for an hour or so, waiting. She didn't tell Tom, choosing to go either early in the morning or just after work, stitching together stolen swatches of time. Watching for her. Expectant.

She'd begun to have physical dreams, dreams in which she felt the tug of the baby's mouth against her nipples, the warmth of letdown followed by the animal pleasure of having her heavy breasts relieved of milk. Then the dreams would take a dark turn, the baby melting into nothingness in her arms, and she would wake, sweating, heart thundering in her chest, distraught. Foreboding registered itself everywhere, from the fall of early light through the window to the way the baby churned inside her, restless.

She startled awake again one morning at five forty-five, just as the birds had started their summer cacophony outside. Tom was still asleep beside her, his face slack and untroubled. She was jealous of him, she realized. He'd never been betrayed by his own instincts.

She kissed him gently on the forehead before pulling on a loose cotton skirt. The baby kneed her insides gently, and she spoke to him without actually speaking. *Stay calm, my little. Just wait.*

Walking up to the cemetery, she actually felt stronger. She would get her necklace back. The day was beginning to break, and it was warm but not yet oppressive.

She opened the little gate and let herself into the cemetery. A reddish fox scampered away, and she gasped. It seemed yet another sign, one she chose to interpret as positive.

She found a large stump covered in strange twists and fingers of lichen in bluish gray and orange. Cora knelt, inspecting this quiet, vegetal world with a line of ants marching businesslike and a white-gray mushroom poking up like a thumb, until she sensed someone walk up behind her. Cora knew who it would be. Groaning slightly, she heaved herself upright and blinked, momentarily light-headed.

"Hi, again," the girl said. She was still wearing Cora's necklace.

Cora studied her. It felt like she was reaching back for something distant, and then she retrieved it.

"Tammy," Cora said finally. "Your name is Tammy."

The girl nodded shyly, pleased.

"We were there together."

The girl nodded again. She was so pale, her arms translucent with their greenish veins running underneath, that she appeared ghostly.

"They gave it to me by mistake," the girl said, tilting her head as she unclasped the necklace from around her neck, handing it back to Cora.

She turned from Cora, looking off over her shoulder as if she'd heard something.

"I come here a lot. I started to see your little boy. Then I recognized you."

An uncomfortable knowledge settled over Cora then. She thought of the girl, Tammy, coming here, and of Martin, his innocent hellos to the little lambs on the smallest gravestones. She had the impulse to touch the girl then, to offer some kind of consolation, but she held herself back, like the girl was a wild creature who might startle.

"I'm sorry," Cora said finally.

Tammy seemed to be looking at something lost in the distance. The sun had risen now, and the first cars were arriving at the office building just behind them.

Tammy tilted her head.

"It's not your fault."

There was a little bench nearby, and Cora moved to it and sat. The girl sat down beside her.

"I'm too old for this now," Cora whispered to the girl. "I'm not sure what I was thinking. Trying again."

The girl shrugged.

"No right age."

Cora nodded, and they sat there for a little while, watching an early-morning bicyclist on the path just beyond them.

"Do you mind?" the girl asked. She placed her small, warm hands on the hard globe of Cora's belly, and as if in response, the baby moved beneath her touch, jabbing a definitive elbow. Cora knew then that this would be the very peculiar sensation that she would soon miss.

The girl smiled at Cora, but her eyes looked watery and tired.

"Well, bye," she said, rising from the bench.

Don't go, Cora wanted to say then, because it seemed then like this girl might be one of the few people in the world who understood. This one girl might at least understand how things might go any number of ways despite all the careful motions of your hands, all your craftsmanship.

"Bye," Cora said instead, so quietly that the girl probably didn't even hear. She had already turned and was halfway to the kudzu-covered stretch of trees into which she'd disappeared the first time. For a moment, squinting into the sun, Cora caught a glimpse of how she'd previously seen the world: an arrangement of gorgeous geometries and contours, light gilding even the most unnecessary objects into things fierce and sparkling and alive. Every form begging to be replicated. Then there was a tightening, more urgent this time, and Cora knew she had to walk home now, slowly, slowly, because the contractions were increasing in frequency as well as intensity. She turned to start back, the shapes of leaf and shadow sparking and trembling behind her.

DARLING

DARLING WAS USED TO SLOPPINESS. SHE WAS USED TO dirty napkins and sticky seats and loosely capped ketchup bottles, mushed french fries, and smeared plates. She maneuvered through the restaurant detritus, avoiding crumpled napkins on the floor like a royal sidestepping dog droppings, and she'd perfected a way of looking down her nose when a patron, jokey and overfamiliar, said, "Darling. Now, that's not your real name, is it?" Darling wouldn't even answer, just cocked her head to one side, tapping her pen on her pad like it was an act of noblesse oblige even to be there, like she hadn't even heard such a question, or was ignoring it out of politeness and fundamental decency, the way one might ignore a fart. She made it very clear she was suppressing her boredom, taking drink orders, reciting appetizer specials, suffering fools. Her silences made the diners—poor, uncouth souls, they'd realize in her presence—blush and stutter a little, these glad-handers and good ol' boys. It wrong-footed them. She stood there, erect and stately in her company-issued lime-green polo shirt, her hair in a neat bun, something goddess-like and ferocious in her face.

"You got some city in you, now," a good ol' boy would say, because she was incongruous, certainly: a switchblade on a heap of throw pillows, a shark's tooth in a bowl of jelly.

Darling would ride that pause out before she'd answer, and again, the good ol' boy wouldn't quite know what to do with the silence. If he were lucky, he'd have his beer already—cold but slightly flat, the good, cheap, American stuff—and he would take a mouthful of it to occupy himself.

"Oh," Darling answered, but only sometimes. "I'm nothing but a local girl."

She would turn with what was almost a swish, although she had on canvas sneakers and khaki cargo shorts, and so the effect was something she managed invisibly, leaving the stunned customer in silence.

This was just how she did things. She was slow to bring out food. She stared at a spot just over her customers' shoulders, never quite making eye contact when she spoke. Yet her tips were always generous.

Everyone knew, in a vague way, that Darling had been disgraced. This fact radiated off her, like nuclear contamination. Now she was no better than any of the rest of them, the dullards who'd stuck around and followed the line as it was laid out for them.

When Clyde first saw she was back, he did a double take, but he knew her immediately. She had the same high-stepping stride she'd had as a teenager —like a show horse, his mother had said. His mother hated Darling.

"Darling Bridges called," his mother would tell him, back when they'd been going out, and she wouldn't have to say anything else, but there would be that tone to her voice. She'd mostly kept her opinions to herself, but his mother was a woman who favored honesty and thrift, washing out and reusing sandwich bags, steeping a tea bag at least twice, coming to a full stop at stop signs. She also favored good, old-fashioned names, like Margaret, Anne, or Jane. Anything else, she'd once opined, seemed like you were putting on airs.

Darling had been Clyde's high school girlfriend. She had the same auburn hair now, only a few grays, almost unnoticeable, at her temples. Her face was still impressively unlined for someone with fair skin. Clyde knew that he had done all right with the years himself. He was a little heavier. Filled out, his mother said, softer all over, like a plushly stuffed couch, far from the rangy kid he'd been back in high school. He, too, still had the same hair—blond, which he'd never taken as a liability until he went out with Darling. Shortly before they'd broken up, she'd said to him, "You know your hair is the exact color as a Malibu Ken doll's," and he'd flushed, thinking this was some sort of compliment, until she'd added, "I just can't take a man with yellow hair seriously."

He'd been self-conscious about his hair ever after. Yellow. She'd had a way of undoing you, Clyde thought, and yet somehow you wanted to keep coming back for more, hoping against hope that this next time you might earn her regard.

"Darling?" he said to her that first night when she passed him where he sat, hunching over a half-full beer at the dimly lit bar.

A mounted television blared at them from above: college basketball, which everyone had real feelings about. The greater Raleigh-Durham area was expanding outward like a blob, more or less enveloping their little town now, and with it came people from elsewhere—research scientists and university professors who didn't mind a bit of a commute so long as it got them more square footage for the dollar.

At first it didn't seem like Darling had even heard. She made a scornful sound with her mouth like she was sucking something out of her molars and pushed her pen back behind an ear. Turning, she looked at him full-on, appraisingly. Clyde could feel all the blood in his body moving like hot soup up into his cheeks.

"Well?" he said, attempting to put a little bravado in his voice. The way her forehead crinkled suggested she was interested, that maybe this was the first mildly interesting thing she'd seen all night.

"Clyde," she said, but her voice was affectless.

"You still lighting up every room?"

She rolled her eyes, then gave him an ironic twirl.

"You still tied to your mama's apron string? She still hoarding her pennies like a mean ol' dragon?"

He scoffed, shaking his head, but he was smiling.

Darling moved away from him then, picking up a little rag she used to scrub at a spot on the bar. The wood was shellacked to such a shininess that you could often see your face in it. The bartender tonight was a man named Mike whom Clyde also knew from school—a former wrestler now decades into hard-won sobriety, one forearm intricate with tattooed kudzu climbing all over it. The good thing about growing up here was that you could get your vices out early: fully vested alcoholic by seventeen, probation by twenty-three, four rounds at Freedom House by twenty-six, then solid citizenship before you hit thirty. It wasn't necessarily a bad thing to get knocked down hard and quickly. Mike repositioned himself farther away, making a show of ignoring them.

One of the stools was out of alignment with the rest, and Darling bumped it with her hip to straighten it. She put the rag back down and looked up at Clyde.

"It's nice to see you," she said, although she didn't make it sound particularly nice.

"What are you doing back?"

"Here for a spell. Supposed to see someone I haven't seen in a real long time."

She looked into his face for a long moment searchingly but gave no further explanation. He dared not ask. Finally, she took her eyes off him, glancing back up to one of the televisions overhead. The restaurant patrons cheered at the conclusion of the game: a win. Someone flipped the nearest TV to a news channel, and there were headlines bannering: drop in stock prices, an impending trade war, an imprisoned billionaire found dead in his jail cell.

Clyde watched Darling's face rotate upward, caught the tiniest hint of a frown beginning in the pinch of her brows, but she put her hand to her hip as if to check her pocket for something and said nothing.

Out back behind the restaurant, Darling leaned against a wall. He was dead, then. That billionaire. Her billionaire. She'd stifled a yelp when she'd seen it on the news, like it was nothing, merely a fact about someone far away. Clyde, on the other hand, she'd been glad to see. She'd actually been waiting for him, hoping he'd show up. It had taken weeks. But once he'd come, the whole rhythm of their encounter had felt off.

Back in high school, Darling had real feelings for Clyde. Not quite love, but a feeling of safety. That was something, it turned out. Considering this, she sat, pacing her breaths. Her pulse was finally slowing. She took a drag of her cigarette, letting her mind go blank. For a long while, she'd tried to give it up, switched to nicotine gum, but lately, she'd given in. Because why fight what fate had in store for you? It was all already there, carved into some dirty stone: your birthright, your fortune. She was done fighting.

Darling wiped an arm against the little half apron she wore over her shorts. Her hands were dry and chafed, the hands of an old woman, no matter how much hand cream she used at night. Once upon a time, she'd had lovely hands—Clyde himself had often said so. At least, he'd liked it when she touched him. Lovely skin all over, soft and firm and unblemished.

They'd had a good time back in high school, she and Clyde, that judgy mama of his notwithstanding. People like Clyde's mother—old-timers with a family name they thought meant something, women who'd paired up with the wrong men and were bitter about it—were the worst kind of people, mean and righteous and set in their ways. Clyde's mother would have been pleased when Darling left. Darling's own mother, in one of her moments of sobriety, had been practical. "Tell him," she'd said, "and he'll do right." It had seemed simpler not to say anything, especially when opportunity dropped into her lap the way it had. She'd moved to New York. Clyde had stayed down here, earning his associate and then his bachelor's, then, eventually, a law degree. He was the sort of man she probably ought to have married. Things could have gone that way if she'd let them.

Across the street, somebody shouted. Darling squinted into the afternoon sunlight and saw old Ed Meyers pushing his bicycle. One of the wheels was bent, and Ed looked a little sun-dazed, listing to one side like a crooked sailboat. Same as always. Catching sight of her, he shouted something about being in the magazines, a movie star, but she rose from the crate on which she'd been sitting and brushed her hands together. Ed paused across the way, awaiting a response, but Darling just turned and went back inside. Her break was over.

When she'd left town, Darling had left of her own free will. Eager and ready, blissed out by all her little dreams, tantalized by the scent of opportunity. She'd wanted to become something. A fashion designer. A singer. A model. The story differed a little depending on who was telling. Even Darling hadn't known exactly, her ambitions at the time large and vaporous. But she'd left town seeking greatness; greatness had sought her out, and with impeccable timing.

Or so it had seemed. Not long after her conversation with her mother, greatness had come in the form of an elegant older woman who walked into the restaurant—Darling had worked there in high school, too—and offered to do a tarot reading for Darling. It was funny; now tarot was all the rage again, but back then, Darling hadn't known exactly what it was—a root vegetable from an organic food store, the name of a French inspector?

The woman had been wearing all black. Her hair was pulled up in a clip, the way Darling imagined sophisticated women with office jobs all wore their hair. She had a beautiful face, even though it was lined, fine wrinkles gathering at the woman's mouth and eyes. She wore lipstick and carried a leather bag that Darling instantly recognized was expensive. It had an important-looking heft to it. When the woman pulled up a seat at the bar, she set the bag down on a stool next to her, where it waited patiently, like it was an obedient child.

The woman waved to Darling and requested a Diet Coke with a lemon. Darling had been both hostess and fill-in busser at the time, not an actual server, but she'd nodded, sliding back behind the bar to get a glass and pouring the Diet Coke for the woman herself. When she slid it over, the woman caught her wrist.

"What are you doing here?" she said, looking Darling up and down. Her eyes were green, green like no one's eyes she'd ever seen. Later in life, Darling would think back and wonder if she'd been wearing colored contacts, but at the time, the effect had been like meeting someone from another realm, one inhabited by witches and green-eyed mermen and elves.

Darling had faltered. The woman had voiced the very question in her own mind.

"What are *you* doing here?" Darling asked, the words escaping before she could think better of them.

The woman tipped back her head and laughed. She laughed and laughed, and Darling could see that she had a long, elegant neck. She was like a gorgeous antique—even with a fine coating of dust, you could look at her and sense the value, the exquisite craftsmanship. Darling was already starting to feel squat and weary and unwell, a hopeless country bumpkin doomed to repeat the cycle of every woman she'd ever known to go before her. Staring at this woman was like staring into her own longing.

"I'm from here," the woman said, still smiling with her eyes. There was a dizzying, mirrored quality to their conversation now, with the woman saying the very phrases Darling was forming in her own mind before Darling could speak.

"*I'm* from here," Darling said.

The woman took a sip of her Diet Coke and then dabbed the corner of her mouth with a napkin.

"I *was* from here," she said. "It's been a long time since I've been back. Things have changed."

Darling nodded as if this all made sense to her. Nothing much seemed to have changed for as long as she could remember. Sure, one big-box chain store replaced another big-box chain store. The river rose, brown and murky as an overflowing septic tank one season, then ran peacefully, almost prettily, in another. But that was it. The same old men ate biscuits and gravy off foam plates over at the place by the Shell gas station every morning, nursing bottomless cups of coffee and talking about hunting. The same tired woman rang her up in the grocery store and got irritated if she had the audacity to bring coupons. Darling pulled up another stool, careful to avoid upsetting the woman's bag, and sat down.

"Look," the woman said, patting Darling's hand. "Let's do a reading. You're familiar with tarot?"

Darling thought it better not to seem a fool, so she didn't respond.

The woman studied her again, then pulled out a deck from somewhere in the depths of her bag, shuffling the cards in such an elaborate and extended way that it felt portentous to Darling. The woman pulled each card out with a little popping sound, fanning them on the counter before them. The Devil stared up at Darling from the middle, bare-chested and frowning, holding a man and a woman in chains.

"Oh, you're special," the woman said to Darling, her voice warm, honeyed. "I knew it. From the moment I saw you."

She went on to describe the cards, her pale, slim hands fluttering over them. Darling felt her head go soft and buzzy, the pleasant kind of waking-sleep feeling she got at certain qualities of sound, certain voices. She would do anything, anything, if only the woman would keep talking. Weeks later, she would try to recall something more specific from the reading, something exactly the woman had said, but there was nothing, only sense memory: the smell of smoke, the soothing sound of the woman's words, the steady click of the ceiling fan overhead.

Darling gazed into the woman's eyes after she'd finished. She would follow this green-eyed woman anywhere, under the hillside, down to meet the mountain king.

"You could do things. Big things. More than this."

The woman gestured to their surroundings, and Darling took a gulp of stale air. There were grease stains on her shirt. Her hands smelled of onions and spilled beer, and suddenly, she felt the need to hide them.

"I dunno," Darling said, because the thing she'd learned so far had been not to reach too far, not to have your hand smacked down so relentlessly.

"It'll take sacrifice."

The woman smiled at her, and Darling thought of those moments of which she'd read, when one of the immortals took an interest in a mortal, appearing in human form, offering something: a gift, always with a catch.

"I can teach you," the woman continued. "You strike me as a bright girl." She paused, taking another sip from her drink and then neatening the deck of cards. "My boss pays well. You'd pick it up quickly."

She tapped the deck once, twice, and then slipped the cards back into her bag.

"I don't have money," Darling said, her voice faltering. "For travel. For anything."

"My boss will handle it," the woman said. "It will all be taken care of."

Darling cleared her throat carefully, terrified of blowing her only chance.

"There's also this," she said, and then Darling had whispered the rest of it into the woman's ear, as if giving it full voice would only make matters worse, because now she'd counted it all out, the weeks on her fingers, and she knew: even if she had the money, it was most likely too late.

The woman nodded.

"We can handle that."

Clyde, whose daddy was nothing but trash, had become a lawyer—but so what? It was a good thing, of course. Showed you could rise above your own blood. It was good to have a degree behind your name, more than one degree, at that. There was something respectable to it. "My son, the attorney," Clyde's mother enjoyed saying. She liked to drop it casually in situations in which there was no cause for it.

What people didn't understand was that you could have a law degree and still be racking up credit card debt. You could have that degree and still not have a job, still have student loan payments higher than any monthly mortgage. For three years after he graduated, Clyde couldn't find work—at least not full time. He did contract work, bought crappy disaster insurance, didn't go to the dentist. When his mom bragged about him in the checkout line over Christmas, it made his face burn. One of his law school roommates had recently emailed a photo of the new home he'd bought inside the beltline in Raleigh, and Clyde had typed out a hysterical-looking all-caps *HAHAHA* before thinking better of it and hitting delete. A lot of his classmates had come from long lineages of attorneys—fathers and grandpas and great-grandpas. Southern gentility.

But now he was doing okay—okay enough to take himself out to lunch occasionally during the work week, okay enough to leave Darling a tip that demonstrated his regard but not so large as to suggest anything.

He walked along the stretch of road between the restaurant and the shopping center in which he rented office space. One car, another car whizzed by him, creating a warm rush on the side of his face. There were no sidewalks. Pedestrians were an anomaly and most often represented the more reckless elements of local society—the homeless or mentally ill, or the under-twelve crowd. Clyde, in his leather loafers and suit pants, his jacket slung over one shoulder, was the only respectable person in town who ever showed up anywhere on foot. It had been something he and Darling had liked when they were in high school, both carless. They'd walked everywhere: to Jason Rodenburgh's party at his parents' house ten miles outside town, to rent kayaks at the lake, back and forth to each other's houses. The soles had literally come off their shoes.

He had a very distinct memory of Darling frowning over a pair of sneakers with a tube of something called Shoe Goo. When he'd walked in on her, finding her absorbed in this careful task, she'd looked up, defensive.

"They're still perfectly good," she said.

When he'd asked to borrow the goo himself, she'd obliged. It was like he'd passed a sort of test.

He remembered the way she'd walked, right on the white line, barely moving to the shoulder when a car passed, heedless of any risk. She liked to feel the heat of them moving past her. It had made him nervous, even then, as an impulsive teenager himself; there was something in her always sidling up to the edges of things, leaning over railings and bridges, courting danger, tilting toward it.

He'd loved her. But she'd been skittish, difficult to read, especially there at the end. Once, he'd sheepishly brought up making future plans together, and she'd laughed harshly. She wasn't the type, she said. She'd seen what happened to all the women around there—fed and bred and forgotten, like the sad old donkeys behind Bob Merritt's place. And then she'd disappeared one day without a word, not even bothering to show up with the rest of them in their green caps and gowns at graduation.

Back in his office, Clyde sat down at his desk and pulled up his email. The fan spun steadily over his head, a soothing, sleepy rhythm. The air smelled stale, of ink pens and strawberry-flavored tobacco mixed with old egg salad. There was always a sweet, rotten odor to the place, no matter how Clyde aired it out; the previous occupant had run a head shop. Once, Clyde had found a small rainbow-colored hand pipe that had fallen behind a radiator.

The old-fashioned bell on the door jangled, and he rose from his chair to look out. Standing in the doorway was Darling Bridges.

Many months later—after she'd lived with them, after they'd felt almost like parents to her, strange parents, yes, but parents all the same—an intimidating man in a dark suit had brought Darling into a cold interview room and started asking about Madeline LeBlanq née Berkowitz.

"Groomed me?" she'd repeated dumbly, thinking of Madeline that day in the restaurant, Madeline's long legs, the way her eyes flashed with pleasure or irritation, how Madeline taught her to massage Robert's feet, just the way he liked. It was an act of kindness, these small, physical niceties—that was how Madeline had billed it—for all his hard work, all his generosity. It hadn't even seemed weird after a while. He just wanted the best for her, to help her succeed. "My sweet, talented girl," he called her.

It had felt like a notable event, being chosen, deemed special by someone who saw her potential. Soon enough, of course, she would realize that she was but one among many. A stable of girls, all dewy with youth, sleek as thoroughbreds.

Sitting there in front of the man in the dark suit, everything that ought to have been obvious about Madeline came into focus. This felt, in its way, like a greater betrayal than anything that had ever happened with Robert. Madeline, her great friend and champion, her confidante. Darling had started to cry.

"It's okay," the man in the suit said. He passed the box of tissues to her. She figured he was used to interviewing drug traffickers, murderers. He looked like he wished Darling would pull herself together. She snuffled, heaving out a strand of snot into her tissue.

Up until that moment, Darling had thought of Madeline as somehow separate from the rest of the experience—her brisk entrances, her keen eye for decorating, her glass of Diet Coke with a lemon wedge, her quick wit, her book recommendations. She'd seen Darling in her worst moments, wrenched apart and squalling and raw, and wiped her face and brought soup and helped her come back to herself and, eventually, to a better self. Darling had loved those winters, the way they'd curled up at the window, their sock feet pressed together while they read the papers. In the evenings, Madeline had poured herself half glasses of wine—anything more was too much sugar, an invitation to migraines. She wore only mascara or lipstick, never both, always the most expensive variety. She'd taught Darling an aesthetics of restraint. Madeline had taken Darling to yoga, had bought her fashionable leggings and tank tops and made Darling throw out her ratty gym shorts. She taught her about waxing and threading, when and where to apply unguents and oils. With Madeline, Darling learned to treat her own body like a costly possession, something to be glossed and maintained. No-nonsense Madeline, who helped Darling when she learned that Darling hadn't been filing taxes. Madeline, who comforted her that first morning, after she understood the price of Robert's patronage. Madeline, who'd taken her to a clinic in the Bronx under a pseudonym—because no, not again, never again—introducing herself as Darling's aunt.

Robert remained central, but also peripheral, making his appearances bright and grand and episodic, like a full moon.

"Modern geishas," Madeline had said once, semi-ironically, standing on a balcony overlooking the city like Evita, lights twinkling beneath her like gems. Darling, inexplicably it seemed to her now, had felt beautiful and proud.

Later, of course, she'd grown to hate him. She'd wanted him to suffer. And yet she'd also pitied him. The poor old monster. A part of her still felt something almost like affection. Prurient reporters managed to find her and call a few times, but for the most part, her name wasn't included. There were other girls. Women, now, telling similar stories.

Darling sometimes remembered the parties with a fondness that shamed her. She'd been such an innocent at first, her skin flushed, fine new jewelry burning her bare neck, her arms chilly in the gossamer-thin dresses. Big cars bearing oil tycoons and banking barons pulled up at the place in Coral Gables or Palm Springs or Montauk. There would be valets at the ready in matching shirts, demure caterers in all black waiting with aperitifs on trays as people walked up the drive, and she and the other girls poised and ready to flitter among the men. Madeline had coached her, giving her little conversational tips, telling her who was well known for this, who ran which investment firm, who'd just bought a Mondrian.

It had been exhilarating. She'd been young and dumb and radiant with her own kind of power. Or so it had seemed. It hadn't been real power—at least not the same as what the men in those rooms possessed.

Robert had a mean streak, a bully's delight in torments and small, nasty fictions. She remembered the first time she'd noted it. Once, after she'd contradicted him openly at a party, he'd made it clear that she ought to escort a particularly hideous European dignitary, stooped and pockmarked, old enough to be her grandfather, to one of the upstairs bedrooms to make him welcome. He wasn't above causing physical pain—he'd broken her pinky one time, on purpose, slowly—as long as he wrought no damage to the face. Their faces, their supple mouths, she knew, were precious to him, in the way that all his belongings were.

Darling stared at Clyde from the entranceway. She was still wearing her work uniform.

"Here," she said, handing Clyde a warm cardboard take-out container. He opened it and saw french fries and a dry-looking burger on a bun. "Somebody placed a to-go order and never picked it up."

He nodded and ate a fry to be polite. It was soggy, limp as a worm. Darling seated herself in the chair across from him. She looked wearier in the harsh light of his office, the fine creases under her eyes visible. A haggard sort of beauty, intelligence in her eyes. Sadness. He felt protective of her, just as he had in high school when she'd whispered to him once about her long-gone father, her mother, bleary-eyed, unable to hold down a job, her loneliness. He remembered her, skinny and quaking in his arms. The other high school girls had seen something in her to revile; he remembered this, the way they'd snubbed and mocked her. Beautiful, always, but her clothes never quite fit, always off by a decade, clearly culled from the Thriftpick. Becky Johnson and Tiffany Joyce and Maddie Ackerson, with their chokers and cashmere sweaters. He recalled the words he'd seen scratched onto her locker. "They're just jealous," he'd said, trying to turn it into a joke, a compliment. She'd shaken her head. He'd felt it then, the need to intervene somehow, although she had not let him. There was nothing, nothing to be done. He felt it now—a desire to perform some act of heroism.

"You wanna hang out?" she asked.

It was the phrase they'd used with each other. He wasn't sure if the words still held the same meaning exactly, but he nodded, grateful to put down the container of damp fries and go with her. They would talk, and it would be good to let the sound of her voice, its familiar lilt, wash over him. He knew already where she'd lead him. When they exited his office, he didn't even bother to lock the door. There was nothing there worth taking.

She headed across the street and he followed, cutting through an undeveloped lot, and then down another neighborhood side street. They turned at a small clearing in the brush and scrambled down an overgrown bank. There. The spot by the river that had been theirs back in high school—so many hours talking, laughing, tossing stones. The last time he'd kissed her, it had been here, and the thought of this moment now filled him with a mixture of dread and longing.

She plonked herself down onto the riverbank as if incredibly weary, an old woman heavy with time. Clyde stood, squinting out over the water, as if looking for something. A groundhog, fat and glossy, scurried away on the opposite bank, and he almost pointed it out to her, excited as a boy, but when he turned to her, he could see she was already watching it, her eyes still registering nothing but exhaustion.

He sighed.

"Like old times," he said, simply to say something.

She didn't respond. He knew that she'd ended up with that billionaire creep, Malinowski. Robert Malinowski.

"You were gone a long time," he said, and then, slowly, as if not to startle her, he lowered himself beside her.

She turned to him, her face lit by the low sun in such a way that she seemed now a heavenly being, all her youthful beauty restored.

"You forgive me for leaving like that?"

He just stared at her, his eyes watering at the fiery corona the sun formed around her. It was a thing he'd never thought she'd bring up so directly, and he—he wouldn't have dared. He said nothing for a long while. She turned from him, toeing a rock with apparent disgust.

"This place," she said, and her voice was broken now, disconsolate. "Always this place. I shoulda said something before I went, at least."

"I'd forgive you for anything."

He spoke in a rush, his words spilling out, overeager, because it was true, wasn't it? He would. She was as marvelous now as ever.

She looked at him sadly, the low sun making him squint and blink, casting her face once more in its blinding, hallucinatory light.

"You wouldn't. Some things are unforgivable."

"I would."

"Look," she said. "I'll show you something."

She stood before him, the red dust rising and catching sun so that it created sparkles around her, and began to unbutton her shorts. This was sudden, much more sudden even than he'd imagined. His tongue went dry as jerky in his mouth. She lowered the shorts so that he could see the plain white cotton of her underwear. It was the same type of underwear, cheap and functional, purchasable in a big plastic sack from Walmart, that his own mother wore. He remembered Darling's bare thighs from high school, the smooth, pale heft of them in his hands, so when he saw what he saw now, he bit his tongue. Blood filled his mouth. He swallowed.

She gestured to her inner thigh.

"You can touch. It doesn't hurt now."

For some reason, he did, feeling the raised dark areas under his fingers. Scars. He'd hurt her. She led his hand upward to the curve of her hip and away.

Clyde tried to envision it: she and the other girls, bare-shouldered in matching white dresses like virgin members of a harvest cult, flutes of champagne, lines of coke. A beautiful place somewhere exotic, just outside Santa Fe, or Park City, the men all powerful, with lacquered hair and dark suits. Everyone laughing, all that easy power. A lighter, the cherry of a cigarette. Flesh burning. Smell of charred meat.

She looked at him hard, meaningfully, like she was trying to tell him something, or seek his opinion. He had to say something. Maybe comfort her, but how. Bile rose sour in his throat.

"You let him do that to you?"

She flinched as if scalded, then pulled up her shorts. His hand fell away.

She didn't answer, but turned from him, scrambling back up the bank they'd climbed down. He knew he'd said the wrong thing. This test: he'd failed it miserably. A clod, a dolt. Climbing back up the bank, she was as limber as a girl.

"Wait," he said. "I'm sorry."

But she didn't answer. She didn't even turn around.

"There were other things," he shouted, ineffectual, desperate. "Things you never told me. You ought to tell me now. I ought to know."

What he meant was *I'm sorry, I love you, I'm sorry*, but there were no words left in his mouth to speak. By the time he himself made it back up into the little neighborhood behind the river, he was breathing heavily, winded. Darling was gone.

The secret, of course, is that if a woman asks another woman in just the right way, she will do things. That is, if she has earned your trust. If she has leaned over you, motherly, stroking hair from your forehead, if she has spooned broth into your feverish lips, if she's brought you fresh packets of ice, her voice soothing, her face attentive. A girl can be lulled into almost anything.

"Please. It will mean so much to him. A small token. It's an honor, really."

The softest treachery. You will want to oblige, when such a woman asks. Darling knows this.

She still recalls the time in middle school, school photo day, when her mother had insisted upon curling Darling's hair. Her mother was almost always in a bad way then, her breath rank, eyes smeary, laughter too loud. Darling remembered how her mother had wielded the curling iron, loose-limbed, reckless, how Darling had wanted to please her. "You'll be the most beautiful girl in school, Darling. The most beautiful beauty. My star." And Darling had squirmed under her mother's hands, tipping her head away from the hot coil, too afraid to say anything, her mother's rising irritation. "Sit still, you brat, sit still." And she'd learned to sit still, to grit her teeth under the mounting pile of curls, the tender pink helix of her ear sizzling under the metal while her mother smiled into the mirror at their joint reflections. "My beauty, my best girl."

It was the hopeful part of him that kept going back day after day to the restaurant, looking for her. But Darling, with her prancing walk, her shoulders thrown back, was no longer there. The only faces he saw were tired and familiar, local women in lime-green shirts and khaki shorts, slogging through the restaurant with platters balanced on their arms, making friendly chatter to the locals, none of them a thing like Darling, it seemed to Clyde. There was the same old smell of ketchup and pine-scented cleaner and grease wafting from the kitchen. It was so dismal it could make a person want to cry.

She hadn't even given formal notice, he learned. Just never showed up for her next shift. Hadn't even bothered to turn in the company apron with its little badges and geegaws.

"Sorry, man," Mike said, scratching a spot on his elbow and turning away, giving Clyde a moment to collect himself and reset his expression. "She's like that, you know? Easy come, easy go. Said she only planned to save up a little, then be on her way."

He had to stay. He couldn't leave; that was loyalty, a place that had a hold on you down to your bones. Good thing he was still here, because people needed him. "Good thing," his mama said, squeezing his shoulder whenever he got that restless look. His mother's savings were gone. Some lowlife had stolen the empty Crisco container filled with bills from the back of her pantry, although who would have known to look there, she couldn't say. He'd always told her it was a bad idea, keeping money like that.

Clyde would earn it all back for his mama and then some, he told her. He was a good man, he told himself. He did right by those who'd let him. Or, he tried.

Robert Malinowski's name faded from the news cycle, an old, dead villain, replaced by others.

A girl showed up in town. A young woman, maybe twenty, twenty-three at most, asking for Darling Bridges. She appeared at Clyde's office one day holding an old-fashioned tweed bag and wearing a baseball cap over her yellow hair. There was a piece of paper she held with Darling's full name on it. There were questions all over her face. She had, Clyde saw, Darling's eyes, Darling's way of walking, as if she were a majorette about to join a parade. He saw something of his own mother in the turn of the girl's mouth.

"Hello," the girl said to Clyde, and Clyde's own mouth went dry at the sound of her voice, his heart plummeting to his feet and then rising again, up, up, up like a balloon.

Clyde took her hand in his, touching it as if she might disappear.

Darling was long gone, but here she was: this new person, with a wry little twist to her smile and a sharp gaze: a shard of glass in a boll of cotton, a sliver of bone in a scoop of ice cream.

She threw her shoulders back and smiled at him, like someone wholly free, unbound to the pitiful muddy river running through town, to a name, to anything.

Clyde was nothing—a buffoon with an advanced degree, a blunderer, saddled with debt and good intentions, but when the girl suggested a cup of coffee, he agreed, ready to follow her anywhere, straight into the sun even, ready to feel himself burst into flame.

THE FILMS OF
ROMAN POLANSKI

MY BOYFRIEND HAD NO INTEREST IN SCARING ME UNTIL I began working with the Devil Boy. After that, he—my boyfriend, not the Devil Boy—paid careful attention to me, planning and executing little jolts. Frightening me became a sort of art. He started small, with silly, generic gestures at first, anything that would elicit a reaction: a rubber roach inside the box of my favorite cereal, a lizard with red plastic eyes waiting as I stepped out of the shower, a relentless series of breathy voice mails from a blocked number. The pranks of a child. Later, of course, he progressed.

He was sweet and timid, this boyfriend of mine, having grown up with terrible asthma and an overbearing father, the combination of which had resulted in his missing months of school at a time, growing quiet and withdrawn, developing all the requisite habits of a future computer programmer. His shyness was one of the things that had drawn me to him. He had the auburn hair of a red setter, and the slow, doleful gaze of an old-fashioned fire-and-brimstone preacher. He told me of long hours spent as a boy in his sickbed listening to voices moving beneath him and the slow drumming of his own heart.

I found gummy worms burrowed deep in my container of yogurt: my boyfriend's doing. I spooned them out and smiled. His efforts were a form of attention, a way of noticing what attracted or repelled me. I'll admit: whether I should have been or not, I was flattered. This electricity between us now, it seemed to mean that something was happening.

We did not talk about it, but I knew. My boyfriend knew I knew. It was one of those things that went without saying. Like the fact that calling him *my boyfriend* was ridiculous. At his age. At mine. I'd considered adopting *beau* or *gentleman-friend*, but this made me sound arch, like I was speaking ironically. I've always been a plainspoken woman of no-iron shirts and comfortable undergarments, so archness did not suit me. I'd tried using *partner*, but this made me sound stilted, like I'd joined a law firm of very meek and hesitant attorneys.

At night, he'd begun stroking my hair again, a thing I liked for him to do before I fell asleep. He hadn't done this in ages, so it felt as if I had earned something. We'd grown more affectionate with each other, more demonstrative.

"You know I'll always take care of you," he said when we fell silent. "You don't have to work with those kids. Juvenile delinquents."

"I have to," I said. "You know I have to."

I had to because it was my job. But what I also meant was that I wanted to—I wanted to see all those children, most especially the Devil Boy. I could not stop thinking about him. The Devil Boy followed me in my thoughts after I'd left the clinic, haunting me like something I'd birthed and abandoned. This haunting left me harrowed, wrung out, compliant.

"You don't have to," my boyfriend responded. He went quiet, his hand frozen just above the pulse in my throat, curled like a snake watching its prey. Our breathing slowed, and we lapsed into the hush of two people drifting toward sleep. Then he hugged me ferociously, with such suddenness I startled.

He laughed and kissed me.

"I'll take care of you," he said, kissing me again, firmly, stealing my breath away.

The clinic where I worked was on the other side of Bolton Hill, walking distance from our apartment. In good weather, I did walk, crossing the bridge and passing the train station, where grimy artists bicycled one direction, DC-bound commuters in suits marched briskly in the other. I picked my way over the uneven sidewalks, where the houses were shaded and beautiful, although often in need of renovation. I'd once dreamed of being the kind of person who owned one of those houses, working throughout the weekdays in order to devote myself on the weekends to the loving repair of my Victorian home. Families lived in Bolton Hill, and I thought of them as families of style and intellect, families unafraid of a little petty theft or of the late-night shenanigans of the nearby art students. I had given up on the idea of forming such a family myself. My boyfriend and I had met one another later in life, and he did not want children. In truth, neither of us had proven very good at taking on long-term projects.

At the far side of the neighborhood, in an area that became plain old West Baltimore, was the clinic where I worked. It was a new site. Our office sat in a repurposed storefront, sad and slumping, with blacked-out front windows for privacy. A falsely cheerful sign with jaunty stick figures promised child and family services. The people who came to see us, our clients, were there under duress—referred, often, by a concerned school guidance counselor or the court system.

My supervisor was a cheerful woman in her sixties named Tawny. Tawny had short, chic steel-gray hair and wore brightly patterned scarves. She had the air of someone who would be good in any number of hypothetical crises, able to staunch wounds or oversee a precipitous labor in the back seat of a taxi. She was warm and practical and fast-talking. She did not attempt to disarm reluctant clients but rather wore them down with her relentless competence.

"There's no magic to this," she'd tell me. "Our clients need bus tokens. Our clients need canned food. Our clients need structure."

A lot of what Tawny did was reinforce positive parenting strategies. No one questioned her advice because she spoke with a hard-won authority. When I offered input, on the other hand, people looked skeptical.

"Have *you* ever raised a child?" one woman had scoffed, although her question was not actually in quest of any answer. "You don't know the first thing."

She grabbed her little boy by the arm then, jerking him roughly from the bookshelf he'd been trying to climb. He yelped, his eyes seeking mine, waiting for me to reprimand his mother, perhaps—to assert myself as the one true adult authority in the room. I felt chastened under his child-gaze, the brutal wisdom of it. I said nothing.

Tawny was quick to emphasize, however, that we had authority. We had knowledge, credentials—just look at the certificates on our wall! Having a baby did not automatically imbue one with parenting skills! Not having had a baby did not diminish one's professional acumen! She'd speak in this vein from time to time, and I knew she was doing it for my own benefit, to bolster me. Tawny herself had raised two children, neither of whom had landed in jail yet, she was quick to add with a laugh.

"They say we're getting a tough one," she told me one fine Friday in autumn. It was warm outside still, but with an edge of the cool weather to come, sunlight filtering golden through the ruddy leaves. Even the grimy parts of the city seemed beautiful. Someone had finally addressed the thriving mischief of rats that had threatened to overtake the alley by our building, catching and hauling away the most vicious. A few mean, fat holdouts still grappled in our dumpster over empty bottles of grape Fanta and the fiery crumbs at the bottom of spent Takis bags, so we were careful to avoid taking our clients out the side door.

I smiled at Tawny and nodded. Fall was my favorite season. My boyfriend and I would sit outside under an umbrella at our favorite café, each reading a book while we ate sandwiches in pleasant, almost telepathic communion. I looked forward to this. I've never minded the smallness of my pleasures.

"James Hadley," Tawny said, and I noticed this time that there was a slight twitch in her eyelid, which meant she was tired, or had had too much coffee, or both. What she would not be was nervous. Tawny was unflappable. She had been bitten by boys just out of juvenile detention, had been punched in the face once by a three-hundred-pound pregnant sixteen-year-old, bore the claw marks of shrieking twelve-year-old girls. After such instances, she'd merely looked at me, unfazed, and asked for an ice pack. The most troubled of troubled children, the wounded, the feral—she'd look them all right in the eye without wavering.

"History of violence?"

She shook her head.

"Not officially." She was frowning, flipping through some of her paperwork. "But one of the homes he lived in burned down. Suspected arson. Eventually, one of the other boys confessed he did it by accident. With another family, one of his foster sisters kept showing up to school with unexplained bruises. No placement has kept him longer than a couple months."

"Psych history?" I asked.

She shook her head again. "He's been evaluated. Didn't meet criteria for ADHD. Oppositional defiant, but isn't that all of them these days?" Tawny shrugged, handing me the boy's intake file to skim.

When James arrived a little later, he appeared undernourished, swallowed by a large blue jacket. He did not look up at us. His foster mother had a harried look, a flightiness to her gestures that suggested she was overdue for a cigarette. I watched Tawny exhale when she saw the boy, surely having imagined someone larger and more imposing. These days there are eleven-year-olds with the heft of full-grown men.

Tawny and James were in the conference room for a long time. I sat at the desk outside gazing into our small lobby, the blue plastic chairs that looked like they belonged in a school cafeteria, fine shafts of dust suspended like glitter in the sun that filtered through the blinds. Usually, I could expect raised voices, a child yelling at his or her parent, the parent's voice rising in frustration, and then Tawny, cool and practical, soothing everyone back down. Today, I heard nothing.

At a certain point, the foster mother walked out of the conference room, shutting the door gently behind her as one would if whoever inside had fallen asleep. She proceeded, tiptoeing almost, to the waiting room, where she seated herself in one of our too-small chairs, clutching her bag in her lap like a shield. I watched as she closed her eyes, breathing—resting, I thought at first. Only then I saw she was softly crying.

It seemed a long time later that Tawny and the boy finally exited the meeting room. The foster mother thanked Tawny quietly, and she and the boy were gone.

Tawny turned to me. Something unintelligible passed across her face. She gazed at me steadily, impassive.

"How was he?"

She exhaled slowly and did not answer at first.

"Fine," she said. "Perfectly polite." She rubbed her temples with both hands. "I'm just getting one of my headaches."

"Sit down," I told her. "Let me get you some tea."

She obeyed me, suddenly childlike herself, docile. I handed her a cup, and she closed her eyes and drank.

You will certainly think it's too perfect when I tell you that my boyfriend and I went to see *Rosemary's Baby* on our first date. There'd been a weekend-long retrospective on Roman Polanski at the Charles. My boyfriend, although he was not yet my boyfriend at the time, had suggested it. I called my sister to tell her I was finally getting out into the world, dangling myself like a piece of less-than-fresh meat in front of mangy lions.

"Good for you," she said to me. "Finally."

When I told her about him—a computer programmer, fortysomething, never married, loved pumpernickel bagels and vintage radio repair and the films of Roman Polanski—she stopped me.

"He actually said that?"

I was puzzled. I wasn't sure which part she meant. He'd sounded nice enough to me. I was pleased with myself, my efforts, and wanted my bravery honored, like a cat dragging back a bloody mouse to its owner. Maybe he was the less-than-fresh meat and I the weary lion.

"Said what?"

"The films of Roman Polanski."

"So?"

"First of all, you don't say *films*," my sister said. "It's pretentious. And secondly, you're allowed to like some Polanski movies, fine, but it's not a thing you advertise. It's not something you include in a dating profile. There are implications."

"He probably wasn't thinking about implications. Just what he likes," I said, knowing this would placate my sister, who had made it very apparent that she believed I, too, lack subtlety or guile.

My sister was silent then, which I interpreted as grudging approval. She was surely glad for me to be seeing anyone. My last breakup had been, unbelievably, eight years earlier. I'd been chopped and gutted like a fish. With my ex, I'd planned beautiful futures: overfull hanging baskets of lobelias, thrifted porch furniture and redone wood floors, a pair of quirkily bright children who wore their old-fashioned names like horn-rimmed glasses. Instead, I'd been left lonely to rot.

And so I found myself meeting for the first time the man who would become my boyfriend. I could tell by the way he shifted his weight, the way his pale cheeks turned as rosy as a little boy's, that he was nervous. He was one of those people who managed to be simultaneously too skinny and yet soft in the middle, his body an unevenly squeezed tube of toothpaste. In his nervousness, he excitedly recounted little facts to me. Did I know that Mia Farrow had been filmed stumbling through actual Manhattan traffic? That this was Polanski's American film debut? Or that the film was supposedly cursed, and that Polanski's pregnant wife, Sharon Tate, had been murdered not long after the release?

I nodded. It was all very interesting, if decidedly inauspicious.

I could sense by the way my boyfriend settled into his seat beside me that he was a person who detested distractions, even if this was a movie he'd seen more than twenty times. His breathing slowed, and I could feel an animal warmth emanating from him, absorbed as he was there in the darkness. His perfect stillness struck me as uncanny, so I was surprised when his hand found mine, just before the Satan rape scene. Like I'd already surmised, he had no sense of implications.

"I really enjoyed meeting you," my soon-to-be boyfriend said to me afterward when we emerged from the theater, blinking like moles in a blaze of afternoon sunlight.

We had hardly spoken to one another, yet it felt like we had survived something quite trying together, a high-camp ordeal. Poor Rosemary, with those glowering Castevets, that black bassinet, and the baby with its horrible eyes.

I understood then that my boyfriend was establishing something from the outset, offering me an implicit contract of sorts. There would be things I might expect if I went along, and other things I might not. I could bid farewell once and for all to my Bolton Hill house with its sets of big and little rain boots in the mudroom, all its busy clamor and bright decrepitude. What my boyfriend would offer me was not a compromised vision of something I'd once wished for, but the acknowledgment that such a vision was a false promise from the start.

"I enjoyed meeting you, too," I said, and my boyfriend kissed me, bold and abrupt, with more appetite than I'd imagined any computer programmer might possess.

When I arrived at work one morning, I noticed that Tawny had transferred the new boy's file to my desk.

"This will be a good case for you," she said. "He's not so bad."

"What about the fire?" I asked her. "The bruises?"

She shrugged and moved toward our kitchenette, pouring grounds into the coffee maker. "You know how some of these placements are," she said, her back still to me. There was a tightness to Tawny's shoulders I'd never noticed before. It would be unlike her to disparage the foster parents we worked with, but she was right: there was huge variability in the quality of the placements. That was merely a fact.

James Hadley was due back that day. I felt more curiosity, more anticipation, than I ordinarily did. Already, I'd sensed that James and I were brethren somehow, both of us castoffs, already tossed into the markdown bin.

The boy's foster mother shuffled in like she'd just finished a long shift somewhere. She looked at me bleakly, and I understood she expected me to fix nothing.

"Come along, James," I said to him. "I'm Miss Beth Ann."

The woman, his foster mother, clawed at my arm, pulling me toward her. Her breath was hot and sour at my ear, and she spoke like the bad fairy at the christening.

"Watch out," she whispered. "He's sly, that devil boy."

I shook off her grasp, hoping James hadn't heard her, and she released my arm.

He followed me, obedient, and took his seat at the table in the conference room. I had a plastic tub of toys and stickers. Even the older children were usually curious about my rewards, but James just sat there at the table, swinging his legs, uninterested. His dark hair covered his eyes.

"I'd like to get to know you a little bit, James," I said.

He nodded.

"Yes, ma'am."

"How are you getting along in your house right now?"

He shrugged.

"You're getting along with Miss Nancy?"

"I dunno," he said, and now he looked at me. I saw for the first time that he had marvelous features. His eyes were burnt gold, a translucent amber, like polished agate. He was beautiful, his boy's face perfect in its symmetry with full pouting lips and dark lashes. *Exotic* was a word I'd been trained not to use, as it implied something colonialist about my own gaze, something that only reinforced certain hierarchies. *Exotic* was a word that othered people—I knew this, but that was the word that kept coming to mind. This little boy seemed both beautiful and rare, like a precious metal, something surfacing from deep within the folds of the earth.

He smiled at me, and I realized, flushing, that I'd been struck dumb gazing at him.

"I miss my mom," he said to me, and suddenly his lower lip quivered. "You remind me of her."

A sound rippled deep in my throat, but I swallowed it. I knew from his chart that he was thirteen, but his cheeks had a baby fullness. A little boy. That was all he was. I recalled from his chart that his mother had lost custody of him because of neglect. She'd had a history of opioid dependence and unstable housing.

"I'm sorry," I said, collecting myself. "That must be hard."

He nodded. Then he reached one hand toward mine, grabbing it. His hand was soft still, a little boy's hand, sticky-warm.

"You'll help me find her, Miss Beth Ann?"

He was holding my gaze with those golden eyes and nodding, so intently that I found myself nodding back reflexively, *Of course, of course*—until I registered what he'd just asked.

"Oh, James," I told him. "I wish I could. I wish it were that simple."

I wanted to promise him that he would see his mother again, that she would get herself together and find a suitable home and take him back, but if I've learned nothing else over the years, I've learned never to promise that.

He jerked his hand away from mine.

"Please?" he said to me, fastening me again with his steady gaze, standing. "Tell me what you want, I'll give it to you."

"James, sit back down."

The room where we met was too small and poorly ventilated, windowless. There were times like this where I felt overheated, sickly, like my head was too full of mucus, my brain bobbing in a viscous soup. It seemed that my glasses were too strong for my eyes. James was very close to me, his hot little hands on my wrist, and I had the sick urge I associate with my migraines.

"Please," he whispered, his voice sounding smooth, knowing, that of a man who can make things happen. "I'll give you anything. I can do that. Anything you want."

I stood up. I was sweating. I might have imagined those words, I think now. I felt unwell. The papers in my lap spilled, drifting to the floor.

"Stop it, James," I said very loudly, speaking as if the loudness of a few unvarnished words would clear my head. "Stop it. Sit back down, please."

He is thirteen years old, I reminded myself: a child. Thirteen, an unlucky number, trouble's precipice.

Now he was curled and crying, tucked against my ankle like a cat, the delicate bones in his wrists and arms visible beneath the skin.

"Miss Nancy hurts me," he said, his voice young once more—helpless, pitiable. "Please. You have to help me."

And what could I do but kneel and comfort him, because he was a child, and one ought to take a child at his word?

When we began dating each other, part of what I liked about my boyfriend was his odd self-assurance. My boyfriend very quickly began to treat me like a clock or an appliance, something reliable and small. I mean this in a good way. After my relationship with my ex, I'd learned there is such a thing as too much hot blood. My boyfriend had very specific ideas, his mind moving in a rigid and orderly way—cool, impervious to argument.

I mentioned James to my boyfriend one day, although not by name. I called him the Devil Boy, because that was how I thought of him. The title was not pejorative—if anything, I marveled at James. I wanted to talk about him.

"There's a child I work with," I told my boyfriend, who was sitting at his computer, sipping a cup of coffee. "I worry he's being abused." I mentioned the house that burned down, along with a series of other troubling, inexplicable incidents Tawny and I had since uncovered. I told him about the boy's current foster mother, who was under CPS investigation. I'd made a confidential report after what James had said to me that first day.

My boyfriend's hands froze on his keyboard as he listened. He frowned. Although he did not speak of it, there had been other difficulties in his childhood, so he took an interest in the hardships of children. This was one of the reasons, he'd explained to me, that he hesitated to be a father himself: He worried about replicating a pattern.

My boyfriend closed his laptop and sighed. "I've told you so many times," he said patiently, the way a good teacher might reprimand a student. "You don't have to keep working there. I'm here now. To take care of you."

It moved me to have someone worry over me, but I shook my head. "I like working there."

"There are other options," he said. "Something part time, maybe. Less stressful."

"I don't want something part time. I want to do this."

"Beth Ann," my boyfriend said, still speaking to me like I was much younger than he was. "You're too trusting. It's dangerous."

I shook my head again. My boyfriend and his computers, his chat rooms and Reddit threads—he had many notions, I thought, but he had no idea.

"It's fine," I said, laughing hoarsely. "I have good instincts."

My boyfriend also made a laughing sound, a hollow one, like someone choking on a bone, and drew me toward him, his hands against my waist in a way that made me feel valuable. A beautiful woman, a person who mattered. Both the subject and the object of desire.

He kissed me.

"A kid like that . . . unhinged. He could start following you home. Stalking you. It could get scary."

"That's the nature of my job," I said. I heard my own stubbornness rise like the blood vivid in my cheeks, my words an official challenge. "I don't mind being scared."

My boyfriend grinned at me as if I'd just delivered a flirty dare, pressing himself against me and pinning me to the bed. His face hovered near mine, and I could hear him breathing more rapidly. Holding both my wrists above my head, he kissed the scoop of my throat like he knew he was both the cause of and the solution to my shivering.

Looking back, I realize this was what started things.

"No one listens to me like you do," James told me the third or fourth time we met. He blinked his yellow eyes, contented, feline.

We sat together there in the conference room while he chewed the eraser end of a number two pencil. His school papers were spread out on the table, covered now in little crumbs and granulated sugar. The last time James saw his mother, she'd taken him to a Dunkin' Donuts. She got a huge cup of coffee for herself and an enormous blueberry muffin for him. His favorite. This was the last time he saw her, he'd told me, and so this brief moment had now become heavy with meaning.

How paltry, I'd thought when he told me, what can be counted as affection. How little it can take: mere crumbs. A muffin.

So I'd started bringing him little treats. Nothing at all, really. I told myself these were but small kindnesses. With my offerings, it felt like I was breaking through to him, accessing parts of him that were honest and true: the hurt motherless boy beneath the supposed villain.

That day, as I followed James out to the waiting area, I handed him back the essay he'd brought to show me, and our hands met, his still sticky from the muffin. For a few seconds, my hand lingered on his. We stood, looking at one another without speaking. Were we holding hands? Maybe. But it felt like more—an exchange of something, a vital energy. Then it ended. He turned from me, rejoining his foster mother. She stood, her eyes skittering away from mine, and started walking briskly. Nervous, I thought as she exited with James. Hiding something, perhaps. Guilty.

It was only after they left that I realized Tawny had been standing behind me, watching.

"Everything okay?" she asked, her voice practiced, no-nonsense. "I can always take back over."

"No, no," I said, flustered. My cheeks were hot, like I'd been caught mooning over a crush, although of course it was not like that. It was not like that at all. "It's fine. I feel . . . very invested in him."

Tawny laughed. She had a rich, layered former smoker's laugh.

"Don't," she said. "That's the first rule in this business. Do what you can, but don't let that happen. I can always take over. There are plenty more."

I nodded, careful to make my face neutral again, a mask of professionalism. But I knew Tawny was wrong: there weren't any more, not for me. At a certain point, you realize that life is a series of doors closing, the world narrowing down, until there is always, ever, only one.

Once they'd begun, my boyfriend's pranks afforded me a means of demonstrating my good instincts, proving that I was not naïve. I became familiar with the sensation of someone watching me. I plucked odd, threatening notes from the front seat of my car with an air of boredom. I knew my boyfriend's handwriting—he didn't even bother to disguise it. I grew accustomed to hearing a knock on the door and finding no one there whenever I was home alone. My keys would go missing and then turn up in strange places: behind the refrigerator or buried in the soil of the ficus in our living room.

When I began to notice things missing from my drawers, items of jewelry replaced with others that were similar yet not the same, photos moved from one spot on the wall to another, I thought to myself not *There's a name for this behavior*, but rather *This is our weirdo love*.

"Did the Devil Boy follow you home today?" my boyfriend would ask in the evening.

"I think so," I'd answer, my voice cocktail-party light, as if we were chatting over finger foods. The truth, however, was that I was out of sorts, pale and tired. I craved sleep. My digestion was off. I awoke in the wee hours burping acid. "Someone's been watching me."

"Be careful. Don't let any bad guys in."

We talked like this, like we were winking at one another, using poor James as a lever on which to hoist our relationship.

My boyfriend took things to the next level gradually: a dead mouse nestled in my work bag, a bat pinioned against my pillow with two earrings I no longer wore. Strangely, fear worked a sort of magic. We did not speak of these pranks, but a closeness grew once more between us. I could feel my boyfriend watching me, sensed his excitement whenever I drew closer to one of his surprises. It was for him, I suppose, titillating.

And indeed, our intimacy had increased in frequency. I am not a woman who talks openly of such things, but my boyfriend seemed to be overcoming an inherent awkwardness, growing more confident. I won't reduce my boyfriend's actions to a mere bedroom game. But there was this—a side effect, an unintended benefit of our bizarre triangle.

At work, I continued to see James.

"I feel like I've always known you," he said to me one day. We were going through some of his school assignments, and he'd paused, looking up at me with those large amber eyes. "I wish I could live at your house, Miss Beth Ann. I wish I could live with you."

He nuzzled his head against my arm, and I let him, even though I'd been trained to avoid such contact. It seemed only natural to allow for such basic human warmth.

James sighed, shifting against me. I'll admit: I'd begun to fantasize about bringing him into our household. A son. I imagined the three of us eating quiet breakfasts together on Saturday mornings or walking down to the farmers market under the big overpass—although so far in the investigation of James's current foster placement, there'd been no evidence of any problems.

"Please? Miss Beth Ann?"

We were in the windowless conference room that smelled like cheap pine cleaning fluid and cheese puffs. I allowed myself the luxury of kissing his dark head ever so lightly.

"We can't," I whispered. "It's not allowed."

This was an oversimplification, but it made things easier.

"Why?" he wheedled.

I sighed. "Miss Tawny makes us follow the rules here," I said. A coward's move.

"I hate her," he said, his voice turning to a whimper. "Miss Nancy, too."

"No, no," I said, shushing him. I drew him close to me. Even at thirteen, he was still such a baby that I could hold him on my lap like I did my four-year-old nephew. His breath was feathery against my neck, ticklish. We had room in our apartment. We hardly used our study; it could become a child's bedroom. James twisted against me, one of his fingers tracing a small circle on my forearm.

"I love you, Miss Beth Ann," he whispered. "I love you."

I cannot tell you the thrill those words gave me. My boy, my own little boy. There was a surge of something, something so pure that even now I don't believe it was sullied by what came afterward. I believe that, however brief, this moment was real.

I held James, letting him cry quietly against me. I held him until his crying slowed, and I felt him going still in my arms. I rocked him gently, shushing him. This, I thought, was how mothers felt when their baby calmed. I dared not move so as not to disturb him. Overcome with exhaustion, I let myself close my own eyes, feeling his warm weight relaxed fully in my arms. We would both take a short rest, I told myself.

When I opened my eyes again, I was aware of something not right: a very specific pressure and suction, new yet also deeply familiar to the primitive part of my brain. My skin felt cool. My shirt was unbuttoned. There was James, his warm lamprey-mouth at work on my nipple. With one hand he tugged my breast downward. I felt his tongue, his teeth careful against my tender skin: a perfect latch. Nursing. A cruel parody. Mammalian and grotesque.

"James!"

He released my nipple with a pop and looked up at me with a malicious little smile.

I was aware now of a wiriness to him, a strength that went beyond his baby softness and reminded me he was on the brink of adolescence. He squirmed in my lap, and I felt the sharp bones of his pelvis pressing against me like a threat. He batted my breast away, almost playfully. I yanked my shirt up, covering myself, and shoved him off.

He looked at me, amused, sneering. I wanted to weep. I wanted to make him weep also. He had ruined it all. He had ruined everything.

The flat of my hand flew toward him, smacking him, hard.

He stepped back, eyes widened, momentarily surprised. And then he grinned again.

I was on him then, all over him, my fists pummeling his face, his thin boy's chest, my fingernails scraping his arms. I slapped his face again so hard there was a red welt on his cheek. My hand stung. He stumbled back, still laughing, mocking me. Egging me on.

A raw feeling like a scream tore through me. Maybe I did scream. What I know is that my hands were operating outside my control—demonic things, fists and claws and talons, and then I was squeezing him, my hands around his neck, and I swear to God, even then he was grinning at me. Like evil. Like the devil himself.

The door opened.

"What in the world."

Tawny stood there, a look on her face I'd never seen before. I released James, my arms falling limply to my sides. I could feel my whole self melting, sweat moving in rivulets beneath my arms. My breathing was ragged, like someone finishing a long run. James looked at Tawny blandly.

The light in his amber eyes seemed to have dulled, but he smirked again—mean and knowing. Two of the buttons of my shirt were still undone, my mouth too dry to speak. I could see the red marks from where I'd dug my nails into his neck.

"What in the world," Tawny repeated.

It wasn't a question, and no one responded for several long seconds.

James eventually sighed like he was bored.

"Miss Beth Ann hurt me," he announced to Tawny. He stood there, staring at her, before making what appeared to be a slight bow and turning to leave the conference room. We followed him wordlessly to the reception.

Tawny and I watched James leave with Miss Nancy. The Devil Boy and his foster mother. She moved like someone much older, stooped, as if bracing against a great gale. He walked, docile, beside her. I'd only ever seen him obey her, although she told us what she believed he did to the other children at home. There were bite marks on his foster sister, a ring of bruises like a mauve collar along his younger foster brother's shoulders.

"I never catch him doing it," Miss Nancy had told me once, a few weeks earlier, shaking her head. "And I think the other children are too afraid of him to tell me. That's the devil for you."

After James and his foster mother had left, Tawny turned to me. She looked stricken, her skin the grayed-out color of an old movie.

"I should have taken his case myself." She rubbed her forehead, frowning. "What were you thinking. What the hell were you thinking." Again, she delivered this not like a question but like a bleak fact.

I'd thought I might explain myself, explain everything to her. But looking at her, I did not.

"I'll pack my stuff," I said instead. "I'll go."

She nodded, turning from me and going to her office, the door clicking shut behind her.

By the time I walked home, past the old train tracks, crunching through a layer of brown leaves, the sun was beginning to set. A siren passed, and then another. That's one thing I've grown used to in this city: quiet is never quiet. The sounds of sirens are always there, becoming a sort of persistent, forgettable background noise. If one is on high alert for long enough, one learns to tune things out. The body becomes numbed to fear, adapted to a constant state of stress.

Stress can also affect a woman's menstrual cycle, causing her to skip a period or be very late. This is a fact, one that I'd been repeating to myself for the past three weeks. Because at my age. Because what were the odds, really. Because in all likelihood it was nothing.

I remembered that early on in our relationship, my boyfriend and I were eating tapas together at a restaurant when he'd mentioned something, a moment from his own boyhood involving a dog and a piece of rope. It shamed him.

"There are certain things you just don't want to pass on. Like a sickness you carry," he said, shaking his head and prodding his fork into the plate of calamari. Like a savage, I'd thought briefly, before softening toward him. He was trying to do the very best he could.

At home, our apartment was eerily cool and still. My boyfriend was not yet home from his office, but one window was open, letting in a waft of car fumes and garbage from the street below. My phone rang. It was my boyfriend, checking to make sure I was home.

"I lost my job," I told him. For the first time that day, I could feel tears welling up. I was not one to cry, not ordinarily. "I got fired."

"It's okay," my boyfriend said into the phone, so calm he was nearly triumphant. "I'll take care of you. I've said that all along."

"I messed up," I said, my voice finally breaking.

"I'll be home soon," he said, and then, fondly, a singsonginess to his words: "Home to my girl. Don't let any bad guys in."

I hung up the phone, needing a glass of water. In the kitchen, a plastic spider inside the water pitcher greeted me like an old friend, a joke told so many times it had worn thin. All the bland whites of the kitchen—refrigerator, countertops, curling linoleum floor—blurred into a hazy nothingness, a shapeless expanse looming in front of me like a long series of blank boxes on a calendar. Endless days, all the same.

I gulped the water so fast my throat burned cold.

Then: a knocking at my door, tentative at first, but growing louder, more insistent, as if the person knew I was inside, expectant, alone. Shave and a haircut . . . two bits. Another little joke, the knock of someone who already had a key.

I knew it must be my boyfriend. I knew that he would hold me in his arms and comfort me, surround me with himself until I could see nothing else— not the bad, rough edges of the world, not anything. Only us, our private jokes, our little intimacies. But for a moment, I pretended I did not know who it was. I pretended I had not already welcomed this stranger, had not already invited him in.

MR. FORBLE

THE TREES SEEMED TO HUNCH CLOSER AS DARKNESS FELL.
Something—a mouse, or maybe a squirrel—emitted a high-pitched shriek, and Marta startled. An owl, she thought. The notion of being seen by something invisible, a creature swooping noiselessly onto its prey, unnerved her. Owls could rotate their heads because of special contractile reservoirs in their cephalic arteries; she'd learned this fact at a natural science center event she'd taken Teddy to when he was little, and it had been one of the facts he'd repeated to her for some time afterward, during a brief obsession with raptors. The path she followed now was washed out, rippling and uneven with knobby roots, so she moved with care, picking her way forward. In daylight, the tree trunks rose white blond to the sky, filtering golden light, but now the shapes surrounding her had turned inky and strange.

"Teddy?" she called.

The sound of Marta's own voice was alarming, too loud.

The birthday party guests would all be home by now, safe in their pleasantly lit houses. There would be evening news reports, light dinners, the rinsing of plates and cups followed by the loading of dishwashers. Back under the park pavilion, the remnants of Teddy's double-layer Funfetti cake listed on the picnic table. The icing was probably studded with mosquitoes and gnats at this point. She'd been in such a hurry that she hadn't even covered the cake, and the thought wouldn't have occurred to Doug, eager as he was to usher his own daughter away. All the other parents had stood there, dopey-eyed, useless, hands resting protectively on the shoulders of their own children for those first few seconds. Wary. You could feel it in the air, or at least Marta could—everyone was looking out for his or her own. The chatter had stopped, the party suddenly over. Later, of course, they'd recovered themselves, the other parents, in a flurry of perfunctory offers to help, but by then, she wanted none of it. She'd dismissed them all, brusquely. Her thoughts were only on finding her boy. You could say this for Teddy: he knew how to make an exit.

Marta walked across the little wooden plank bridge that she remembered from other visits during daylight hours, recalled how it crossed a little creek in which springtime minnows darted. The creek dwindled to almost nothing in the summer. "Where do the fish all go?" Teddy had asked her once, the water then nothing but a reddish-brown thread. She'd shaken her head. "They disappear."

Marta's face was starting to ache already. Gone was the numb feeling, and now she felt a dull throb, the sensation of her flesh starting to swell like fruit past its ripeness. She touched her nose and cheekbone lightly, wondering if something was broken. There were fourteen bones in the human face: another fact she knew because of Teddy. She could picture him, only a few years earlier, his face boyish still, beaming up at her, offering these morsels like a cat presenting its owner with dead mice. Facts pleased him. "How precocious he is!" everyone said to her. At a certain point, Marta had realized that *precocious* was a word that carried its own malicious little twist. What at age six is precocious, by age thirteen becomes simply odd.

Up ahead, there rose a set of steps carved into the hillside—an ascending series of large, smooth stones laid into the packed earth. Marta and Teddy and Rick had taken the dog out here many Saturdays back when Teddy was younger, back when Rick was still living and they were a unit, a family. They'd watched as the dog scampered joyously ahead of them, leaping two paws at a time, snuffling underbrush. The path was a loop. There was a little bench at the top of the rise where the three of them would sit together, drinking water from canteens and eating bagels Marta packed. It was some of their best time together. Teddy had enjoyed it, or so it seemed. He'd enjoyed it as much as he enjoyed anything; it became part of their weekly rhythm. This was before Rick's diagnosis, before his long decline, before Teddy had started spending every minute he had alone in his room, going wherever boys went on their computers these days—online games featuring bright terrain and anachronistic weaponry, chats with friends in Sweden, message boards cluttered with cryptic posts. Places she did not want to know about.

She'd tried. Therapists, tutors, parenting books. No one could fault her efforts.

Marta almost expected to find Teddy sitting there at their old bench, waiting for her. Crying, maybe. When was the last time she'd seen him cry? Probably in third grade, after Kaitlin Richard's boy played that prank. One of many he'd endured, but this one could have killed Teddy. Kids didn't appreciate the seriousness of allergies. Kaitlin had called her, of course, apologetic. Kaitlin had punished Michael, done everything a good parent ought to do. And Marta had understood on some level. Teddy invited prankery, mischief; he stood out among the other boys in his class, a serious little old man, long-jawed and morose. Puberty had hit him too early, rendering him a halfling, more satyr than human boy. His responses, even to her, were always slightly offbeat. Sometimes she got the feeling he did it on purpose, taking a perverse satisfaction in provoking meanness out of others, like it proved him right.

Recently he'd become more obstinate, refusing family dinners, burrowing away in his bedroom. She offered to take him for haircuts, new clothes.

He declined, barely looking up at her, his face awash in the bluish light of his laptop. So when he'd asked her for a birthday party, the first in years, she'd been delighted. There he stood in a yellow-pitted T-shirt, his hair mussed, a line of dried saliva visible down his chin. She'd been so delighted she'd hugged him, not even minding how he stiffened, or that smell of his: sour and faintly murine. A birthday party. Of course. He would have a birthday party. She would make sure of it.

But did thirteen-year-olds still have birthday parties? Marta was vaguely aware that the other kids Teddy's age had transitioned to inviting a couple of friends out to dinner, or to the new cineplex with plush reclining seats, or over for a pizza and game night. She'd asked him if he might not like to invite some friends for dinner and a movie night instead, if that's what his classmates were doing.

"I want a party like when I was a kid," Teddy had told her. "Like when I was little and Dad was here."

She'd winced when he'd said this. Doug had been over at the time, grilling salmon on the patio. Perhaps that was what led Marta to respond so enthusiastically.

"Of course," she said. "We can go to the park just like we used to. Your favorite cake and everything."

Teddy looked back at her blandly.

She recalled a moment a few years earlier when she'd found Teddy in her bedroom, poring through his father's prized baseball card collection, the old photo album of their honeymoon open on the floor beside him. A photo of young Rick in bathing trunks beamed up at her. Rick had treasured those baseball cards, would have been thrilled to see his son admiring them. Teddy was a good boy deep down.

On the porch, Doug and his daughter, eleven-year-old Emmeline, were laughing while the fillets cooked. They looked like an advertisement for something summery, fabric softener or clean white bed linen. Oh, to have such a normal child! Doug always corrected her gently when she said this. He was a family therapist and quick to point out the diversity of individual gifts. "That's easy for you to say," she would respond, "seeing as you have a normal child." The air was delicious with the scent of salmon on the grill, teriyaki glaze. Teddy, of course, refused to eat salmon. There were basically only three foods he ate: Goldfish crackers, hot dogs, and oatmeal. She'd stopped fighting him on it. It wasn't worth the battle.

"Marta," Doug said, entering from the porch with the grill tongs still in hand. He pecked her on the cheek, and Teddy flinched.

"We're planning a birthday party," she said brightly, gritting her teeth into something like a smile.

"Fantastic!" he responded, always game. Doug was, on the face of it, a very good sport.

But the party had been the opposite of fantastic, and now here she was in the woods, alone, as it grew even darker. There was a bit of ambient light from a distant neighborhood, and a sliver of moon was up, but even so it was difficult for Marta to see more than a yard ahead. Her face pulsed steadily, like a living thing she carried separate from herself, bruised and humming.

"Teddy! Let's go home, please!"

Something grabbed her foot—a cruel, hard hand jerking her down—and she flew forward, smacking the ground so hard that her breath was knocked out. She lay there, stunned.

She'd prepared so hopefully, with the cake, the streamers, the snacks Teddy had requested: SunChips and cotton candy ice cream and Mountain Dew, things he said the other kids liked. But then, for the entirety of the party, Teddy had appeared aloof, distracted. He'd barely talked to the other boys, sitting by himself on one of the park benches. His eyes rose expectantly every now and then, surveying the parking lot for some late arrival. It was like none of it, none of her efforts, even interested him.

At one point, when the other guests were playing cornhole and badminton with more enthusiasm than she'd expected—because the rest of these boys and girls, his classmates, were not such bad kids, really, when it came down to it—she'd grabbed Teddy by the elbow, jerking him toward her.

"What? What's wrong?" she'd hissed at him. "What are you waiting for?"

"Nothing," he'd said, pulling away from her, his voice gruff with tears. And she knew then he'd been wishing for something she was incapable of providing, incapable of even fathoming. All this—the party and streamers— was for naught.

Marta let the good side of her face rest on the ground where she'd fallen. Maybe she would just lie here all night. She had no idea where she'd left her phone; it probably sat, useless, beside the remains of the cake. She could feel the looping tree root that had snagged her foot, her ankle turned at such an odd angle that she could barely consider it without feeling queasy. Already she could tell it would not bear her weight.

The woods around her held a foreboding kind of quiet now. Marta felt the steady throb of her face and ankle but refused to cry. A sound like firecrackers went off somewhere in the middle distance, puncturing the silence.

Then came a crunching of leaves—footsteps, someone coming up the path behind her—and she could tell from the heaviness of the tread that it was not Teddy, but rather someone fully grown. Whoever it was, she could hardly lift her head to look at him.

It was Teddy's thirteenth birthday. All at once she felt very old.

After the party stopped abruptly—not the way he'd planned, but still—everyone stood there like morons with their plates of birthday cake and cups of soda, their sugar-sticky mouths hanging open like dummies, plastic spoons poised midair. Teddy had looked at them, wanting to howl in amusement, even though he could feel the tears welling up in his eyes. He'd shouted something stupid—the first words that came to him—about his mom being a bitch, an idiot, forcing out a hoarse laugh. Before anyone could respond, he'd fled. He'd run up the familiar path, agile and sure-footed. They'd come here all the time with the dog when he was little. Then he sat there for a while at the top of the rise, hidden just behind a cluster of trees, catching his breath and waiting for his mother to come find him.

None of it had gone off. Nothing he'd planned. He was uncertain what he wanted now. For his mom to come and wrap her arms around him, murmuring words of comfort? *Oh, my sweet Teddy, my special one.* Even though he'd hit her. Hard. She loved him stupidly and could not help herself. Teddy attributed this to some fixed rule of evolutionary biology, the cell's love for its cellular line: bullshit. He hated her for it, hated himself for craving solace from her. It felt pitiful, the way he lapped up his mother's soothing—something written into his genes, a dumb biochemical inheritance over which he also had no choice.

Maybe she would understand implicitly, not even expecting him to apologize. Or maybe she would be accompanied by Idiot Doug. Doug of the graying hippie ponytail and all-season Tevas, with his Kabbalah bracelet and therapy talk. Everything with Doug was about *appreciating dialectics* or *wise mind*. It was all enough to make you want to punch him in the face, an urge that Teddy had always resisted. Punching Doug in the face, however satisfying, would have accomplished nothing.

Teddy had learned to watch Doug with the same immobile calm he'd beheld in the copperhead they'd once found sunning itself in their front drive: slit-eyed and motionless, biding its time. The less he reacted, the more Doug danced, desperate for friendship, approval, any reaction. It was pathetic. In a small way, withholding made Teddy glad. Of course, ultimately, he'd ended up punching his mom instead.

He was growing bored sitting there. It was a little surprising no one had come to find him yet. A crew of ants had been hauling the dead body of a wasp near his feet. He watched for a while, studying the elegant machinery of the wasp's wings, its beaky proboscis, the up-close tiny horror of its face. Teddy placed his hand down nearby, letting the ants crawl over his fingers. It was a strange sensation, not unpleasant.

An evening bird gave a hiccuping call off in the distant underbrush. Maybe his mother had given up. Maybe she wasn't coming, just like the guy hadn't come. You couldn't trust half of what you found on the internet. His mom always said that. And yet he'd always had good luck sourcing things online in the past: weed, acid, a surprisingly realistic-looking Russian passport, some kind of sketchy supplement called Dick Enhancer that came in a little white envelope with a crude sketch of a rearing stallion on it. Why not expect that the guy would come through, too?

He'd had excellent customer reviews: *Trouble. Havoc. Mayhem. Your hands kept clean! Mr. Forble delivers.* Naturally, the listing had caught Teddy's eye. The guy had a felon's inventiveness—nothing too large or too small. All for a fee. Teddy could get the money; he had his dad's old baseball card collection. "Take good care of these," his mom had told him, way back when Teddy still wore footie pajamas. "They're going to help us pay for your college." But the guy online had taken Teddy's money and no-showed. The reviews were probably all fake. Although maybe, apart from having lost the baseball cards, it was for the best that he hadn't come. Teddy considered this, poking the anthill with a stick. And yet—the thought of their faces. For one satisfying moment, he could have sat back and just watched. He would have called things off before it went too far.

Flicking the ants off his hand one by one, he heard her voice.

"Teddy!" his mother shouted, and the way she said his name made something hurt inside him, like a hard crust wedged in his throat. Reflexively, he froze behind the nearest tree, as if he were still a child and they were playing hide-and-seek.

He'd hit her hard, his fist landing on her face with a sickening smack. It had felt exhilarating, just for a moment, like a release of some pent-up bodily need—finally taking a piss after holding it so long your whole gut ached. Something like that. Even after the guy hadn't shown up, even with his disappointment that the whole thing hadn't gone off as he'd envisioned. Hitting his mother hadn't been part of the plan. But he'd felt a physical high for a split second. She'd flinched, turning away and pressing a hand to her nose. When she'd turned to look up at him afterward, though, he'd seen the worst thing of all: she wasn't surprised. She'd been expecting this from him his whole life. There was a resignation on her face that he recognized. Resignation, and dumb, bovine, unimpeachable love.

He'd watched Doug tighten his arms around smug little Emmeline. Emmeline with her straight-As and summer musical camps and too-cheery voice. Emmeline, who sang to animals and said hello to every passerby, like a nauseating cartoon princess. There was the way Doug's lips curled upward then, too—the look of someone who found the whole thing slightly amusing, someone suppressing an I-told-you-so.

Teddy should have finally punched Doug as well and been done with it, but instead, he'd thrown the jug of lemonade against the wall and ran. The jug—plastic and half full—landed with a heartless *thwat* that even Teddy could appreciate was anticlimactic.

A low rumble passed overhead. It could have been thunder, but he knew that there was a back road just over the rise, beyond where the trail ended. A truck, he thought, and for some reason he shivered. It was getting cooler now that the sun was setting. He'd left his jacket in the car.

His mother appeared on the path below.

She was moving slowly, unsteadily, off into the brush away from the trail. She looked winded and baggy, and this only made him angrier at her, her weakness a personal affront. He squinted to bring her into his sights, pulling back his trigger finger on an imaginary rifle and letting his bullet find its target. Bull's-eye. He nodded to himself.

As if on cue, she stumbled, smacking the ground with a heavy thud. He sucked in his breath, fighting the urge to call to her. He felt a pang of something that wasn't quite sadness.

There was a *pop-pop-pop* in the distance, like an engine backfiring. His forehead went cool and slick, as if he were coming down with the flu, his armpits gone sticky.

It was hours after the time they'd agreed upon, but he was struck with a sense of certainty.

Mr. Forble was coming after all. Mr. Forble was already here.

Michael sat in the front seat of his mom's car fiddling with her satellite radio. He had a sick feeling, a mixture of the cake and caffeine and carbonation roiling in his gut, but probably also because he got a kind of sick feeling whenever he saw that kid Teddy. He'd tried to explain it to his mom, but she didn't understand, or else felt too guilty. She was still so hung up on that prank they'd played with the peanut butter in Ms. Pendergraff's third-grade class. It hadn't even been his idea, but he'd been the one designated to carry it out. How were they supposed to have known? They weren't trying to kill anybody. It was a joke. And look at Teddy—he turned out fine. Or, maybe not *fine*, but peanut butter wasn't his problem.

"Of course we're going," Michael's mom had said when the invitation arrived. "We're going, and you're going to be happy about it."

Sometimes, when Teddy looked at him, Michael could swear he was wishing him dead. That's what Carter Blanchard always said: "Teddy Yarborough over there shooting death beams out his eyes again." Then they would all laugh, him and Carter and Tyler and Dylan and Griff, releasing the tension, and it would feel okay, but seriously, that kid Teddy could give you a creepy feeling. He was too big for his age, all hunched up in the classroom desks like a weird narc. He already had facial hair, or at least a dark line of fuzz over his upper lip. Michael was an avid and jealous student of the signs of puberty in others. His own underarms were still perfectly hairless and smooth, like nectarines, but he'd learned to laugh and deflect.

He could see his mom walking in a loop over by the trash cans, near the big sign that showed a map of the intersecting trails and trailheads. She was on her phone. "It's work," she'd said. "I might as well take this here. We can wait a second, just to make sure Teddy's mom finds him. Just in case they need anything. You sit tight." It was never just a second, though. He watched her, pacing around the recycling bins, gesturing with her hands. He could see the nervous way she kept brushing her hair back, a tic of hers. All the other party guests had already left. The only other car in the lot belonged to Teddy's mom.

Michael turned the radio to NPR, his mother's preferred station, and let the smooth voices comfort him. He never bothered to listen to what they were saying, but it was pleasant hearing the familiar chiming musical interludes, the voices polished and calm, intelligent-sounding. Verbalizing the world into a kind of order. Sort of like his mom. She was all right, really. She did important work for the school board, and people in town respected her for it.

Once, when Carter and Dylan had both been at his house spending the night, Carter had said to him, like it was a revelation, "Dude, your mom's actually kind of hot." And he'd tackled Carter, rolling with him like two puppies on the floor until finally things had resolved into breathless laughter. It was true, although uncomfortable to admit: she *was* kind of hot. But Carter was just saying it the way he said a lot of things, to get a rise out of people. Carter had also told them that Teddy was having sex already—with Ukrainian prostitutes he hired online, big-titted sluts with hairy legs, according to Carter, which was hilarious. A lie, certainly. But with Teddy, you could almost believe it.

Michael's mother was sweeping one hand through the air in a slicing motion now, a gesture he recognized. He was aware of a dull rising ache from his pelvis, a fullness in his bladder from all the soda. Walking back to the bathrooms over by the picnic shelter seemed an impossible task, though. Maybe he would just hold it until he got home.

He wondered if Teddy's mom had found him, if Teddy had apologized. He'd heard a crunch like a seashell under the heel of a shoe when Teddy had hit her. "Damn, son!" Carter had whispered under his breath, and ordinarily, Michael would have laughed obligingly, but he hadn't felt like it.

Prior to that, the party hadn't been so bad, really. It reminded him of the parties they'd always had in elementary school—wholesome fun, the entire class invited. There'd been that awkward moment when he'd run into Teddy in the bathroom. Michael, baby-faced and good-natured, a little chubby even, was well aware of which way the power tipped. His only advantage came when he moved en masse with the other boys. Man-to-man, Teddy was more imposing.

Teddy was leaning against the wall near the urinals when Michael walked in. He'd glanced up, nodding curtly at Michael. The bathroom was bare and cold, filled with spiderwebs and the husks of dead insects piled in the corners. Michael wanted to pee and get out.

Teddy moved away from the urinals to the sink, focusing on the video playing on his phone. Michael stood for a few seconds, nervous, trying to relax his mind. He always got pee-shy. Finally, he went. Zipping his fly, he walked over to the sink.

"Happy birthday, Teddy," he offered feebly.

Teddy continued to concentrate on his phone. At little intervals, he laughed, and Michael could see orange bits of food caught behind the tines of his braces.

"If you want soap, there isn't any," Teddy said without looking up.

Michael shrugged. He rinsed his hands off anyway, wiping them on his jeans.

"Whatever. I think your mom brought sanitizer."

Teddy's gaze was still locked on his phone. He grinned, amused at something Michael couldn't see. Flashes of color reflected off the lenses of his glasses. Michael wanted to leave, but Teddy was blocking the door. The others would be wondering what was taking so long. Carter tended to crack jokes whenever someone spent too long in the bathroom. "Trouble changing your tampon?" he'd say, which was stupid but always left Michael red-faced.

"Look," Teddy said, thrusting his phone in front of Michael. "Tell me what you think."

It took him a second to piece together what was happening in the clip.

Movement, flashes of color, fleshy shapes—once he was oriented, he could identify the specific body parts in motion. Then he saw someone sitting in a chair, begging to be let go. The video was grainy, the lighting poor. A jangly soundtrack. Laughter at one point, a goading voice.

Michael was growing increasingly uncomfortable. He wanted to look away, but Teddy was very close to him, so close that Michael could smell his unwashed odor. The phone was right in his face. Michael shifted himself away.

"Wait for it," Teddy said, moving closer, his breath in Michael's face. "There."

"Oh, God," Michael said, pushing the phone back reflexively. He leaned away from Teddy, pressing his hands to his knees, breathing like he'd just finished a race in gym class. A wave of clamminess passed over him, his vision narrowing so that he blinked hard, trying not to pass out. "That's not real, is it?"

Teddy was full-on grinning now, the entirety of his silver orthodontia revealed. He slipped the phone into his back pocket, opening the bathroom door so that the late afternoon sunlight fell in an oblong shape onto the concrete floor.

"You're not so bad, are you?" Teddy said, his expression inscrutable. "Spineless. But gentle."

Michael didn't answer. Were Carter Blanchard saying this, it would clearly be mockery. With Teddy, he wasn't so sure. Michael wanted to leave. And never watch that video again.

"Anyways, have a good birthday," he muttered.

He was halfway out the door when Teddy grabbed him by the shirtsleeve.

"Hey, I like you, so I'll let you in on a little secret," he said, and he whispered into Michael's ear, his breath ticklish. "Tell your mom you want to leave early. Before the cake. Before the piñata. Tell her you don't feel good or something. Trust me."

He released Michael's shirt and winked.

Michael had barely seen Teddy for the rest of the party. He'd whispered to his mother at the first opportunity that he wanted to leave, that he felt sick and needed to go home, but she'd shaken her head. "Uh-unh, sir. Not today. We're staying."

And so they stayed. The singing of "Happy Birthday" had sounded a melancholy note in Michael's ear, and the lighting of the candles on the cake added a touch of menace. He'd felt jumpy, overly alert, ready to bolt.

But then nothing had happened.

He saw it in Teddy's face, though: Teddy had been expecting something. It hadn't just been a joke, what he'd whispered in the bathroom. It had been a genuine warning. And after whatever it was hadn't taken place, after the candles and the cake, Teddy, in frustration, had punched his mother. Boom. Right in the jaw.

You had to feel bad for Teddy's poor mom, the way she'd looked, bug-eyed and afraid, and yet, Michael had experienced a wave of relief. The party was finished. Done. They could all go home.

He could go home, that is, if his mom would ever finish up her phone call. It was dark now. The lights over the parking lot came on with a pop and a click. Michael could see his mother, still pacing over by the picnic hut, phone pressed to her ear. He pressed the radio button again, finding a pop station. Some cheesy song was playing, a happy song about being happy, and since no one was around, he turned it up.

The music was loud enough that he didn't hear the truck pull into the lot. When he glanced up again, there it was: a rusted reddish Ford one space over from him. He turned the music down, careful to keep his eyes straight ahead.

In the side-view mirror, he saw the driver's-side door of the truck open and a very tall man slide out. The man wore jeans, a dark shirt, and boots. Michael could see that he walked with a mincing sort of limp. He carried a long stick—a baton? Or some kind of cane?—that was black and gnarled. He waved to Michael, but Michael kept his gaze straight ahead, pretending not to see.

And then the man was rapping on the passenger-side window with the stick. Michael wasn't sure whether to answer or to call out to his mom, who had moved out of sight. He remembered a snippet from the video Teddy had shown him—one specific and horrible frame—although why this should enter his mind at just that moment, he couldn't say.

He took a breath, turning to look him directly in the face. Before the man even spoke, Michael felt a tingling in the soles of his feet. The man had arrived like an answer to a question Michael hadn't realized he'd even asked.

"Hello, little guy," the man said through the window. "I'm late."

Emmeline's roommate is scraggly-haired and morose, a techy kid from some rural backwater who, instead of going to class, forever sits in their dorm room wearing noise-canceling headphones and cackling over YouTube videos. While Emmeline is out forming friendships, trying out for the fall musical, meeting up with classmates for study sessions in the library, Emmeline's roommate posts comments: on video clips and Instagram posts and Reddit threads and multiplayer gaming sites. Her name is Flo. She has long, pale, mosquito-bitten legs—a wonder, since Emmeline has never seen her go outside—and large, unblinking eyes. "Psychopath eyes," one of Emmeline's friends said, although Emmeline shushed her, because Flo is not so bad really, and because Emmeline believes she has known a true psychopath, although she does not mention this. When people ask Emmeline about her roommate, she shrugs. "She's an Internet commenter," Emmeline explains, like it's a vocation. For Flo, it is a vocation. All hours of the day, Flo's face is bathed in the bright light of her laptop screen, aglow as if she's in the presence of something holy.

It is freshman year: first-year, as they're supposed to call it. For Emmeline, the university is something from a dream—lush green lawns, stately buildings with columns and domes, libraries filled with a solemn quiet as pages are softly turned. It all inspires in Emmeline a kind of awe. She is bright and well adjusted. She has earned this; this is what her father, three hours away, tells her over the phone. She can hear the whistle of their pet cockatiel in the background and knows her dad is in the kitchen. She pictures him: pony-tailed, in jeans and sandals, like an aging community-theater Jesus. It is just the two of them, plus the cockatiel, whose name is Petey. She wonders if her father is lonely. It has always been her tendency to wonder about the inner lives of others, even if she is careful to conceal this, to appear buoyant and harmless so as not to make people uncomfortable. Her life has been more or less charmed; she knows this, and she knows, too, that this makes her curiosity a little unfair.

So one warm fall night when she comes home to the dorm crying after a cast party, she hopes that Flo won't notice—not because she is ashamed, but because it feels like a thing over which she ought not to trouble Flo. Her sadness is genuine, but it is also mundane, and even from within it, she can hold on to the awareness that it is small. It will pass. She will feel happy again.

Flo glances up when Emmeline walks into their room. The room is dark, Flo's side a morass of empty potato chip bags and stray articles of clothing. A video is playing on Flo's computer. Emmeline, stubbing her sandaled toe on a massive sociology textbook, cannot help but kick the offending book out of her way, issuing a great, frustrated moan. Insult on top of injury.

"What's wrong?" Flo asks, pushing back her headphones so that Emmeline can see her ears for once. They look raw and pinkish, almost private, Emmeline is so unaccustomed to seeing them. The sight fills Emmeline with tenderness.

"Oh, nothing," she says, wiping under her eyes, where she can feel her mascara running. "Dumb boy stuff."

Flo nods knowingly, then pats the corner of her bed.

"Here," she says. "I'll show you something interesting." She types into the search bar on YouTube, and a number of videos pop up in the results.

She turns to Emmeline and clasps her hand, as if it is a thing Flo has studied in theory but not had opportunity to practice. Emmeline appreciates it, nonetheless.

"You've heard of Mr. Forble, right?"

Emmeline can see in the YouTube results the thumbnails and descriptions of videos: *Mr. Forble Visit 1, Mr. Forble Visit 27, Mr. Forble Comes to Kentucky, Mr. Forble Takes Manhattan*. Now she recalls. It is one of those recent viral memes, another internet hoax, like the one about a horrible bird-faced woman daring children to commit suicide.

But looking at the results on Flo's computer, something funny and familiar pulls her. Flo pivots the laptop toward Emmeline, and she leans closer. She rests her hand on Flo's touch pad and selects one video in particular. There is something in the frame: a face she might have seen before, or an expression she recognizes. It is nothing, but she hesitates.

"Mr. Forble," Flo says, nodding toward the screen. "People say he's all about vengeance."

Emmeline clicks on the clip, and it is blurry, a chase scene through a field, someone running after someone until there is a muffled sound, the footage swinging wildly from sky to darkness, followed by a strange, low laughter.

"Weird," Emmeline says, and she has stopped crying now. It's the laughter she recognizes. It is the laughter that's familiar.

"There are better ones," Flo says, and she brushes Emmeline's hand away gently, scrolling down through more results. *Mr. Forble Comes to Dinner, Mr. Forble Airport, Mr. Forble Prom, Mr. Forble Office Party #3, Mr. Forble Meets the Parents*.

Emmeline has placed the laughter now. It is the wild, angry laughter of someone trying not to cry. It is the laughter of her former stepbrother—or her former almost-stepbrother, the son of her dad's girlfriend—creepy Teddy, who disappeared after he punched his mother at his birthday party. Teddy had legitimately scared her, Emmeline recalled, and when he'd run away, she hadn't been as bothered as maybe she should have been. Things ended between her dad and his mom not long afterward; relationships cannot withstand certain stressors, certain losses, her dad had said. The truth is she'd sensed tension between her father and Teddy's mom long before the disappearance. Weeks had passed, months, with no trace of him. "Poor Teddy," her father said, but she could tell that he'd been a little relieved.

"They say Mr. Forble comes when you call," Flo says, and she smiles a little sadly. "But there's always a catch."

She selects another clip and shifts in her chair so they can both easily see. It is a bare room, empty but for a chair. A boy sits, his hands bound. The video is well done, Emmeline must admit, authentic-looking and eerily reminiscent of a recurring nightmare from her own childhood. What happens next looks almost real. Emmeline recoils, but forces herself to keep watching. She hates watching stuff like this. But it's nothing—a simulacrum, a deep fake, low-fi guerilla horror.

Flo exhales. "See?"

Emmeline swallows before she speaks. Her tears have dried now. She's pleased with herself not to have been duped.

"Play it one more time."

THE FIELD GLASSES

FOR WEEKS MY SISTER CLARA HAD BEEN WARNING ME
that there was something in the woods that wanted to eat the children.

"Hush, Clara," I said when I found her staring off, trying to discern whatever shape lurked out in the pines and lindens beyond our back porch. "Come inside."

She startled and turned, and I saw she'd been using the field glasses. They were lovely, unusual—hand-carved from smooth blond wood. I hadn't seen them in years.

"Here," she said, almost sheepishly, handing the field glasses to me. They were mine. I would put them back, tucking them away in the drawer where they belonged.

A deer emerged, eyeing us warily before bolting back into the foliage. Clara tensed beside me. She was, of course, frightened of deer. She was frightened of everything.

"The deer won't hurt anyone," I reminded her, touching her hand, but she wouldn't look at me.

From the time we'd been young girls, Clara had possessed what teachers and doctors had at first called simply an overactive imagination. This had been both magnificent and terrifying—Clara calling me over to whisper secrets she'd heard from the ants scurrying to and fro on their mound, Clara big-eyed at the portentousness of how a late summer shadow quivered, Clara interpreting the voices she heard murmuring within the grumble of our dryer. Everything, for Clara, was too acute, too vivid—always a mystery to be unpacked. She became a medium for messages I was too dull to discern.

I was boring by comparison. Eleanor, the grounded twin. Clara, the creative, sensitive one. Throughout our childhood, our mother dressed us like matching dolls in ruffled pinafores with big pink ribbons in our hair. We sang sister-sister duets together at the county fair, stepping daintily over sawdust and wood chips in our patent leather shoes. We sang like songbirds, our mother said. Like something celestial. A pair of angels, the old judges remarked. Always, as children, we were reminded of our exalted twin-ness.

On the porch, Clara tightened her grip on the railings as if she were on a roller coaster preparing for a sudden plummet. I watched her face, a hundred different emotions flickering over it in quick succession, something I'd only otherwise seen on the face of a sleeping baby. In such moments, she was lost to me, attuned to another plane entirely. She blinked rapidly then and turned toward me.

"I don't know, Ellie," she said slowly, carefully, as if waking from a curious dream. "I just don't know."

I led her back inside, and we sat together for a hot cup of our favorite rooibos. Like our mother, I believed in the power of a cup of tea to soothe, but Clara was sensitive to caffeine. I'd also put out the little jam cookies Clara was partial to. We were two proper ladies in this way—frugal in our habits yet still prone to small indulgences. *Old maids.* I imagined the neighbors, with their Priuses and laughing broods in soccer cleats, referring to us as such.

Two nice, old-fashioned storybook spinsters who just happened to live in this wooded neighborhood filled now with young families.

"Oliver shouldn't bring Peter," Clara finally said. "Now isn't the time. He wouldn't be safe here. Not with that thing in the woods."

I coughed on my cookie. Oliver was our cousin, Peter his young son, whom we adored. Peter came to stay with us every summer while Oliver traveled for work. His visit had been planned for months.

"There are plenty of children in the neighborhood, and they're all doing just fine," I said. "You're overwrought."

Overwrought was a word our mother had taken to using in speaking about Clara, her sudden fits and preferences, her cloudbursts of emotion.

She shook her head, the cup of tea trembling in her lap.

"I'm not," she said. "I promise. I'm not."

She appeared so fragile sitting there, my sister, my other half. Even now in her late sixties, my sister had kept her long, smooth legs, her knees still knobby and coltish, giving her an almost girlish look. Her hair was still ash blonde, like my own. She had a long nose and pale lashes and watery blue eyes: my mirror self. We were—are—identical, except for the pale, jagged scar on my sister's arm that I do not share. There is also the faint but persistent tremor in my sister's hands, whereas mine are firm and steady.

"Shh, shh."

I took my sister's cup from her and placed it gently on the table, wrapping my arms around her. This, I thought, is a sensation that few others get to experience: the sensation of comforting one's self, her body both utterly familiar and yet foreign, both known and unknown, like hearing your own voice on a recording. She sank against me, her head dropping to my chest, and once again, it occurred to me that we shared, as sisters, the physical dailiness of spouses. She shivered in my arms, and I wondered if she needed one of her pills.

Outside, I heard the caw of birds, the chirp of frogs calling from the creek, and suddenly felt aware of all the other living creatures.

She looked up at me with worried eyes, tracing the seam of her scar up the length of her arm. This was her habit whenever she was troubled, rubbing as if she might massage her arm back to its former smoothness.

"There's something hungry out there," she whispered again. "Something that would eat a child."

Likely, I would have forgotten these words soon enough. There would always be another fear, another premonition, that ebbed and flowed with passing months. This one, too, would have melted into the haze of unretrieved memory had it not happened that, only a few days later, the first child was bitten.

Where one ends up begins to feel inevitable, and so now I can say that it feels like I was always meant to end up here with my sister, two peas shriveling in their pod. But there was a time when things looked otherwise. There was a time when I was young and bold and in love.

At eighteen, I went off to the state teachers college, and Clara stayed home with our mother. She was too delicate, our mother said, to take on such demands. Not so for me, practical Eleanor. Stalwart, sturdy Eleanor, who loaded up a borrowed truck with suitcases and drove three hours away to the mountain town where I would be free. I wore my face like one who is undertaking a great and solemn duty, but in my heart, I exalted.

The secret is that it feels good to cut loose one's twin after having borne her for so long, like discarding a garment grown too small. No longer was I Eleanor, twin of Clara; I was simply Eleanor. I missed her, certainly. I missed our mother. But I read wonderful books and stayed up late laughing with my dormmates and drank too-strong drinks until I was giddy and graceful in the arms of boys from the neighboring college. I wore lipstick. I was kissed. The world opened swiftly and gently with its offerings. Sometimes, only rarely, did I think of Clara, warbling at the piano for our mother, alone.

It was there I met Preston. He was handsome like a young senator, with his dark hair arranged in a swoop above his forehead, his square jaw and generous smile. He was studying biology, a naturalist at heart who favored long tromps through mud and weedy creek beds. We fell in love, Preston and I. By the time I returned home to complete my student teaching, we were engaged. We were to marry within a year, after he completed his master's degree.

But then my mother got sick, and Clara and I quarreled. Preston and I broke our engagement. Mother died. I've stayed here ever since.

Still, a part of me believes that Preston is a good man, even now, after we haven't spoken in years. He remains, a faceless presence hovering just above me, in all my best and worst dreams.

Clara and I were working in our garden that morning before it got hot—she, trimming the rosebushes, while I pulled at the weeds that sprouted around our perennials. Our garden is the pride of the neighborhood. I like to think of it as part of our effort to live up to our role as two maiden ladies—maintaining our beautiful garden, offering lovely Halloween treats for the trick-or-treaters, delivering homemade shortbread to our neighbors whenever they bring home a new baby, ordering more wrapping paper from school fundraisers than we could ever possibly need. We are overlooked and yet integral to the workings of our little woodland grove. The children wave to us shyly, as if we are ancillary characters in their fairy tale.

"I need a drink of water," Clara told me, wiping her brow. She is sensitive to heat, and her medicines are dehydrating. I nodded, still clawing at a stubborn hunk of dandelion, and Clara vanished inside.

Minutes passed, and I was absorbed in the satisfaction of weeding. Clara did not return, but this was typical. Often, she became waylaid in the course of a simple task, and I would only find her later, thumbing through a magazine, staring out the window at an ordinary squirrel, or fast asleep on a couch.

Then I heard a child's yelp.

I paused. Often the sounds of children playing seem to me like howls of terror. It was probably a shriek of delight. But then the child screamed.

I shucked my gardening gloves and ran toward the sound, around the back of our house.

I found a dark-eyed girl of about four crying, holding her arm. I recognized her—the child of our neighbors two houses down, although I couldn't remember her name.

"It bit me," she said, holding out her chubby arm for me to behold. There, unmistakably in the plump flesh, were teeth marks and a faint beading of blood. The child's eyes filled with tears, and I knelt to encircle her at the waist, to offer comfort. There are some instincts that still have not left me.

"Shh, shh," I whispered. "Let's go wash this and find your mother."

The screen door clanged then, and there was my sister, bearing cotton swabs and a bottle of hydrogen peroxide.

"Coming, coming!" Clara shouted, holding the bottle aloft, her cheeks flushed.

The child flinched almost imperceptibly, drawing herself closer to me. I witnessed something primitive, an animal terror, in her eyes.

"It will only sting a minute," I said. "She needs to clean it out."

Clara smiled reassuringly, extending a cotton ball toward the little girl, but the girl twisted and pulled away.

"No!" she yelped, stomping on Clara's foot.

She ran from us and was gone. Clara took in a quick breath, splotches of pink rising up her neck.

"She was scared," I offered quickly. "We should go let her parents know." Clara nodded.

I looked out to the woods that stretched behind our house. The heat of the day was rising, swelling from the sunbaked ground. A distant bird cawed, but all else was quiet. In the trees, nothing rustled. Nothing moved.

"I told you," Clara whispered. Her voice was so quiet I could barely make out her words. "Peter shouldn't come."

I brushed a strand of hair from her forehead and led her inside before walking down the street to speak with the neighbors myself.

Soon afterward there were signs posted. *Beware of rabid animal.* No one knew for sure if that was actually the animal in question—perhaps it was a raccoon, or a fox, or a feral dog. What but a rabid creature would demonstrate such unprovoked aggression?

The affected children—there were three of them now—were all receiving postexposure prophylaxes just in case. Their descriptions of the animal varied—short, tall, hairy, fast, eyes like a rabbit, razor-sharp teeth—and weren't tremendously helpful. The children were all young enough to be unreliable.

"I'd like to catch it," my sister told me one morning, turning from our kitchen window. Toast crumbs trembled at the corner of her mouth, and I could see a faint smear of raspberry jam on her cheek, giving her a carnivorous look. "I really would." Her eyes gleamed like a bounty hunter, this sister of mine, alternately quaking and ferocious. "I'd catch it and bring back its hide. Problem solved."

"Someone will take care of it," I told her. "Animal control is searching. Everything will be fine by the time Peter arrives."

She looked away from me then.

"Clara? What is it?"

I heard her exhale, and then she was looking at me again, her jaw tightening.

"I already called Oliver. I told him not to bring Peter."

A muscle in my arm twitched, and I realized I was fighting the impulse to grab her.

"But, Clara. They already had tickets. It would have been fine."

I'd imagined the picnic we would take by the river walk, the bubbles we would blow on the porch. There was a little train for children two towns over, and I thought we might drive there one day, for a train ride and ice cream. I'd already imagined the sweet solidness of Peter's hand in my own, the two of us drinking lemonade on the back porch at the end of a day filled with laughter.

"Oliver was able to cancel the tickets and still get a refund."

I could have cried. But no, not in front of her. Not in front of Clara. I wouldn't. Even though Peter would already be so much bigger than the last time we'd seen him. Even though if we waited until next year, I could only imagine the coolness with which he would regard us. Children forget. They lose their comfort with you, like trained birds reverting to wildness. I thought of last summer—how he'd found his ease with me, how by the end he had run into my room every morning, jumping into my bed to wake me, his little body like warm bread, the sweet stickiness of his grubby hands. "I love you, Cousin Eleanor. I love visiting you," he'd said, the heat of his face glowing at me like a small sun.

Clara studied me with an appraising look.

"Besides, you spoil him," she said, her mouth twisting, the words sour to the taste.

I turned to pour myself a cup of coffee so as to hide the shaking in my hands. Clara had a different way with Peter, a different way with children in general. She spoke to them like tiny, obstreperous adults. They looked up at her quizzically, fascinated but nervous. I knew she loved Peter, but she possessed none of the natural ways of bonding with a child, of calming him. I had a flash of memory then: last summer, Clara standing at the doorway to my room, her lips a hard line, Peter jumping on my bed. "You woke me. You two woke me." She'd said this and walked away. Peter had looked at me large-eyed before we dissolved into giggles.

For not the first time, I thought that Clara was capable of a certain jealousy.

She touched my shoulder then gently. I sloshed a bit of coffee on the counter.

"I'm sorry, Eleanor," she said. "But I didn't want anyone to get hurt."

My mother believed that Clara is prescient. It was Clara, of course, who told my mother she was sick, that something grew within her, a grotesque fruit on a knotted vine, and that this thing would kill her. She foretold this long before the doctors found anything on her scans—before, even, my mother had developed real symptoms. Something was growing, wrapping its gnarled tendrils around my mother from the inside and strangling her.

It was Clara who called me, summoning me home just before my final college papers were due. I was able to make arrangements, turn my assignments in early, and be at the hospital for the meeting when the doctors finally told my mother what they'd found.

After my mother was discharged to spend her final months at home and we were leaving the hospital, it was Clara who crumpled. It was Clara who fell against a hamper of dirty linens, batting wildly at the air as if fighting off an invisible swarm of bees.

"You can't leave," she'd cried. "You can't, Ellie. You can't leave me all alone."

My mother and I had had to call another nurse to help us calm Clara, to give her one of her pills and push her in a wheelchair, head lolling, to the car.

It was also Clara who had warned me about Preston. He'd been so kind, I thought, to come to us as soon as we heard my mother's diagnosis. He offered to start his summer research late, to stay for several weeks and help.

Clara shook her head to me one evening, pulling me into the den while a late summer storm broke outside.

"He isn't good, Ellie," she said. I remembered her pulling me aside with similar warnings in childhood—a witch was loose, there was a dark spirit trapped in our attic, yellow eyes peering at her from outside the playroom window—her voice always that of a true believer. Her eyes flashed with the heat lightning outside the bay windows. "I don't trust him."

"Why would you say such a thing, Clara?" There was nothing but kindness in Preston. He was gentle and considerate, the sort of man who noticed a person's preferences and remembered them. His hands were large and chapped even now that he was a graduate student—a lifetime working on his parents' farm outside Lenoir, he told me—and I loved those hands for both their strength as well as their restraint. He was a person you could imagine being a father to someone small and vulnerable.

"He looks at me, Ellie," she whispered, her voice a hiss. "He looks at me in a way he shouldn't."

A high-pitched sound escaped me. I grasped her by the shoulders, pleading, wanting her to unsay these things, begging as I might beg a prophet to revise a prophecy.

"Impossible," I said. "You're imagining it."

"He's brushed against me when we're alone," she continued. "Touched me. More than once. He acted like it was an accident. But I felt him." She shook her head. "And he's watched me in the shower. Through those glasses you got him. I see him standing outside under the fig tree."

Something hot and sour rose up inside me, but I swallowed it down. Preston was an avid birder. I'd gotten him those field glasses, specially made for him, carved out of basswood and engraved with his initials, for our one-year anniversary, just before he'd proposed. He'd loved my gift. He'd told me it was the sort of gift that could only come from someone who truly knew him.

"Liar," I hissed. "You sick, jealous liar."

Her eyes grew bright then. I was not one to challenge my sister so directly.

"I can't wait to leave here when all this is done," I added, words I knew would hit her with a specific cruelty.

She shrugged then, a smirk growing on her lips.

"Fine," she said. "You'll see."

And we didn't speak for long weeks after this, maneuvering like distant roommates during the time that my mother wasted and died.

That summer of the rabid animal, Clara began taking long walks again, returning only when the sun dipped low in the sky. She'd reappear in the backyard covered in beggar's-lice and burrs, her hair frazzled with twigs and leaves. This was a thing she'd done at times in the past, and so it was less troubling than it might have been. She brought back special pine cones or fern fronds, bluish rocks the smooth shape of eggs, items marked by no particular magic I could discern, but clearly valuable by some system of her own devising.

I'd wake in the mornings to find her already gone, a dirty mug in the sink the only sign she'd been there.

"She's eccentric, your sister," my mother had always said, as if this were an allowance we made for her, a special dispensation exempting her from any task at hand.

I carried on without her. I tended the vegetables in our plot. I took my part-time shifts at the county library, lovingly tending the broken-spined books, taping back together pages torn by greedy toddlers. I purchased our groceries in the evening and fixed our dinner, saving a plate for her beneath plastic wrap.

Finally, after several weeks, I asked her, "What do you do out there all day, Clara?"

She sighed, gathering her thoughts, it seemed, to offer me a thoughtful response. But then she turned to me, blinking slowly, a dazed expression on her face.

"What?"

"Never mind," I said, because it was impossible to talk to Clara in certain modes. It always had been.

I went upstairs to brush my teeth and get ready for bed. More children had been bitten by then—a five-year-old boy and his six-year-old sister looking for blackberries, a three-year-old who'd been playing in his sandbox. They'd said the animal leapt at them so quickly it had seemed to come out of nowhere. Parents were no longer letting their children play outside.

I brushed my teeth until my gums bled, an old, bad habit. I have beautiful teeth, neat and well-shaped and smooth, perfectly even from the time they grew in. I smiled a bloody smile at myself in the mirror, only it was not a smile, not really, but rather a baring of teeth. A growl. Clara's face, I thought for just a moment. Clara's face snarling back at me.

I thought then of the last night I'd seen Preston, before my sister's words had proven true.

My mother had been very ill then, the hospice nurse visiting regularly. I had been late at a library meeting and had stopped at the bakery on the way home. My mother was eating very little at that point, her mouth and throat ulcerated and raw. She only had a taste for one thing: frangipane tart. She would take one bite, her eyes rolling back in her head blissfully, until she broke into hoarse coughing. I'd picked up a slice on my way home. I was humming to myself.

The truth is I was not as unhappy as I should have been. I had Preston, a man who cared for me. My mother was sick and dying, but even in this I saw the promise of peace, the promise of being freed of something at long last, the prospect of her death rising before me like a set of great black wings. Even my sister's stony silence was bearable—almost a blessing, really.

But when I pushed open the door to the house, I knew something was wrong. There was a strange quiet. No music playing, no sound of Clara clattering through the kitchen cupboards.

"Clara?" I called. "Preston? Mother?"

I moved through the kitchen, the dining room, the living room, then the upstairs. There was silence: only the steady tick of my mother's old grandfather clock following me up the staircase.

Then there were voices, speaking quietly at first, but growing louder, more urgent. I heard a shout, the sound of something toppling, and then my sister appeared, rushing from her room, holding her arm aloft as it streamed blood. A bright, steady trail followed her on the beige carpet.

Preston followed her, his face stricken.

"Clara!"

Preston and I said it simultaneously. He caught my eyes, his face bewildered.

Clara stumbled into my arms, whimpering, her arm staining my shirt with blood. She was wearing, I noticed, a dress of mine, one of my favorites, navy with a bright repeating pattern of cherries.

"My God," I whispered. "We have to get this stitched up."

"I told you," Clara said, her eyes flashing accusation. Preston shook his head.

"Eleanor, no, I can explain," he said. "It wasn't—"

"Leave now. Leave us alone," Clara said.

I could not speak a word.

By the time we'd gotten back from the hospital, Clara's arm stitched up, Preston and his belongings were gone—everything except for the field glasses. These he'd left on the kitchen counter—a sign of contrition or guilt? Or simply a sign that he'd given up, that we were finished? I've never known. I tucked those beautiful field glasses deep into the back of a kitchen drawer, unable to give them away, but unable to bear seeing them.

For months after, years, I wondered what had happened. Could I have been so blind? Had Preston had another side all along, a shadow self? And my sister, holding her streaming arm. My cherry dress ruined with blood. She said nothing else about it afterward, and the dress disappeared.

I was waiting the following evening for my sister to come home. I sat on the back porch of our house, watching as dark oranges and lavenders flooded the sky. The high-pitched chirring of crickets grew into a sound so persistent it was easy to forget. I sipped a bit of my mother's sherry, an appropriately old-ladyish drink, something I allowed myself now and then.

I'd brought the field glasses. Their weight was strange and satisfying in my hands, and I touched them gently, as one might touch a relic for fear of it crumbling. I looked through them, and the blur of green sharpened to individual leaf and stem.

My phone rang, and it was my cousin Oliver. I put down the glasses and answered his call.

He told me about Peter, how he missed me, how sad he was that the trip had been canceled. He asked about the rabid animal in our neighborhood.

"They haven't caught it yet," I said. "No one knows. It may be a feral dog. An opossum. A raccoon."

He sighed.

"Well, there's no reason I can't just ask you now," he said. "Peter and Sally and I, we were planning to invite you back with us, if you were interested. We've got the guesthouse out back, and it's a perfect little apartment, now that Sally redid it. And you're just so great with Peter. It could be like a live-in nanny arrangement. We would pay you, of course. We could try it for six months to see, no pressure."

He paused. My hands had grown so sweaty the phone slipped in my grip.

"What about Clara?" I asked.

"There'd be room for her, too, of course," my cousin said. "If you wanted. Although the guesthouse is small. It's up to you."

"She's doing very well here. She's used to it. And she's never loved children like I have," I said, my heart already juddering in my chest. The sherry had gone straight to my head, and I felt a little dizzy. "You and I both know that Mother always babied her. There's an agency that checks in. Besides, it might be good for her to have time apart from me. To be more independent."

I heard the call of something deep in the woods behind our house—it was a stark, lonely sound, wolfish, although there were no wolves as far as I knew in this area. Someone had once claimed to see a mountain lion. I'd heard weird stories of mountain lions making off with toddlers, owls swooping down on napping babies, coyotes snatching sleeping children from sleeping bags, stories so far-fetched they could only be true.

"Oh, good," Oliver said. "Clara was so certain you'd say no."

After we said our goodbyes, I poured a second glass of sherry. The conversation with my cousin, the sherry—it was all giving me an overwhelming feeling of clarity. The clarity was warm and soft, and relaxed me at my shoulders. I felt I understood things, at last. The sun had sunk behind the tree line now, a mere ember.

I knew then that I would leave. I would leave for good one morning soon, and I would say nothing. Clara would return from her strange ramblings in the woods and find me gone, the field glasses resting quietly on the kitchen table. She could have them. They were hers.

There was another call, a different animal this time, joining in mournfully with the first, their voices rising in a strange duet, and I determined it must be two dogs, something wounded and wild in their voices. Through the darkened trees, I imagined or heard the crack of branches. Something hungry out there. I waited for a figure—my sister, a deer, some other animal—to emerge.

RIDING

IT WAS SPRINGTIME, THE AIR CHOKED WITH POLLEN, a time of year that used to mean many travelers on the road, heading to the mountains or the beach, crisscrossing the state in minivans and SUVs and convertibles. Now the roads were eerily quiet. I was driving. I'd already turned off the interstate, onto one of the more desolate state byways. Only scraggly trees and the occasional shuttered shopping center stood watch: an old Food Lion, Sal's Autobody, a long-defunct restaurant with a green awning called China Wok. It was like these surroundings were part of an abandoned stage set on which I alone existed. I drove fast. The quarantine could make a person feel simultaneously vulnerable and powerful.

I was going to see my grandmother because she was dying. An ordinary fact from ordinary times: it was what grandmothers did. It was the way of things, predictable, this slow-wave dying of grandmothers. No one would make too much of it. Condolences, yes. But a sadness, not a tragedy. And in this instance, my grandmother was not even dying of the virus. She was dying of one of the many familiar kinds of decay, one that predated the novel contagion which had, of late, swept over the world like a brushfire.

Checking my odometer, I relaxed my foot on the gas. It would be best not to attract the attention of the highway patrol. I had several items in a bag beside me—acetaminophen, omeprazole, grape-flavored electrolyte drink, a box of saltines, a bag of mandarins. I was bringing my grandmother food and medicine. That's what I would say if stopped. My excuse. It was impossible to find a local pharmacy or grocery store that delivered as far out as she lived.

When my grandmother had last called me, she'd been crying. "I don't want to do this," she'd said. "I don't want to go." It stunned me to hear her so broken, the whimper in her voice. My grandmother had always been stoic and tough as a scrap of leather, a loner at heart, fiercely loyal only to her own blood. But deep down, she was tender, fearful. From the time I'd been very young, people had compared me to her. Two peas. "I'm lonely, Janet. I'm so lonely," she'd wept into the phone.

After the first quarantine, things had reverted, gradually, to a limited sort of normal. And then came the second quarantine, the third, the fourth. Now we'd grown resigned to it, this way of living, entranced by the light of our laptops, like mole people, rarely emerging. The only ones getting out regularly these days besides essential workers were the Masquers—an urban legend, a group of young people who might or might not exist. The Masquers couldn't bear the uncertainty of a wait, couldn't stand holing themselves away indefinitely. Impatient, they'd come up with their own solution: secret gatherings, first conceived as infection parties, held at undisclosed locations. The original concept had been to invite one person already known to be infected, who'd preside over the festivities like a May Queen in the days of old. You might die as the result of such a party, or live with the assurance that you'd suffered and were immune—but for how long? Months? A year? Soon enough, the parties came to be just parties, an act of rebellion against the lockdown, against the virus itself. The gatherings were known as Red Masques, inglorious marvels of nihilism and psychedelia, if you could believe the rumors. Selfish bastards, people said. Fools. Animals. But there was fascination in their voices, a trace of envy.

The woods were dark around me, and the overhanging branches cast wavering shadows on my left arm. My grandmother lived in a rural area, just outside a small town in the northern pocket of the state, near the Virginia border: a quiet place in ordinary times, now nearly deserted.

Behind me, another car appeared. It was a long, plain sedan following too close. My little car was the brilliant red of a fresh manicure, a small indulgence that had once pleased me. The road was otherwise empty, but this sedan was tailgating. I glanced back in my mirror.

Something sprang from the woods. A blur of gray fur, dashing across the road. I slammed my brakes and felt the thump—a soft mass tumbling against the undercarriage of my car, the crunch of bone in flesh.

And then the crash from behind. I buckled forward, snapping against my seat belt. The other car had rear-ended me.

I sat for a moment, letting my heart slow, then pulled the car to the shoulder. The driver of the sedan did the same. I did not want to see the animal I'd hit lying dead on the road, a tangled mess of bloody fur. The thought curdled in my stomach. I also did not want to see another person traveling through such an isolated area. The pandemic had brought out an extra skittishness around strangers, amplified the wariness already there.

In my rearview, I could see the driver of the other car was wearing mirrored sunglasses and a ball cap. I watched this person step out of their car and approach mine.

"Hey," the other driver said, tapping on my car window. "What happened?"

It was a young woman. Her ponytail was pulled through the ball cap, which featured a decal for a trucking company. She was dressed in a heavy corduroy jacket and thick, multipocketed work pants despite the warmth of the day.

"Something darted out," I said, loud enough for her to hear with my windows still rolled up. "A stray dog, maybe."

Tipping one shoulder toward the road, she spoke. "It's gone now. Must not have clipped it too bad."

This seemed impossible given the impact. I'd felt the animal's carcass rolling under my wheels. I shivered. The woman watched me, impassive, offering no apology for having followed so close in the first place.

"Come on, let's check your car out," she said abruptly.

I reached numbly for the bandanna mask I wore over my nose and mouth when out in public, realizing then the most obvious oddness of her appearance: she wasn't wearing any mask herself. It was startling to see a human face in full, not on a screen. Below her sunglasses, she had full lips, a mole like a tiny dot of paint on the left corner of her mouth, and small white teeth that shone when she'd smiled. She stepped aside to allow me to open the door, hitching her pants up. I wondered then if she was out of work these days, hard up for cash, if this had been an intentional hit. Not everyone had the luxury I had of working from home, bathed in the soft ethereal glow of videoconferencing. I'd read recent stories of people manufacturing small traffic accidents in order to rob people.

She laughed hoarsely, taking the measure of my reluctance.

"Hey, I don't bite," she said. "Virus-free, I swear. I'll stand back."

For someone so slight, she held herself with authority.

After covering my mouth and nose, I followed her to the back of my car. It was worse than I'd have thought, the whole back end crumpled, tailpipe dangling. I looked at her, but the young woman just gazed back at me, unfazed.

"Best if I tell you now that my insurance is lapsed," she said calmly. "I'll have to make this up to you some other way."

The wrinkle of displeasure on my forehead must have been obvious. She lifted her hands in a what-can-you-do gesture.

"Come on," she said. "Where ya headed? I'll give you a ride. I've got a buddy with a tow truck. Won't even have to let the authorities know."

Her car, long-snouted and golden green as a crocodile, sat there, undamaged. A large gray cloud glided over us like the keel of a boat, its shadow settling there, darkening everything.

"I'm not going far," I said. "I'll try to drive it."

"Better not." She frowned and kicked at part of my back bumper, which fell to the ground with a thud.

"I can wait here." We both knew, of course, that everything was half staffed these days. I might wait hours, and I'd have to notify the police first, make an official report. The first fat drops of rain began to splatter on our shoulders, my poor car, the sparse grasses along the roadside, glazing the highway to a black vinyl shine.

"Come on. It's not a good time to be a woman sitting on the side of the road."

Like there'd ever been a good time for that, I thought, but she was right. The young woman turned and opened the passenger door of her car, motioning for me to get in.

There were two people sitting in the back seat. A boy in dark sunglasses, fair and thin-lipped, wearing a skull and crossbones T-shirt, and another slightly older boy, heavyset with brown sideburns and a goatee wearing the sort of dark glasses I'd seen my great-aunt wear after cataract surgery. I say "boy," but they both might have been in their late teens, early twenties at most. I accepted the offer of the passenger seat, and the boys nodded from the back, like they'd been expecting me to ride with them. Neither was wearing a mask. This bothered me, of course, but I hardly felt myself in any position to speak up.

"Name's Longshot," the skinny, fair-haired boy said, not bothering to offer me his hand, a habit we had all long dropped. "And this here's Rogue."

"Janet," I said, although my voice came out meek, muffled, the triple-thick bandanna still over my mouth and nose.

A memory came to me, of a trip I'd taken once long ago with my then not-yet-husband, back when we'd been very young, first dating. I turned to the woman in the driver seat, who looked even more childlike now, her thin shoulders hunched up, the bluish veins visible in her skinny neck.

"You look like a bandit," the fair kid said. "Janet the Bandit."

"No banditry. Just going to visit my grandmother," I said, turning to the woman, hoping she'd introduce herself. She'd pushed her sunglasses up on her head like a headband now that the rain was falling harder, and I could see her eyes: large, brown, with preposterously thick lashes. She was beautiful, her features delicate-looking, like those of a porcelain doll. I wondered if that was why she compensated by wearing such thick, mannish clothes. She blushed faintly, reading my gaze.

"Crow," she said, turning away from me to steer, easing the car back onto the road. "We'll call you Bandit. It's better."

I felt that same itchy memory again: that time with my now ex-husband, back when we were first dating, a July more than fifteen years ago. We'd gone on a road trip in a terrible hand-me-down RV my ex's father had given us. It was rust-eaten and unreliable, prone to breaking down, and sweltering to sleep in during those summer nights. The whole interior stunk of spilled Coke and mildewed towels. After it puttered to a stop somewhere in northern Florida, we'd finally decided to hitchhike—my ex's suggestion. Back then, Dan, my ex, had been handsome and persuasive, even in his filth, his stranded-on-the-side-of-the-road frustration. We'd eventually been picked up by a van of young women driving back from some sort of concert/spiritual conference. Hippies, we'd called them, although it was long past the time of true hippiedom, and the truth was they'd been following a heavy metal band whose front man had achieved guru-like status. They had long, snarled hair and bright, unwashed faces, their breasts hanging loose in smocked tank tops and their bodies ripe with musk. Their van was sweetly redolent of pot, air-conditioned and positively luxurious compared to the RV.

Dan and I ended up traveling with them for a full week, making our way up through the South, parking and pitching tents guerilla-style. Both of us had been graduate students in economics, but Dan had always had an aesthete's dreaminess about him, an openness to adventure. We whiled our way homeward with those women. I remembered long, hazy stretches of highway, the underwater sensation their oversweet brownies gave me, the wonderful leadenness in my limbs every evening as we sat around a campfire, sharing a bottle of cheap, potent booze. It was like Dan and I had stepped outside of time, like none of that time riding in the back of the van while the hippie girls flirted benignly with us, reeling us in with languid proficiency, officially counted.

"Got a lot of friends," Crow said, squinting into the road as the rain thickened. "Could probably find you a reliable ride whenever you need."

From the back, I could hear the guy in dark glasses making an odd humming sound. He hadn't spoken since I'd gotten in the car. I rearranged the bag of offerings for my grandmother at my feet.

"You seem like a nice lady. Why aren't you home with your family?" the blond kid asked, in a way that suggested he did not think I was nice at all.

"Don't have one. My husband left me."

"For another woman?" this kid, Longshot, asked, scratching behind his ear. He reminded me of a stray dog that used to show up at the back of our apartment when we lived in the city. There was a way that dog had paced, nervous, hungry, eager for something. A desperate friendliness in its eyes. And then it had mangled the hand of one of the neighborhood children.

"You don't have to answer," Crow said quietly, eyes still on the road.

"Or another man?"

I shrugged.

"He got spiritual. Found God."

There were a bunch of them like Dan, all living together at this place outside Asheville, washing clothes in buckets and hanging them out on a line, raising chickens and calling one another Brother and Sister. The last time we'd talked, Dan had balked at my use of the word *commune*. Yes, it was communal living, but the word *commune* carried connotations, Dan thought. I already knew better than to say *cult*. He was there of his own free will, Dan was quick to emphasize, and besides, they didn't believe in hierarchy. Dan and the other brothers and sisters farmed and did Holotropic Breathwork, letting their lungs carry them into states of divine dismantlement. I'd visited the farm with him just once. We spent the day apple-picking, then ate stew from a giant tureen that evening. Afterward, there were songs sung swayingly around a bonfire, like we were kids at a summer camp. All those voices mingling, the circle of faces behind the flames—it was enough to make anyone's eyes well up. At the time, I wondered briefly if Dan had arranged the whole evening for my benefit. A tactic. But no, it was merely what they did every night—one of them, Sister Anne, I think, told me. I left after that, refusing to spend the night on a bunk bed in one of the shared rooms. I couldn't bear feeling any more of whatever it was Dan felt there.

"It's good to see you," Dan said to me the last time we'd seen each other, letting his eyes drift heavenward. He'd let his hair grow long by that point, so that it curled in gray-brown ringlets on his shoulders, and his eyes had lilac bruises beneath them, his cheeks hollowed out by farm labor and a diet of homegrown carrots, mustard greens, and speckled eggs. "You should visit again." We'd met at a chain pancake restaurant off 40 in Asheville to finalize some papers. It was dinnertime, the other customers all depressed-looking, ready to blunt their sorrows with stacks of carbs. He'd become scrupulous, I noticed, about not calling me by name. *Janet.* As if this might invoke some of our former intimacy.

"Maybe so."

I dragged a triangle of pancake through syrup, letting the tines of my fork scrape the plastic plate. The virus had just started up then, and little did we know it would be the last time we'd set foot in any sort of restaurant for a long while. Back then, it was still one of those things we took for granted.

"It's not like I didn't ask you to join me," Dan said. I saw his hand rise, maybe to take my own in it, offering me some kind of succor. I jerked my chair back, distancing myself. "It's not like I didn't love you."

You had to give Dan credit. He'd gone devout before so many of the others, the ones who'd fallen back hard on superstition when the pandemic ramped up—desperate, carrying around crucifixes and little icons to stave off the plague.

The rain had become so hard that it was a sheet of water, a blinding torrent, and Crow could only inch the car along.

"Of all the excuses," Crow said without breaking her gaze on the road, "God's not a bad one. Hard to compete with. God." She said the word like it was a new flavor, a concept she was testing out. She squinted through the windshield. "You could say we're looking for God, too. Listen to me, now I'm just talking." She made a little half-laughing sound. "Good ol' God. Smiting sinners."

I didn't say anything.

"You're a real cool customer, huh."

The way she spoke it was not a question.

I thought again of the time Dan and I had traveled with the hippies. On that last night, under a giant, melon-colored moon in a farmer's field in South Carolina, the loveliest of the young women had invited Dan and me to wander off from the rest of the group to stargaze. She'd spread an old quilt out on the ground carefully, then pulled me gently toward her. Her hands were soft. Dan sat on the other side, so that I was sandwiched between them. The hippie girl was close to me then, very warm, an odor of crotch and lavender emanating from her that was not entirely unpleasant. "Look at the sky," she'd said, and Dan and I had looked: a sparkling magnificence flung across the blue-black depths. When she reached over to stroke the back of my neck, then my arm, I felt myself lean toward her, as if she were exerting a gravitational force. Her fingertips on my arm were electric, like air before a summer storm, sending a tingling all the way up to my neck and down my spine. For a moment, I simply watched. I could witness the whole scene as if it were someone else's arm being caressed, a pleasure to which I was somehow privy.

When Dan cleared his throat, I stiffened. It was my arm she held again. A terrible warmth flooded me. The whole scene felt off to me then, contrived and artificial. Even with the bad weed and alcohol, I was trapped inside my own head. My woodenness shamed me. I pulled away from her and rose to my feet. I think I told them I needed to pee. I walked several paces away in the dark brush for a long while, pretending to relieve myself, hoping something might have shifted by the time I got back. When I returned, there were Dan and the girl, a naked tangle, pale limbs entwined in the moonlight. I froze momentarily, then turned to walk back to the van by myself, where I pretended to sleep.

It was, Dan said afterward, once the girls had vanished in their van like vapor, both meaningless and also the ultimate compliment, a demonstration of his total indifference toward anyone but me. A sort of mortification of the flesh. The parts that mattered, the parts I laid my claim to, were his heart and mind. His spirit. His love for me was such that these carnal dalliances held no weight at all.

Longshot laughed hoarsely, then leaned forward to pick something up.

"Janet," he said so that I turned.

I flinched.

Longshot laughed. He wore a horrifyingly convincing wolf mask, the lips peeled back in a snarl, incisors dripping blood. The muzzle was perfectly painted, the fur realistic. It was an adolescent boy's Halloween-store wet dream.

Crow scoffed.

"Stupid," she said to Longshot, then turned to me. "We've all got one." She paused and made a cartoonish howling sound for my benefit. "Full moon party tonight. You could come with us if you want." She'd managed to pull a cigarette out of a crushed pack in her breast pocket and was lighting it now, her wrists guiding the steering wheel. The sun was back out. When she rolled down her window, the air smelled like wet earth and leaves.

"Oh, no," I said. "Thanks, but I ought to get this stuff to my grandmother."

"Your loss. It's magic. Like nothing you've ever seen," Longshot murmured, his eyes going shiny, the bluster gone out of his voice. He'd taken off the wolf mask again and was smoothing out his flaxen hair, his fingers delicate, almost girlish.

The suspicion I'd had about this little trio all along took on more shape. I imagined such a party: the press of young bodies, a delirium of dance, the rubber masks growing slick inside until they were finally shucked. A brute freedom. The dreamy way Longshot spoke reminded me of Dan, how he'd spoken of those off-the-grid carrot farmers in their rough linen, with their morning prayers and meditation, their sharing circles in the evening, and communitarian principles of love. "No one can own another person's body," Dan had chided me. "You can't even own your own body." A good excuse for recklessness, I'd thought, for letting the unruly body run wild. I wondered now if the virus had made it out there to him and the others on the farm yet, putting a stop to their morning chants, their evensong.

"You don't worry about getting sick?" I asked, tossing that question into the silence, a coin down a wishing well.

Crow laughed and lifted up one arm so that her sleeve fell away. She tilted her wrist so that I could see the delicate skin was inked with a tiny blue pattern: the indentation of teeth from a tiny mouth. Or stars. I'd heard of this, too—a tattoo the Masquers all received.

"Already been sick," she said. "Three weeks I was laid up. Felt like looking death in the face till I came through."

She turned to me and smiled, and I saw the glint of one canine: gold, pirate-like.

"You sure you can't get sick again?" I asked.

Crow laughed.

"Who's sure of anything?"

Longshot spoke up from the back. "I already had it, too." He lifted one wrist for me to see the blue mark. "Been partying for a little while. But Rogue here, he's getting his cherry popped tonight."

"You really don't wanna come with us?" Crow asked. Although her eyes remained on the road ahead, her voice was not more than a whisper, strangely intimate, creating a sense of privacy between us up front. "You don't have to go to your grandmother's." She raised an eyebrow, letting her hand fall on my knee, haphazardly. Her fingers traced a series of smooth circles along my thigh, a practiced move, automatic. An invitation.

There was a gnawing in my gut. A wave of nausea. I shook my head.

"You're not that old. You've got decent odds," she added.

"I'm old enough. Still hoping for a vaccine."

Crow took a drag of her cigarette and exhaled out the window.

"Suit yourself."

A spill of yolk-yellow light fell before us between gaps in the trees. Just ahead was a russet barn and a field in which cows grazed. They didn't even glance up as we passed. I recognized this stretch. We were getting closer.

"Why go to your grandmother now?" Longshot asked. "You might infect her."

"She's dying anyway," I said. "Not from this." I gestured vaguely out the window, as if the whole sky were visibly awhirl with viral particles. "She's lonesome. Lives in a big house off Harford Mill Road all by herself."

"I think I know the house you mean," Longshot said, pointing to our right. Something had registered in his face, and I saw a new alertness there, like a hound catching a scent. "Near the intersection with Fourteen. Purple mailbox, sits way back up a long dirt drive."

That was indeed my grandmother's house, notable because it was the largest for miles, but something in his eagerness told me to withhold confirmation.

"Oh, not that one. It's farther down," I said, my voice false, unconvincing. "There are several out that way. Hard to see them from the main road."

No one answered, but I felt an energy being transmitted silently, little pings I couldn't quite decode.

"What's she like?" Crow asked softly. She turned for a moment and smiled at me a bit, her eyes genuinely curious. I felt a complicated feeling I now recognize as very simple: I was lonely and I wanted to be liked.

I pulled out my phone, on which I had saved an old photo of my grandmother. In it, she was younger, near my age, holding a bunch of roses. She wore a simple blue dress and was laughing so hard that her eyes were almost closed. I pointed the phone toward Crow so she could glance quickly and then to the guys in the back.

"Wow. You look like her."

"Yeah," I said. "But that's where the similarity ends." A hard knot was rising up through my chest and throat: the inexplicable longing to cry. I hadn't cried in ages. "I mean, I love her, but she's kind of a nut. Guns and conspiracy theories. She got even more paranoid after her third husband passed a couple years ago. Keeps her house stockpiled for doomsday. Forwards me crazy fake news whenever she can figure out how to turn on her computer."

"Sounds like a real peach."

"Sounds like a real bitch," Longshot said.

Something twisted inside me, although nothing I'd said was untrue.

"Oh, she's actually pretty harmless. And she's been good to me. She's endearing once you get to know her." I could hear how I sounded, both shit-talker and apologist. Pathetic.

Longshot scoffed.

"Still sounds like a real bitch to me."

I didn't respond. Crow caught Longshot's eye in her rearview mirror, and I saw her shoot him a look—irritation, or an unspoken question for which there was no answer. Rogue stared ahead in his dark glasses, inscrutable. He hadn't spoken a word the whole time. For the first time, I noticed his pallor, the sheen of sweat on his brow, although the car was cool and comfortable enough. He didn't look well. Green at the gills, my grandmother would have said. Carsick. I hesitated even to ask.

Rogue coughed sharply.

"He okay?" I finally asked.

Longshot laughed another rough laugh and gave Rogue a playful shove, which moved him not an inch. He sat there, like a lumpen figure shaped from clay. Longshot, on the other hand, seemed to be in especially good spirits now.

"This ol' buddy of mine," he said. "He's fine. Just playing it cool until we get there. Taking it easy. Resting up. These things are real intense. It's like—" And here he raised both palms like an old-timey preacher trying to convey something ineffable, something so wonderful it went beyond words. "Gorgeous. Indescribable. You'd have to experience it."

"Where will you go when it's done?" I asked.

"Everywhere," Crow answered. "Anywhere. There are abandoned houses all over now. Off someone goes to the hospital, poof. Plenty of houses for us to make ours."

She arched her back then, stretching languorously, demonstrably, tipping her head to one side so that her neck gave a pop. She put her sunglasses back on, now that it was bright again, and it was like a curtain had once more been drawn between us.

A whirring filled my mind, the sound of a laptop overheating. That was how I'd come to think of myself, I realized, in purely functional terms: machinery, mostly reliable. A mechanical heart, a lifetime of saying no, safe with nothing but my tired old fear for company and protection. A new panic was rising in me: I no longer wanted to take leave of these strangers. I no longer wanted to be left alone. Maybe I would go with them after all, join their pack, pulling the stinking plastic wolf mask down over my face and rebreathing my own hot breath. I'd follow them deep into the woods, howling at the moon, letting myself fall into a mosh pit of revelers. Let whatever might happen happen and put an end to all this dread.

"I think I want to go with you." My mouth had gone cottony, my words nothing more than a whisper. "To the party tonight."

"Oh, yeah?" Crow answered without even glancing at me.

Longshot spoke from the back seat.

"One problem. I forgot we only have three masks." He lifted them up for me to see, as if proof of something. Like the pelts of roadkill, the masks flopped, snouts flaccid, eyeholes horribly empty. Beside him, Rogue looked even paler, full droplets of sweat rolling from his forehead and down his cheek.

"I've really gotta take a piss," Crow announced. She spoke now as if from a great distance, the opposite side of a ravine, a far-off ridge.

There was nothing nearby: no rest stops or gas stations in sight, only woods and empty stretches of field.

She pulled the car over. Longshot and Rogue opened their car doors and stepped out. I sat, my still seat belt buckled, unable to move.

"Everybody out," Crow said, although only she and I remained in the car.

There were wildflowers blooming in patches just ahead. Dark crimson and heavy-headed, they nodded slowly.

"I'm fine," I said, aware of my voice, the pleading in it. "I'll just wait here in the car."

Crow looked hard at me. Even from behind her sunglasses, I could feel her eyes. I knew I wouldn't argue with whatever she said.

"Go pick some flowers for your grandmother. That'd be a nice thing to do."

She pointed. It was not a request. I got out. Crow did, too, locking the doors behind us. I imagined I saw the slightest flicker of regret cross her face before she turned from me, scrambling down the bank to find a spot to relieve herself in the brush. Longshot sat on the hood, sipping a can of beer. Rogue sat cross-legged in the weeds, flushed and silent.

I began toward the patch of flowers, but something held me back. Hesitating, I turned around. Longshot was watching me.

"Go on, Bandit," he said, shooing me away lazily. "Go."

The flowers, vulgar splotches of red amid the long, bland grass, bowed in the breeze, awaiting me.

By the time I'd picked a small bouquet, Crow and the two boys were already back in the car.

"Sorry," I called from the distance, waving. "I'm coming."

But Crow was already turning the key in the ignition.

I began to run. She saw me and gave a little wave but didn't stop. Deliberately, unhurriedly, she eased the car back onto the highway. There, in the flattened weeds where Rogue had been sitting, sat the bag of goodies for my grandmother. I picked it up and clutched it to my chest. I stood, watching as the sedan rose over a crest, blinked once in the sun, and disappeared.

Then I began walking.

I walked a long while. It had grown hot at this point, unseasonably so, the sun low and strong, catching particles of pollen in the air like suspended motes of gold. By the time I turned onto the road on which my grandmother lived, I was sweating profusely, thirsty and overheated. Almost feverish. There was a funny catch in my throat that I attributed to the pollen.

Once, back when Dan and I had still been married, after he'd first suggested we move to the farm but I'd resisted, I'd woken in the middle of the night to find him sitting on the edge of our bed in the darkness, gasping.

"What's wrong?" I'd asked him, touching his shoulder gently, thinking he'd had a bad dream. "What is it?"

He shook his head, curling over, letting his face fall onto his knees. I heard a low, muffled sob. I rose from the bed and approached him, kneeling so that my mouth was by his ear, murmuring soft words of comfort until he finally lifted his face again. I wiped his wet cheek in the dark.

"I saw something," he said to me shakily. "When I went to the bathroom just now."

A bad dream, I thought then. Nothing more. Something easily dispelled with light.

"Come show me," I said, taking his hand and leading him back to our dim bathroom, lit only by the seashell night-light plugged into the wall. I watched the two of us approach in the mirror, our reflections there: me, big-eyed and ghostly, an illuminated skull staring back; him, turned away, unable to look straight-on, nothing but mussed hair.

"See?" I whispered. "It's nothing."

Not two months later, he'd left me for good. For the farm. I found the note on our kitchen table, filled with a strange hodgepodge of Dan-phrasings and New Testament verses, Bhagavad Gita quotations and Talmudic gibberish.

I finally started up the long, dirt drive that led to my grandmother's house. Midway up, I was struck by the feeling of being watched, certain there must be someone there, waiting—crouched, hidden, ready to spring out wearing a mask of gray synthetic fur with a rubbery sneer and crudely bared teeth. Hideous to behold. But that was silly. Only my grandmother's house, with its large, dark windows, stared back. This house would hold many people comfortably under its roof. It had generators and its own well, supplies of canned food and ammunition: a tantalizing usefulness suddenly very obvious to me.

When I reached the front porch, I stood, hot, coughing, at her door. It was quiet. Not even the sound of birdsong. A stack of newspapers sat, waterlogged, on the mat, and I had the sense of being somewhere utterly foreign, a place I'd never once set foot before.

I lifted my hand slowly to press the bell, to see who would open the door.

DEAR SHADOWS

THE LAST TIME KATIE HAD TALKED TO COLIN REYNOLDS had been in the spring of 2000 in a sad little rental house with a banana-colored refrigerator, sparse lighting, and abundant water bugs. They'd ended up there on the west end of town after a party. Their conversation—brief, inconsequential, yet overinflated—had been a prelude. Soon thereafter, they'd been making out on a bristly orange couch while Mazzy Star played in the background—not his choice, but hers. Everyone knew what you were up to when you put on Mazzy Star, which wasn't new or cool or particularly interesting even back then, but definitely communicated a certain willingness, a certain agenda. When Katie thought of it now, the scene was like one from a bad movie, but a bad movie you treasure and keep going back to watch, guiltily. Colin had been part of a group that signaled their appeal by dressing as if they'd grabbed items of clothing at random while blindfolded in a thrift store—somehow, they all looked amazing—and who traded socialist zines and recordings of Tuvan throat singing. Katie, with her sweatshirts from the

Gap, her Keds, her toothy, obvious smile, had admired them: all that style and insouciance, the way they walked across campus grimacing, nodding under their headphones, elbows at odd angles like marionettes. Colin had an air about him, even then, like he was on the verge of generating something monumental.

In short, she'd felt lucky to be with him that night. Also, Colin had had a girlfriend. The girlfriend was beautiful and interesting, which, by the transitive property, suggested that Katie herself might also be beautiful and interesting—and wasn't this the deepest longing at the heart of all other longing? The whole thing had seemed startling and rare, like a glimpse of a meteor traveling through a dark sky, until Colin's housemate had arrived home early from his shift at the college radio station, interrupting them.

She might have missed the article completely if Rand hadn't left the new issue of the *New Yorker* out on their kitchen table by his cereal bowl. Thank God it wasn't a whole feature-length article, just a review, but still—the *New Yorker*! "Colin Reynolds's Dreamy-Eyed Dystopia" was the title, and there was a tiny photo insert of him, so unchanged that Katie almost couldn't bear to look at it.

"It's your boyfriend," Rand said, his voice gentle and yet mocking in a way only Rand could achieve. "You gonna try to catch up with him tonight?"

Katie sighed, picking up Rand's cereal bowl and putting it in the sink. Rand was her roommate. She was too old to have roommates. She was too old to be picking up other people's cereal bowls. She was too old to be seeing shows in clubs. Katie swiped a cloth across the counter. Her life at this point could be reduced to a series of mundane actions, rote tasks out of which she strung together her days—what a depressing way to think. But in truth, she was boring. Sure, she could churn out a few nice sentences on whatever new restaurant had sprung up, or opine briefly on the latest controversy involving a local politician. She was a hack, a solid hack. But she wasn't *interesting*. Something inside her had been turned off. She couldn't even remember the last time she'd read a book, or felt deeply moved by a song. The number one most interesting fact about her was that she had once slept with the now famous Colin Reynolds. That was it. She wasn't a complainer. But the lack of anything else notable was sad when she stopped to think about it.

Katie hadn't heard from Colin in years, not since he'd sent a single-emoji reply to an article she'd forwarded him on a whim in 2013. But a few weeks ago, when she'd emailed him, he'd responded.

She opened the cabinet, pulled out a new filter, and placed it into the coffee maker.

"I'm going. What time are you finishing up today?" Katie asked over her shoulder. Her cheeks were a little warm, so she didn't want to look at Rand. "Wanna come?"

"Nah, I'm closing. Go on without me."

With that, Rand was out the door, leaving Katie alone to wait for the coffee to brew. There were three of them: Rand, Katie, and Laura. Housemates. The arrangement had begun a few years ago, when they were still young enough for it to seem temporary, an amusing pit stop on the joyride to somewhere more grown-up and official. Laura had finally found a boyfriend and so had recently made herself scarce, although occasionally Katie found piles of her laundry strewn along the hallway, like cairns. Sometimes in the wee hours, stumbling down the darkened hallway to the bathroom they all shared, in the thrall of a half-remembered dream, Katie could still imagine that she was headed somewhere else, somewhere else entirely.

When she opened her email again, however, and saw there were no new messages, the hopeful buoyancy within her plummeted.

Katie had sent her last message to Colin two weeks ago. Citizens of modernity checked their email within that span of time. Maybe Colin, as a musician, was not a citizen of modernity. Maybe, his life being constantly thrilling, he'd already forgotten their recent exchange.

She was forgettable, after all. Pleasantly so, like inoffensive background music in a shopping mall. She'd retained her big, overly honest smile. Disarming, Rand had called it once. Homey. Her looks were like Fourth of July picnic food—who could find fault with that? Katie had spent her whole life looking *friendly*, which made people want to talk to her, and which was ultimately wearisome. And being described as *friendly* was really a mixed compliment at best. Even back in college, when she'd been interested in creative pursuits, had desperately wanted to appear brooding or mysterious, filled with deep and impenetrable knowledge, she'd looked cheery and capable, like a rosy-cheeked ranch hand.

> Hi, Colin,
> I'm guessing you're surprised to hear from me. It's been a while! Congrats on all the recent success! You guys are huge! You're, like, the one legit famous person I know now! ☺ Anyways, I was planning to try to catch the show when you're in town and was just going to see if you wanted to grab a coffee or a drink and catch up before or after? Gonna write up a little something on the show!
> xo, Katie

To her surprise, he'd actually replied the very next day.

> Katie!
> You were always such a dear friend to me. I've actually been wanting to speak with you. Let's definitely meet up. I'll be in touch closer to when I'm in town.
> CR

She'd responded to this message with a speed and openness that must have been off-putting.

> Oh, Colin, you don't know how good it is to hear from you! Yes, you were a good friend to me, too. I always felt that, even though we weren't as close in the end. . . . Yes, please let me know what works for you! I'm shamelessly available! ☺
> xo, K

She'd meant for this response to sound tossed-off, light, funny-at-her-own-expense—which was the brand of humor she did best—but rereading her messages, the obvious desperation pained her, all that forced cheerfulness. She was like a chipper flight attendant handing out pretzel packets. She was a fool. She'd read in another article that Colin was dating a rising star on the art scene, a winsome pixie with blonde bangs and vintage lace shirtsleeves who made tiny, elaborate cross-stitch scenes depicting famous atrocities—Jonestown and the Tate murders and the like. Her work was now on display in the Whitney, had been lauded at the Venice Biennale. The girlfriend was at least ten years younger. It was slightly nauseating.

She filled her travel mug and paused at the window. A blue heron flew to the drainage ditch behind their house. The heron settled on its stalklike legs with an awkward grace and seemed to look at her. She'd seen blue herons out there before on occasion, and they always seemed like lucky omens.

As if right on cue, her phone buzzed with a text message. Colin would still have her number, wouldn't he? A hard, painful bubble was rising in her throat. She picked up the phone and read:

Meet me at Perla's when you can. I've got some dirt on Colin.

The bubble in her throat burst with a painful sensation. The text was from Deb, her friend, her former coworker at the alt-weekly where Katie still worked.

The heron lifted off with a great ungainly flap from the ditch. It looked like a thing that should not be capable of flight, and yet it flew. Katie wanted to wave to it, but instead, she put on her jacket and walked out the door.

Katie had first met Colin in a creative writing class. Of course that's where they'd met. Katie had erred on the side of earnestness; Colin, obscurity.

"You write like my dad," Colin had told her after one of their early workshops.

"Is that a compliment?" she'd asked, studying this silent, dark-eyed boy.

"My dad's a youth pastor."

"Oh," Katie had answered, and then she'd laughed to disarm the situation. That was her—allowing someone to insult her and then attempting to put that person at ease.

"The kids are really into my dad. He makes an impression."

Colin had fallen in step alongside her as they walked out from the English building, a blunt, ugly structure that sat on the otherwise picturesque campus like a stubbed toe. It had been autumn, their third semester, and Katie was still worrying over things such as: how to drink alcohol, how to talk to people, how to be in the world. So much, she was realizing, depended upon the face you chose to present. College provided an opportunity for reinvention, but what if there was nothing to reinvent? What if you were simply the same, toothy, good-natured girl with a melancholy soul and a jean jacket that you'd been in eighth grade?

They were crunching over leaves as they walked now, the afternoon cool and golden. Katie had a moment of fleeting awareness that this would be a day, a moment, for which she would someday feel nostalgia. *My college days.* It was like what she'd seen in college catalogs, students walking together, talking over ideas.

"You write the way people talk in my dreams," Katie offered. "It seems like I understand, but . . ." She trailed off, drawing the shape of a child's cloud with her hand.

He stopped and turned to her. She stopped, too, a terrible heat spreading from her throat to her ears.

"I don't mean it like that," she said. "It's beautiful, the way you write. I just don't always get it right away." He was studying her, those big, dark eyes. He was wearing suspenders, which looked quirky and ironic on him, rather than old-mannish. He had a perfect nose and a mouth that was full and lush and almost feminine.

Colin laughed, a dry little sophisticated laugh, and Katie had felt a wave of relief.

"You're funny," he said. "I like you. You're delightfully obtuse."

She must have made a face because he put his hand on her arm then.

"No, no. I mean, it's winning, really. Refreshing."

There were shouts and laughter in the smaller quad ahead of them: a group of students in oversize flannels playing hacky sack. He accidentally brushed against her, and Katie's palm tensed and then relaxed against his. For a moment, she thought he might hold her hand.

And then there was Thea. Katie would always remember the first time she met her because the dislike was so instantaneous and pure. Thea wore baggy jeans and a spaghetti-strap tank top with an unbuttoned men's shirt over top, along with purple Doc Martens, all as per the dictates of fashion in that era. But Thea's face was timeless. Her smile was sudden and radiant, like lightning.

"Baby!" she yelped, leaping into Colin's arms.

It was like Katie was no longer there. She'd been subsumed into the background—an oak, an academic building, a blade of grass under the hacky sackers' feet. For a long, sun-dazed moment, Katie had just stood there, silent, while Thea kissed Colin. She'd been waiting, she supposed, for an introduction until it became clear that none was forthcoming.

"Who are you, anyway?" Thea finally asked, pulling away from Colin and straightening the strap from her tank top.

"Nobody," Katie had answered, which, of course, she'd realized just in that very moment was the absolute truth.

She and Colin, Colin and nobody. She felt herself rendered blank and genderless around him—a stopgap, a sounding board, a faceless body in the room.

And yet, they continued to find themselves near one another afterward. This was the beginning of, well, if not a friendship exactly, a regular acquaintanceship. They seemed always to have at least one class together each semester. And even if they didn't exactly pair well in the traditional sense, Katie liked to imagine that they were artfully mismatched, like two disconnected objects somehow delightful in their proximity: a feather and an antique spoon, a marble chess piece and a kettle, a geode and an empty jar. Something other than a moody heartthrob and a wide-eyed nobody.

When Katie arrived at Perla's, Deb was sitting outside at one of the picnic benches, thumbing through her phone, an empty coffee mug and a crumb-covered plate on the table. Deb was scraggly and bucktoothed and charming, always pulling her sagging pants back up her narrow hips. She smelled like cedar and Old Bay and had the louche air of an off-duty Blackbeard. Deb rose and stretched when she saw Katie.

"K T!" she said, putting her phone down. "Looking good, kid!"

Katie allowed Deb to hug her and took a seat.

"Can I get you something?" Deb asked.

Katie shook her head.

A cluster of girls with backpacks passed by. Summer school. Still, Perla's was much less crowded than it was during the academic year. She and Deb were townies now. It felt like they'd known each other forever. Once upon a time, ages ago, in a different millennium, Deb had had a crush on Katie, and sometimes, in her moments of deepest loneliness, Katie imagined the relief she might have now had she only been able to reciprocate.

"You're not gonna fuckin' believe it," Deb said, her eyes crinkling with light and intensity Katie hadn't seen in ages. She was leaning in close now, gesturing for Katie to lean in close to her, too. "You're finally gonna get your revenge."

"Against who?"

"Against whom," Deb said, laughing. "You're a fuckin' editor now, kid." She lifted her coffee cup as if to take a sip, but there was no coffee left, and so the heavy mug just clacked against her teeth. Deb sipped the air as if this fact didn't register. Even though she was only one year older than Katie, she had a way of speaking to Katie as if she were still a bright-cheeked schoolgirl.

"Colin, that's who. That dickwad. For the shitty way he treated you and the way you've been mooning over him all these years."

"I haven't," Katie offered, but her voice was weak tea. A passing truck created a momentary breeze, ruffling the hair on the back of her neck, but it was already too hot. She felt alive now, alert to the possibility that Colin might show up here, too. Famous people still drank coffee. This had been a haunt of his.

Colin hadn't really treated her shittily—or at least, no more shittily than any other nineteen- or twenty-year-old guy might. They'd hooked up once. It had meant more to her than to him. When his girlfriend Thea had heard about it, he'd let Katie take the fall. Cut off contact completely. It was but one of the many vibrant humiliations of youth. What could you expect from anyone at that age?

"K T, come on, darlin'," Deb continued. "You can lie to yourself, but not to me. And don't take my word for it. Look." She leaned across the table so that she spoke right into Katie's face. "He's a fuckin' creep. Bona fide."

She lifted her cell phone, which had been facedown on the table, so that Katie could see the email.

"Hashtag Me Too is coming for you, motherfucker," Deb said, pulling the phone back before Katie could even read it.

"My God. What'd they say he did? Rape someone?"

Deb thrust her phone forward again.

"Read the email."

Katie read.

"Wait, hold on," she said. "Who sent this?"

"Anonymous," Deb said. She paused for a beat, looking thoughtful. "Still thought I was music editor at the *Standard*." Deb had left—or been let go, depending on the person you asked—to pursue her own ventures, which Katie understood to mean dabbling in cannabis cultivars, drinking too much, and attempting to launch a failed kratom bar in the Outer Banks. Now she did some freelance grant-writing and tended bar at one of the fancier restaurants, which apparently paid better than the *Standard* anyway.

Katie laughed, a hooting, delirious laugh to cover that fact that she couldn't actually find words, couldn't actually find her breath. This was worthless. An empty smear.

"Useless," she finally said. "I'd be accused of libel."

Deb sat back, crossing her arms across her chest. She shook her head.

"You were always blinded by that guy," she said. "There's a phone number. Call it."

She passed a sticky note to Katie. Katie stared at it.

"So you're not coming tonight," she said.

Deb had already stood, smoothing her pants.

"To watch you butter him up like a dinner roll? God, no." She turned to leave. "Before you write your puff piece, at least call and check this out."

Deb was gone then, leaving Katie there with the sound of summer traffic up the main street and the rustle and murmur of people walking outside with their cappuccinos and laptops. A man passed by, and for a moment, Katie mistook him for Colin—the same build, the same color hair—but then he turned, and she saw he had a beakish nose and two pinched little eyes. He was so close to beautiful that she almost pitied him, until she remembered that he was a man, and therefore it mattered not nearly so much if he was beautiful or not. Colin's looks were always superfluous to something else—an assuredness that Katie admired and envied. The world, as he lived in it, was his.

"What would you wish for?" Colin had asked her once during their college days. "If you could do anything by the time you're twenty-five." They'd been lying on their backs on the burled gray carpet of Katie's sophomore apartment floor, their sock feet tracing patterns on the moldering wall. Occasionally, Katie's toes would brush against his, a moment shocking in its intimacy. Surely this was not allowed. Surely were Thea to walk in and see their sock feet dancing on the wall, her face would register profound dismay. These conversations, this connection—it all must mean something.

"I don't know," Katie had said, glad that they were watching their own feet. Had he seen her face, he might have read what her wish was. "What about you?"

"I want to make something lasting. Something beautiful and true," he said, and then he'd turned to her and smiled so radiantly that she'd wanted to dissolve right then and there.

"Me too," she'd said. And she'd managed to summon so much enthusiasm that it almost seemed as if she meant it, but even then Katie had known, if she were honest with herself, that she truly was not in possession of such audacity. Her respect and awe were such that she would have been content to be an acolyte alone, to rest in beauty's presence, its nearness both a pleasure and a necessity, a blaze against which she might cup and warm her hands.

Not long after this, she had lingered in their classroom, stalling while Colin spoke with their intermediate poetry professor, an ancient and widely beloved woman with half-moon glasses and a white bun atop her head. They'd been discussing a poem, a poem by Yeats, one of her favorites. *The light of evening, Lissadell, great windows open to the south, two girls in silk kimonos, both beautiful, one a gazelle . . .*

"I love that," Katie had offered breathily. It was a feeling like intoxication, what certain sounds could do to her back then. "Just those lines alone."

They'd turned to her then, both the professor and Colin, and she'd felt it: the nakedness of her own admiration, like a kind of raw desire. She'd blushed.

"You, my darling, are a true reader," their professor had said. "You have a reader's soul." She'd smiled at Katie then, and so had Colin, and for a brief moment, she'd felt understood by them, appreciated, like a spotlight had fallen on her and her alone.

But then their professor had turned to Colin and spoken to him seriously. "Appreciate that. Readers like Katie are few and far between. They are the ones for whom we write."

Colin looked long at the professor, like he was taking a silent vow, finally opening himself to a truth he'd long suspected. It was like watching someone else propose to the person you loved.

Katie could not tolerate it—the sharp prick of shame, the prop to which she'd been reduced. She'd hurried out of the classroom then, unable to explain what had upset her when she'd run into Deb at the library later.

"We disagreed about Yeats," she'd finally said. "It was stupid."

Deb, confident and wry even then, had rolled her eyes. "Dude was a grandiose asshole."

Avoiding the offices of the *Standard*, Katie meandered through town wearing her earbuds, listening to both of Colin's albums. This was the perk and the privilege of her long tenure at the paper: what she did not make in money, she made up for in flexibility, in the ability to let time drip slow as lake water off her fingertips one moment and then pull an all-nighter to meet a deadline in another. It was a hot, muggy late afternoon, the air chowder-thick. No one passed by on the bike path along the railroad tracks. People everywhere were indoors, safe in the dull bliss of air-conditioning. Katie's tank top stuck to her back, sweat dripping into her eyes.

She played one of Colin's earliest songs a second time, a breakthrough track chosen by *Pitchfork* as one of the best of the year. She'd reread old posts on *Stereogum* earlier, trying to see Colin from outside herself. The truth was she didn't entirely understand the appeal of Colin's music; it had a distant, overheard quality, like laughter from another room, something nice to fall asleep to. It reminded her of when she'd seen Low with him in college— lugubrious and long, a show Katie had felt she ought to like more than she actually liked. She'd always preferred things that were more upbeat, if one could consider Elliott Smith upbeat. She'd been so sad when he died. By that point, she and Colin were no longer communicating.

"Not a true genius," Colin had said of Elliott Smith, early in the course of their friendship. "Good, but not great. If he weren't so sad, he'd probably just make straight-up pop music."

This had been a game with them: good versus great. So many people Katie admired, artists whom she might have elected to greatness, were not deemed worthy by Colin. Those who made the cut had some indefinable quality she could never quite comprehend. Thomas Mann, yes, Baudelaire, no. Aretha Franklin, yes, Etta James, not quite. Keats, yes, Shelley, no. Yeats must have made the cut: Colin's second album was called *Strike a Match and Blow*.

Reaching into her bag for a lip balm, she found the paper on which Deb had written the phone number. Katie stared at it, noting the comforting familiarity of Deb's handwriting, staring until the numbers swam, turning strange and meaningless.

On an impulse, she pulled out her phone and dialed, moving to a patch of shade under an awning.

It rang three times before a woman's voice answered.

"Hello?"

The voice was familiar.

"Who is this?"

"Who is *this*?"

"I got your number from an email. About Colin Reynolds. My name is Katie."

The person on the other end exhaled.

"Katie. This is Thea."

After all these years, all of her carefully nurtured hatred, Thea's voice sounded thoughtful and not unkind. Sorry. Thea's voice sounded sorry.

"You must already know what I'm about to tell you," Thea said carefully. "It was an open secret. Lord knows what he tries to get away with now."

Katie listened to what Thea said, closing her eyes in the triangle of shade. Drops of sweat gathered at her hairline and slid down her nose. *Bitter*, Katie whispered to herself, and it was balm. *Vitriolic, spurned, hateful.* She thought these words but did not dare interrupt while Thea talked.

"I just don't know," Katie finally said when Thea had concluded, and then she clicked to end the phone call. There. She'd done her duty. Now she felt a little dehydrated, faint.

A cluster of children were licking cones of Hawaiian shaved ice near the car wash on the corner. A little boy, his tongue blue, waved at her, and she felt strangely abashed.

Surely Colin would email her back, suggesting some meeting time or place before the show. Or did he expect her simply to wait for him until after his show, along with all the other fangirls, barely out of adolescence? She and Colin were *old friends*. She was not a groupie, not a lurker. No. The prospect of crowding in with a bunch of long-limbed, self-serious twenty-one-year-olds sylphs in Buddy Holly glasses was unthinkable.

She started back down the block toward the club where Colin would be playing, passing for the third time now the tour van parked in front. Colin's van, certainly. Was he inside? And if so, what would he be doing? Writing songs? Eating a turkey sandwich? FaceTiming his pixie girlfriend?

"Katie? Katie Thompson?"

She froze as if struck by a physical object. She could not move. Pausing the music on her phone, she pulled her earbuds out and turned to look.

The man watching her was indeed Colin Reynolds. He stood, leaning against the side of the tour van, dressed in a dark shirt and jeans, ordinary clothing that belied his extraordinariness. A hank of hair fell over his eyes, and he moved toward her, through the shimmering summer heat like a swimmer moving through murky water. Like a mirage. All of Thea's poisonous words instantly dissolved, and it was the year 2000 again. Katie could not help herself. She threw up her arm and waved.

Katie waved like a drowning person. It was a full-body wave, so dire and uncool that a couple passing on the sidewalk exchanged amused little eye rolls. But she didn't care. She didn't care because Colin was walking toward her.

"Katie?"

There was a note of pleased disbelief in his voice, and this gratified her.

Up close, he looked almost exactly the same, but there were little lines around his eyes, a few silver hairs at his temples.

"Colin!" she said, her voice gone girlish and artificial, the sort of voice she couldn't help but fall into when she'd read her poetry out loud as an undergrad.

"I've really been wanting to see you," he said, and then, with the tiniest frown, the flicker of some almost imperceptible dissatisfaction passing over his face. "Katie Thompson. After all these years."

Then he was hugging her, and whatever she thought she might have read on his face had vanished, and they were smiling at each other, and she was following him up the steps into his van.

In the days immediately after she'd slept with Colin, Katie traveled through the world enveloped in a soft haze. Her roommate at the time had noticed the faint marks along her neck and commented. Katie found the word *hickey* repulsive, too reminiscent of her guffawing classmates back at the rural high school she'd fled. *Love bites*, she thought instead, studying herself in the mirror. Her eyes were serious, staring back at her in the dim bathroom with the drippy sink. Her mouth, her whole body, had a bruised feeling that seemed somehow precious and wonderful to her for days. Wasn't this how it worked? You made the suggestion of yourself and were wanted, then left glazed and tattered in the aftermath. She seemed different now—more potent, imbued with something profound.

Katie had wanted to contact Colin over the weekend—this had been, of course, before the days of texting—but she hadn't wanted to ruin anything with her eagerness. Besides, his actions had communicated everything: the two of them on the orange couch, the tick of the wall clock like a blind chaperone, "fade into you" sung like a hymn of such solemnity you just couldn't stand it.

And so it punctured something small and hopeful within her the following Monday when Colin didn't speak to her in their creative writing class.

He hurried into the classroom at the last possible moment, eyes downcast. When she tried to catch his glance, he seemed caught up in something else, distracted by a faint shape only he could discern on the ceiling. Ordinarily, they tended to catch each other's eyes throughout the workshop, sending carefully timed looks when other students offered stock feedback. *I liked the way this flowed*, or *The speaker was really relatable.*

It was almost like there was something out the window, beyond where the ground staff was applying fresh mulch in the quad, something that only Colin could see, that only Colin knew would soon arrive.

And then it did.

The door burst open midway through the workshop, at the point in that April afternoon when people had begun to feel a sleepy sort of malaise with the pleasant lull of the professor's voice after Benny Tallberg had read his villanelle aloud, the soft rustle of shuffled papers.

Thea.

Katie could still remember what Thea wore that day: chunky sandals with rugged heels, a scoop neck shirt with a denim skirt, hoop earrings, pigtails braided into two loops. She was crying terrific tears, and the overall effect, this clash of fashion and desperation, gave the impression of a wayward Delia's model who'd witnessed a terrible traffic accident.

"You," she snarled. "You."

Her face was snotted, and she spoke between huge sniffles. Everyone in the classroom was visibly alarmed. Katie braced herself against her chair, ready for hellfire and damnation. Waving one accusatory finger, Thea approached Colin.

"You," she said. "How could you? You asshole."

Of all the people in the room, only Colin looked perfectly calm. He'd folded his hands neatly on his desk and stared back at Thea evenly. She stopped in front of his desk, her arms fallen limp at her sides, a gesture of futility. She stood before him, awaiting some rebuttal. But Colin, holding her gaze, said nothing. The seconds moved, slow and viscous, like mercury in a glass.

Thea turned, as if seeing Katie for the first time, and her rage seemed to renew itself.

"Stay away from him," she said. Her voice was a harsh whisper now, and Katie could see the cords of her throat pulled taut like that of a much older woman. "Stay the hell away from him."

And with that, Thea left the room, and it was like whatever slow-pouring moment that had held them finally broke.

"Let's take five," the professor said, and if Katie was not mistaken, there was dismay and mild irritation in her voice, but also, far worse, pity.

The implication of this horrible confrontation in the classroom was clear. Everyone knew that Colin had a girlfriend, which made Katie the loser, throwing herself at someone unattainable.

Thankfully, it was almost the end of the semester. Katie skipped the final two class meetings, although she did still turn in her portfolio to the professor. She earned, to her further shame, an A, an A presumably born out of pity.

Katie dropped her English major after this. The thought of turning up in classes again with people who'd seen this confrontation, of being carefully ignored by Colin, was unbearable. Her credits transferred to the school of journalism.

The one or two times she passed Colin after that, they exchanged nods of acknowledgment, like soldiers on opposite sides of a demilitarized zone. There was no discussion of that moment in the classroom, or of stories or poems or music or anything else.

When Katie ever spotted Thea on campus, she either fled or hid.

All these years since, Katie had nurtured a special hatred of Thea, an enmity that resulted in occasional internet stalking. Thea was married now, working in PR in Atlanta, sleek and glossy and hateable in a different way. And why not hate her? She had stolen something from Katie— something that Thea herself probably never valued, probably never even understood.

"Make yourself comfortable," Colin said to Katie, throwing aside a stained hoodie and an empty Dr Pepper bottle to make room for her on a bench seat inside the van. "Can I get you something to drink?"

If Katie didn't know better, she would say he seemed nervous. She could see a bluish vein in his temple, and then there was the uncertain way he kept swallowing, and the overall jitteriness of his movements. Gone was the old swagger she remembered.

Her throat was dry, and so she accepted a bottle of water, twisting the cap off and fumbling it immediately to the floor. He shrugged, and so she left it there. The van was filthy. There were clothes strewn everywhere, empty bags of chips and granola bar wrappers, a grayish pair of crew socks lying on a seat next to a blue plastic toothbrush. The whole place smelled of male sweat and hot sauce and cigarettes.

"I was hoping to hear back from you," she said.

He turned away from her, fumbling with a safety pin that had been lying on the window ledge.

"Yeah, sorry. It's been a weird time."

He looked at her, square in the face. The light from the window was strong and unflattering. He looked weary and unspecial, ordinary.

"I'm excited to see the show . . . write something up. I'm still at the *Standard*, you know? And I like it. It's pretty great. Not the poetry we dreamed of." She chuckled here, and God, she sounded idiotic and nervous, prattling on while he watched her. "But it's writing, and it's a job, and I like it."

"Listen," he said, and he touched her hand very softly, with a kind of deference, it seemed. "I wanted to talk to you about something. It wasn't that big of a deal. We were kids. I mean, I don't want to sound defensive, but Thea—you remember Thea? She's trying to make it a thing."

She frowned at him.

"The way things were back then. You know—guys. Like we could sometimes get a little ahead of ourselves?"

Something registered, and Katie stiffened. The way her wrist had throbbed afterward, a thing she'd written off as a byproduct of his enthusiasm. The way it had hurt sharply when she'd peed, a sort of knife-torn feeling she'd carried within herself for days, feeling grave and adult. But these were picky details. Why bring them up now? It was like studying a lovely face too closely. You could ruin it, focusing on all the tiny hairs and pores and blemishes.

"So I wanted to apologize . . . if I, I don't know, made you uncomfortable in any way."

She studied him, an anxious thrum rising in her ears.

"It's just . . . I finally have this girl, Sheila, and I'm crazy about her. And my music—I'm making what I want to make. People want to listen. I've got a lot to lose."

Katie couldn't respond. A carefully curated scene that she'd returned to time and time again in her mind was slowly reconfiguring, each element taking on a different cast. The sad little rental house with its banana-colored refrigerator and water bugs and orange couch. The clock on the wall ticked in accusation now, the hideous couch abrading the bare skin of her lower back, and Colin's hands clutching the meat of her thighs, relentless, too insistent. Her own voice—"wait, what are you doing, stop"—melting into the Mazzy Star she'd selected because she had wanted this, right? She'd wanted this very thing. She'd wanted to see it through. Colin had put the song on repeat, and now it played back in her recollection like a taunt.

"I'm sorry. You probably haven't even thought about this in years. I just mean, God, if I was pushy or whatever. I'm sorry. Fuck. It was a different time, right?"

The van was sweltering. She looked to see if there was a window she could open, but there was not. She had a looping sensation in her head, like she might pass out if she didn't get fresh air soon.

She got up and grabbed hold of the door handle.

"Wait. Katie. You're not . . . I'm sorry. We were dumb kids. Please."

"No," she said. "Stop saying that. That's not how it was."

His hand clamped down on her shoulder, but she shook him off and jerked the door open.

He called to her, but she ran. The sun was much lower, but it was still hot, and the late afternoon air tore like a sheet of steaming fabric as she ran through it. She ran back across town and along the railroad track and stumbled down the scrappy embankment behind one of the new developments until she found herself at the edge of the creek. It was a drainage ditch, really. The very ditch where she'd seen the blue heron that same morning. There was a trickle of putrid water and empty beer cans, colorful bits of trash like the conclusion of a party. She sank onto her haunches, pulling out her phone and keying in her passcode onto the screen to unlock it.

It was growing late. Almost evening. Colin and his bandmates would be setting up soon, doing sound check, popping bottles of beer with the guys who were playing as opener. *The light of evening, Lissadell, great windows open to the south.* She let the phone rest against her cheek for a moment, but then clicked it back to sleep, returning it to her pocket.

A squirrel scrambled up the opposite bank, and Katie found herself waiting for the blue heron to return, like a long-kept promise coming to fruition. But there was nothing, only the squirrel, and a tiny gray bird chirruping behind a clump of dry brush.

The light of evening fell slantwise now through the trees, and depending on how she looked at the drainage ditch, the underbrush, the trees at precisely that moment, it was all either humdrum or utterly wild and vivid and lovely.

The little bird flitted off, and it was quiet.

With a breath, she could burn it all down.

AMO, AMAS, AMAT

NOT LONG AFTER THEY MOVED INTO THE GREEN CRAFTSMAN on the east side of town near us, we began to hear things about the Milandrofers. Mr. Milandrofer was the new Latin teacher at the intermediate school. His wife was from another country—somewhere stark and recently war-ravaged. Everyone had seen Mrs. Milandrofer wandering the grocery store with a dazed expression on her face, pulling brightly colored cereal boxes down to better behold them, only to return them to the shelves again, blinking as if the whole experience was just too much for her.

My mother thought Mrs. Milandrofer was beautiful, and I suppose she did have the sort of thin, extraterrestrial quality one might associate with fashion models. I'd heard Mrs. Milandrofer spoke no English, but when I mentioned this to my mother, she called me rude and asked me how many other languages *I* spoke. None, I said, which was why I'd signed up for Mr. Milandrofer's Latin class. "Ah, Latin is wonderful, little rabbit," my mother said, kissing me on the forehead. "You're becoming an intellectual." It was never entirely clear when my mother was mocking me. She had grown up in Tennessee, near a small liberal arts college where her father taught, and from which she'd absorbed many vague notions about the value of intellectualism.

It was my mother, of course, who had gotten me the scholarship that allowed me to attend the private school where Mr. Milandrofer taught. Proper schools, she said, came at a price and provided a classical education. Mr. Milandrofer was a classicist, thus estimable by my mother's measure—although in appearance, he was nothing extraordinary: short, with cheeks the hue and texture of lunch meat, and a gelled frond of dark hair covering his bald patch. Given the disparity in their looks, we assumed that Mrs. Milandrofer, with her long arms and gloomy-gorgeous skeleton face, must have married him only to escape the cold winters and long breadlines of her native land. Maybe he'd gotten her from a bride catalog, my friend Jenny Henderson suggested. At first we were all fond of Mr. Milandrofer, despite the fact that he was nervous and bug-eyed and unlike anyone else in town.

It was from Jenny that I learned the Milandrofers had a child, a little boy named Robert.

"They're weirdos," she told me.

Jenny lived with her mother and stepfather two doors down from us, and she liked to be in the know.

"Mrs. Milandrofer locks herself in her room to cry all day, and the boy has something wrong with him that makes him dumb and fat," Jenny explained, smacking her grape gum authoritatively. "They play opera music really loud, and there's a door no one is allowed to unlock." Jenny was being homeschooled, so she wasn't Mr. Milandrofer's student, but, being a neighbor, she'd been invited over for a cup of tea with her mother shortly after the Milandrofers moved in.

The house was dim, Jenny told me, and filled with small, dainty objects— doilies and ornate lamps with pull chains and porcelain figurines of shepherdesses and little boys playing lutes. Jenny and her mother had had to sit on a stiff, straight-back velveteen couch while Mr. Milandrofer—friendly, anxious, rosy-cheeked—spoke to them and Mrs. Milandrofer brought out tiny plates of dusty cookies and little ceramic cups of tea so weak it tasted like bathwater. Jenny said the boy, Robert, never ventured out to say hello, but she saw him peeking at them from the darkened hallway on occasion, a pale and curious mushroom. When they stood to leave, Jenny's mother inadvertently hit a side table, knocking over a decorative plate depicting a London street scene of red double-decker buses. Mr. Milandrofer responded with a level of distress he could only barely conceal, but even as he reassured Mrs. Henderson that it was no problem, his frantic eyes read otherwise. Indeed, Jenny and her mother could see the dismay in his face as he hastened to usher them out the door before Mrs. Milandrofer returned to the room.

"She never said a word the whole time," Jenny said of Mrs. Milandrofer. "I think she's mute." Mrs. Henderson had wondered why a mother of a young child would have a house full of so many delicate knickknacks in the first place. Such things belonged in the houses of childless couples or prim elderly ladies, she said, not families with children.

We were sitting in Jenny's backyard the afternoon she told me all this. It was not long into the school year, and I had been to Latin class for only a couple of weeks but was already a little taken with Mr. Milandrofer. He certainly wasn't handsome, but there was a look of such gentle concern on his face, such a sense of amused expectation when he spoke to us—"Salvete, discipuli!"—that it stirred me. When I'd turned in my most recent Latin translation, he'd called me to his desk after class, shaking his head as if there were no words sufficient to convey his pleasure.

"What do you want, Margaret?" he'd asked finally, beaming over me, looking beneficent but weary, like someone who has seen great hardships but still retains the capacity for surprise. "What do you want to be someday, a bright girl like you?"

I hadn't quite known how to answer. No one but my mother had taken such an interest in me before. There I was in eighth grade, less grown-up than the other girls, who'd already taken to carrying around little elegantly wrapped tampons in their purses and putting on practiced smirks whenever adults came into their vicinity. My mother worked shifts as a home health aide. She still gave me bowl cuts and dressed me in dungarees, wheat-colored unisex shirts, or puffy sweatpants stained with brown soda that had been handed down from my male cousin. Money was tight, and she viewed me as a child still, an appendage, not a person. Early on, she told me to go to school for as long as I could, collecting degrees like berries on a summer day until I had so many I could overwhelm the world with my knowledge. "No bedpans for you, little rabbit," she said. Her father—in his eighties now, hemiplegic and lodged in a nursing home—had taught English literature at that small college back in Tennessee. Although my mother had been estranged from her father since before I was born, I'd seen a photo of him when he was young: proud and professorial in his tweed vest and glasses, holding his scuffed briefcase.

Now, with Mr. Milandrofer looking expectantly at me, I felt the need to convey to him our common cause.

"I want to be a college professor," I said. "Or a teacher. At a school like this."

He smiled, raising an eyebrow and stepping back, as if to further inspect my intellect.

"Perhaps of Latin?" he said. "You're off to a good start."

"Perhaps," I said, and the word felt good on my tongue, nice and crisp and so much better than plain old *maybe*. It felt like Mr. Milandrofer and I were already speaking to each other as adults.

"You know," Mr. Milandrofer said, "I could use some assistance. Organizing the textbooks and such. I don't know if you might be willing to help, during lunch, perhaps?"

I felt the tips of my ears going incandescent: so Mr. Milandrofer had surmised my difficulties. He'd passed by me a few days earlier while I was sitting in the arts building hallway, eating my peanut butter sandwich, alone.

To give me a moment to collect myself, he turned and straightened the spine of a volume of Catullus on his shelf. "I don't know," I said, my voice growing hoarse with the threat of tears, the way it did whenever someone was unexpectedly kind.

"If you're too busy, I understand," he said over his shoulder, fiddling with the spines of the Catullus, the Ovid, the *Roma Est Magna*. There were books of Greek poetry, too—hefty and serious-looking. "But I could use the help."

"I'm not all that busy," I said, and Mr. Milandrofer turned back to face me, smiling so broadly that his eyes shrank to two dark commas on his face.

"Wonderful," he said, and he clapped his hands so that the chalk jumped out of its tray behind him.

I forgot myself and smiled full-on at him, allowing my crooked teeth to show. It felt like one of those moments. Like even though he was a middle-aged teacher and I merely his student, something had bloomed, fragile and precious, between us. And even in the end, after all the things people said, long after the Milandrofers had moved away, this was a moment I kept for myself, unsullied.

My mother was my best friend during those years. This is always a dangerous and questionable thing to say, but it was true. Jenny Henderson was the only friend I had who was my own age. Our mothers worked together, and after school I would go to Jenny's house, where we'd wait for them to finish their shifts.

"Omnia Gallia in tres partes divisa est," I said for Jenny's benefit. She was smarter, so sometimes I liked to lord over her the things I picked up in class.

We lay on our backs in Jenny's backyard, flicking acorns over a fence and studying the sky. One lazy, anvil-shaped cloud drifted overhead. I looked to see if Jenny seemed impressed. She possessed the motley knowledge of an autodidact with a library card and an instinct for mischief. Her mom worked as much as mine did, so her homeschooling amounted to Jenny marauding the interlibrary loan system, watching PBS, and wandering feral through the neighborhood. There'd been some behavior issues back in her old parochial school, my mother said—I understood this to mean Jenny had been kicked out—and the public schools were too dangerous. Full of knives and oxy and pregnant teenagers.

"Show-off," Jenny said. "Latin is bullshit."

Instead of flicking the acorn over the fence, I flicked it toward her face. She gave me a shove. Jenny was scrappy and brave, untroubled by anyone else's opinion, nothing like the other girls at my school.

"Latin is the language of law, science, and logic," I recited.

She laughed.

"Come on. Let's look for dildos."

Jenny stood, brushing leaves off her shorts, and I rose to follow. She was obsessed with contraband, most recently dildos. She'd found one once, abandoned in the wooded gully behind the houses. There was a patch of scraggly woods behind Jenny's neighborhood that abutted an abandoned housing development called Nottingham Bend. These half-built Nottingham houses stared out, impassive, through the trees. Often Jenny and I scrabbled down the embankment, wandering through the adjoining woods. Hobos lived here, Jenny told me, and she could sometimes hear their hobo sex cries at night.

"You're a pervert," I told her.

When Jenny first showed me the dildo—big as a man's fist, florid and rubbery, with hyperreal veins—I felt nauseated.

"You're just not used to men," Jenny said, her voice going rich and delicious with secrets, the voice she used whenever she had special knowledge to impart. "Men have certain needs. There are things they have to do."

In addition to her stepfather, Karl, Jenny lived with an older stepbrother, Todd, who was a student at the community college and who, people said, sold pills. Todd and Karl were a mostly invisible presence in the household whenever I was there, but, like wild animals, they left traces of themselves—stained socks, athletic shorts, muddy work boots, half-eaten bags of corn chips—like scat along a forest trail.

It was true I wasn't used to men. Their proximity elicited a jangly alertness in me. There had been times I'd felt Todd's and Karl's eyes on us—not me, really, but my mother, who was, by all accounts, still beautiful. She'd had me at eighteen, derailing a promising academic career. My mother had been a debate champion, brilliant in every way, a full scholarship to a fancy university awaiting her, until my arrival threw things off.

Jenny rolled her eyes whenever I spoke of my mother with admiration. But I couldn't help myself. My mother still carried herself with a certain pride, wearing red lipstick to work and toting around a copy of a Dostoyevsky to read during lulls. Compared with her, all the other mothers I knew looked rumpled and overstuffed, like badly-slept-upon pillows. Jenny insisted my mother was a snob, her small efforts acts of pretension.

"Come on," she said.

We picked our way through the bushes behind Jenny's house, down through the dead honeysuckle branches and pine straw. We'd lost the original dildo. Jenny had known better than to take it home, so we had buried it under leaves by a large oak down at the bottom of the gully. A hobo must have reclaimed it, Jenny decided.

A bird called, rising with a flap from the branches above us. The bare beams of the half-built houses in Nottingham Bend loomed over the next crest. No one knew if these houses would ever be finished now that the Anheuser plant had left town. Jenny hoped Nottingham Bend would remain abandoned. She wanted to meet these so-called hobos. The way she described them, they were a merry band of misfits whiling away their days with gaudy dildos and dog-eared *National Geographic*s, family-size bags of Doritos, and old paperbacks and cans of Milwaukee's Best. I imagined them, swearing and tattooed, full of banter, manning the sterns of the empty houses like jolly pirates.

To Jenny, the gully between her neighborhood and Nottingham Bend was a prospector's paradise. We had found all sorts of human flotsam and jetsam down there—ratty army blankets, a ziplock bag full of old Canadian pennies, and, once, a whole, perfect birthday cake iced with the words HAPPY

BIRTHDAY, MIKE! Jenny swore she'd met someone there once: a skinny man in a fisherman's vest who'd been smoking a pipe and reading a copy of *On the Road*. He'd talked to Jenny about his life philosophy and hopping railroad cars, she said—details so generic they left me almost certain she'd made the whole thing up.

"I found a shopping cart the other day," she said now. "And an old green refrigerator with a bottle of gin in it. I'll show you."

I followed her, picking my way over the large stones that were strewn along the gully like irregular steps. A trickle of dirty water flowed beneath our feet. Over to our left, a lone squirrel snuffled in the leaves, inspecting an abandoned red Solo cup. When we were younger, Jenny and I had pretended this was a great canyon. We'd hopped from stone to stone, talking of wizardry and elves. Now we hunted for dildos, pages torn out of old girlie magazines, interesting hunks of machinery, train-hopping strangers.

There was a rustle of leaves around the bend. Jenny hissed, pinching the flesh of my arm to stop me from talking. I froze. In truth, I was terrified of stumbling upon one of Jenny's hobos.

We stood there for a second, but now the only noise was from a distant lawnmower. Then the rustling started again, like the sound of a small animal burrowing into its nest.

Jenny gestured for me to follow.

A little boy, maybe five or six, was sitting on his haunches in the leaves. When he heard us, he looked up, and I saw that his face was smeared dark, like that of a predator feasting after a kill. He clutched a partially gnawed chocolate bar, big as a cutting board, the kind you might give as a novelty gift.

"Robert?" Jenny called out, and the boy shot us a look of guilt and terror and clutched the chocolate bar closer to his chest.

"It's okay," I said, realizing now that this must be the Milandrofers' little boy. Just as Jenny had said, there was something vacant about his eyes. Instinctively, I tried to make my voice soothing. "Did you get lost? Can we take you home?"

Robert nodded, docile, dutifully wrapping the chocolate back in its foil. As we scrambled up the embankment, he allowed Jenny to hold his hand.

I followed the two of them to the green house. At the door we knocked and knocked again, but there was no answer. Finally, Robert simply opened the door and we all went inside.

"Where's your mother?" Jenny asked.

The house was quiet except for the ticking of a clock in the hallway, and, as Jenny had said, it was dark. The walls were cluttered with decoration: framed images of angels perched on puffy clouds, a poster of Monet's *Water Lilies*, a black-and-white movie still of Humphrey Bogart and Lauren Bacall, a framed copy of the Lord's Prayer in looping cursive script. There were no family photos, no school photos of Robert. The living room was so crammed with objects that it looked like a junk shop. An old radio stood in one corner next to a coatrack made to look like a pear tree. A collection of commemorative thimbles hung in a little glass case above a peach-colored settee. I picked up a music box with a dancing bear atop it and traced a line through the film of dust.

A door opened. I heard the clatter of keys in the kitchen, followed by the sound of footsteps.

We turned to find Mr. Milandrofer standing in front of us. Robert ran to him, throwing his chubby little arms around his father's waist, smashing his chocolatey face right into Mr. Milandrofer's pants.

"Jenny? Margaret?"

A shadow fell over his face like a curtain over a window.

"We found him," Jenny said, pointing to Robert. "In the woods."

Mr. Milandrofer's expression remained inscrutable. He was still wearing the pale blue shirt I'd seen him teach in earlier, but it looked rumpled now, yellowish stains under his arms.

"Where's Mama?" he asked Robert.

Robert pointed one grubby finger to the ceiling.

"Sleeping," he said.

"Thank you, girls," Mr. Milandrofer said, then ushered us toward the door. "Mrs. Milandrofer gets bad headaches sometimes."

Once we were outside, he handed us two lollipops from his pocket, as if we were good children getting a treat from a bank teller.

We licked our lollipops all the way back to Jenny's house, where we found my mom and Jenny's stepbrother, Todd, drinking glasses of Coca-Cola in the kitchen.

"Where were you?" my mother asked, and her cheeks were bright, like she'd been laughing hard. Her eyes shone in that way they did when she was receiving a particular type of attention. Todd turned on the tap and filled another glass with water, taking a gulp.

"Your mom's not home yet, kid," he said to Jenny.

"We found the neighbor boy," she announced. "He was lost in the woods and we rescued him."

My mother's eyes still shone with a feverish light, but her cheeks were returning to their normal color. "Well, aren't you two girls just brilliant things," she said, her words light as confetti. "Wouldn't you say so, Todd?"

Todd grunted his assent, but I saw something in his face: the way his eyes followed my mother as if awaiting her approval, the way he touched her wrist quickly, communicating something not meant for the rest of us to see. It was all over in a matter of seconds. Jenny did a performative little twirl, but it was my mother, standing there in the late sunlight streaming through the kitchen window, who looked shining and divine, like someone out of Mr. Milandrofer's poetry. Her wine-dark lips parted and she laughed, clutching her white arms, my radiant, god-born mother. Jenny tugged my sleeve, but I ignored her like she was nothing but a housefly brushing against my elbow.

When my mother heard I was helping Mr. Milandrofer at lunchtime, she was pleased.

"You learn your Latin, little rabbit," my mother said. "You know, my daddy read Latin and Greek. He was fluent in Italian, French, and Spanish, with passable German, too."

I coughed and said nothing. It was hard for me to understand how she could speak so proudly of her father. And yet I'd learned better than to say anything bad about him in front of her.

From her crossword puzzle—she liked to do them whenever she had the time, "to keep the mind agile," she'd told me—my mother looked up at me and took the capped end of her pen between her teeth. Talking about her father always made her go soft-eyed and sad.

"Never forget yourself because of a man," she said, dropping the pen and letting her gaze drift to something invisible on the horizon.

I understood that my mother meant my own father. I knew little of him other than that he'd been a graduate student of my grandfather's. Older. Married. He'd left when my mother was eight months pregnant with me. My father's departure—and my arrival—had been the reason why she moved away.

Ever since then, my mother had tempered any attraction she felt toward men with a hard suspicion. She probably would have been wary of Mr. Milandrofer had she not yet met him. She didn't say so, but I could tell by the way she'd nodded after giving him the once-over that he was suitably unsexed by his double chin and doughy features, the bad mustache he wore, his poorly tucked shirts. He was simply a teacher. Harmless.

Besides, everyone knew Mr. Milandrofer was pining for his wife. People spoke of this: how she'd married him only for the green card, and how poor, smitten Mr. Milandrofer was now desperate to win her love. You just had to look at all the little gifts with which he'd plied her to see. "He's besotted," the owner of the local deli said after Mr. Milandrofer called again and again to special-order a particular type of sausage, something that Mrs. Milandrofer had loved in her childhood. When people saw them together in public, they noticed Mr. Milandrofer's solicitousness, how anxious and attentive he seemed.

"Go study your Latin," my mother said, waving a hand at me. "Make Mr. Milandrofer proud."

After that, Mr. Milandrofer didn't mention the time I'd dropped Robert off at his house. We spent most of our time at school together quietly. I'd grown accustomed to this: the comfortable silence of our shared lunch breaks punctuated every now and then by an observation on a particular passage from one of the Latin texts or a tricky declension. Mr. Milandrofer let me pore through his books while the radiator hummed and rattled behind us.

"You know," he said one day, "if there are things you ever want to talk about—" He paused, removing his glasses and rubbing his watery eyes. He was eating tuna salad, and he placed the fork down on his desk thoughtfully. "I want to be a trusted adult. Someone you can ask questions. About worries. Or feelings."

I felt a dark, muddy warmth blossoming at my chest and spreading upward. "What feelings?" I said.

"I ran into your friend Jenny Henderson again," he said, looking out the window, as if he were changing the subject. "She's a nice girl. A spitfire."

I nodded.

"You two seem quite close."

"She's basically my only other friend," I said—and immediately blushed at my choice of words. Yet if Mr. Milandrofer picked up on the implication, he didn't show it.

"Adolescence is an overwhelming time," he said. "Just promise me you'll come talk to me if you're feeling confused. Or if you're feeling alone."

"I will," I said.

"Thank you, pious Aeneas," Mr. Milandrofer said, and he snapped the plastic lid onto his empty lunch container. The room smelled of tuna, but I was accustomed to this. The food Mr. Milandrofer brought to eat was always hearty and disgusting—mayonnaisey raisin-pocked salads, bachelor food, meals I knew no loving wife would ever pack. Certainly I wouldn't have packed them for Mr. Milandrofer.

He got up, walked over to me, and gave me two pats on the head. When he called me "pious Aeneas," I knew he was pleased with me. The book open on my desk showed an illustration of two young Roman men in togas who appeared to be wrestling each other. Mr. Milandrofer's hand fell over it, his fingers tracing the contours of the sketch. Right then we were reading bits of Vergil in translation in class, then trying them in the original. To inspire us, he'd said. Advanced work, a challenge. The other students grumbled. The funny kids called Aeneas *Anus* and Dido *Dildo*, and the class laughed like this was a big hoot. They preferred the days when we draped sheets around ourselves as togas, celebrating Saturnalia and discussing Roman culture. Once, when handsome Justin Giddings, a lacrosse star whose parents were both attorneys, stood in his chair, shouting "Veni, vidi, vici" in falsetto and sashaying his hips, I'd watched Mr. Milandrofer smile patiently, although I could swear I heard him curse under his breath.

"You and I, we are a team, aren't we, discipula?" he said to me that day during lunch. It was a thing he'd said before, but he said it that day with extra emphasis, like we were fellow Trojans battling a sea of Justin Giddingses, who loped around the school with all the infuriating grace and indolence of young laureates.

Jenny had been colder to me in recent weeks, more aloof. I was used to this: her moods, the way she lit up from within with pleasure or irritation. When I arrived after school, the doors to her house would be locked and she would be nowhere to be found. I would search the neighborhood, wandering and calling until I found her: in a neighbor's backyard hammock, or inside one of the abandoned houses at Nottingham Bend, her eyes glowing like a wild creature's from the dark.

That particular day, the door to Jenny's house was locked. Jenny had always loved being outside, but we'd also spend time in her house—watching TV or eating popcorn while we listened to music in her bedroom. Now she was never there. She only wanted to be outside.

I found Jenny sitting in the base of a hollowed tree down in the gully.

"Hey," I said.

She didn't look up at me. I saw she'd been drinking one of the fruity wine coolers her mother kept in the refrigerator. Her mouth was stained pinkish, like that of a child with a glass of Kool-Aid in summer.

"You were hiding from me."

She took a swig.

"Want to play Truth or Dare?" Jenny asked.

I sat down beside her.

"It's not that fun with just us."

"Sure it is. Choose."

I knew better than to allow Jenny to dare me.

"Truth."

"Who do you *like*?" she asked, putting emphasis on the last word, tossing the empty bottle of wine cooler across the gully, where it landed with a soft thud in the brush. She didn't meet my eye.

I thought of Mr. Milandrofer, his sweet, dorky smile and mustache, the way he smelled of coffee even in the afternoon, the way his voice rose in enthusiasm, his mustache lifting when he smiled, revealing his small, perfect teeth. I cleared my throat.

"Justin Giddings, I guess," I said.

Jenny snorted. "Justin Giddings is an idiot," she said, yet something had broken open in her voice again, sun parting clouds, and I knew she was not unhappy with my answer. We were still friends. She touched me lightly on the back of my neck, and I shivered. "You're a fool," she said. "A silly little fool."

"Who do *you* like?" I asked, mock-angrily.

"I don't choose truth," Jenny said, her expression gone sly. "I choose dare."

"I dare us to go to your house and watch TV."

"Dare me to go to the Milandrofers' house," she said, her voice airy and reckless. "Dare me to sneak into their creepy old house and see what those weirdos do when no one else is around."

"I don't dare you to do that."

"Dare me to go find your *boyfriend*, Mr. Milandrofer," Jenny said, her voice singsongy, sickly sweet like cough syrup.

"No. That's not the dare."

But Jenny was already off, tearing through the leaves, scrambling up the opposite hillside.

"Wait," I shouted. "Jenny."

She turned, laughing over her shoulder once more, then disappeared above the crest of the hill. I went after her, knowing the dare was already in action.

There was nothing to do but follow her into their house.

I entered from the backyard through the patio door. Inside, the Milandrofers' house was quiet and dark and still. I moved through the kitchen, where plates were piled high in the sink. An opened can of tomato soup sat on the counter next to a half-empty sleeve of store-bought chocolate chip cookies.

"Jenny?" I whispered, tiptoeing through the hallways and into the living room, which was even more stuffed and haphazard than I remembered.

"Jenny?"

Someone padded down the stairs and into the living room, and I started. It wasn't Jenny. It was Robert.

He peered at me from behind a chair, holding a ratty blanket in one hand and an orange Popsicle in the other.

"Hi, Robert," I whispered, kneeling down and making my face friendly.

Robert took a long, slow slurp of his ice pop and then, removing it, stuck out his orange tongue. It wasn't a rude gesture. He smiled a sticky orange smile and looked up at me.

"Have you seen my friend? Jenny?" I gestured to the darkened hallway beyond the living room.

He gazed at me, unblinking, sucking on his lower lip. I was beginning to wonder if he even understood. Then he turned from me, moseying through the living room dreamily, lifting up his mother's miniature ballet dancer, her tiny bejeweled elephant, for inspection. Then, at the doorway, he paused, as if waiting for me to follow.

I did, creeping after him as he went up the staircase, appalled at Jenny's audacity. We made our way down a long hallway, passing several closed doors until we reached the one at the very end of the hall. Robert opened it, and I saw another set of unfinished stairs.

"She's up there?" I asked.

Robert just looked at me, long and slow. He took another lick of his Popsicle, then began climbing.

I followed him into a large, unfinished attic with a pitched ceiling and a planked floor. The room looked like a nursery in a storybook orphanage. It was filled with white bassinets and cradles, a dozen at least, arranged in neat rows under the eaves. In a rocking chair, Mrs. Milandrofer sat holding a lifelike baby doll in her arms. She wore a green silk robe with fuzzy slippers and had drawn two high, arching lines above her actual eyebrows, which had been plucked to nothing. She looked like a washed-up old movie star, someone marked by glamour and tragedy.

Robert ran to her, grabbing the green tail of her robe, and she rose from the rocker, putting the baby down with a shushing sound. I stood immobilized at the top of the steps, hidden behind a large chest of drawers. I had the sense I'd barged in upon a moment of private, personal necessity, like accidentally walking into an occupied restroom stall.

"Babies," Robert said flatly.

"Babies," Mrs. Milandrofer echoed. Her voice was high-pitched and strange, the voice of someone who did not speak often. She picked up another baby doll, patting its bottom soothingly and whispering consolations into its ear, before replacing it gently in its cradle. She murmured a strange word, once, and then again, and I understood this must be the baby's name.

She moved to a tiny white cupboard painted with pink rosettes and opened it gently. Inside were little bottles and rattles and blankets. She selected a bottle and a blanket for one of the baby dolls near the dormer window.

I watched her move through the room, lifting each plastic doll lovingly from its bassinet, cooing and adjusting blankets. Robert followed her, dull-eyed in his red sweatpants, sucking at some orange goo on his finger.

She spoke in such a low tone to the dolls in their bassinets that I couldn't make out her words. I guessed she was speaking in another language, something harsh yet lilting that made me imagine rolling green hills and rushing waters—somewhere far from here, with actual wilderness instead of gullies filled with trash behind abandoned subdivisions.

Mrs. Milandrofer knelt toward one of the bassinets and scooped up a baby doll. Holding it against her shoulder, she patted its back gently. "Shh, shh," she whispered, before putting it back down.

Robert followed her, murmuring to himself. He tugged at her arm. When she did not respond, he pulled up his blue shirt, exposing his belly, smooth and white and fat as a moon, and started jumping up and down. He sucked at the hem of his shirt, making a sound like *glob-glob-glob*.

Mrs. Milandrofer sighed. Turning off the attic light switch, she took Robert's hand. I pressed myself back against the wall, further behind the dresser, to hide myself as they passed me on their way back down the stairs. Mrs. Milandrofer closed the attic door behind her, and I let out a breath. I was alone—except for all of Mrs. Milandrofer's babies.

I looked into one of the nearby cradles. A baby doll stared up at me, one plastic eye open, a cracked seam running down the front of its face like a scar. I picked up the doll and it rested, hollow and light in my arms. A bead of sweat rolled from one of my armpits down my side. The attic was hot, the air musty, and my throat had gone dry.

I moved quietly down the stairs back to the attic door, but when I tried to open it, I found it could only be opened from the outside. There was no inside handle. I pushed at the door, beat on it with my hands. Panicking, I called to Robert, to Mrs. Milandrofer, to anyone, but there was no answer.

I walked back up the attic stairs. Looking out the little dormer window, I saw Mrs. Milandrofer and Robert outside. It was starting to rain. She wore a black raincoat and a pert little hat. Robert had on a jacket printed with yellow ducks. From the attic window, they looked unreal, like tiny mechanical figures. The window wouldn't open; no one would be able to hear me from outside.

Even though the attic was stuffy and warm, a chill fell over me. All was very still.

For a long time I sat there, with all of Mrs. Milandrofer's precious babies surrounding me, silent in their swaddling, while the sun dropped and the attic light grew thinner and thinner, until finally I saw Mr. Milandrofer's car pull into the drive. Then I ran down the steps to beat upon the attic door again, kicking and shouting again, my voice growing hoarse, until Mr. Milandrofer either heard or sensed something was wrong. It was he who finally opened the door.

"Margaret?" he asked. "What in the world are you doing here?"

I was starting to answer when I saw Mrs. Milandrofer standing behind him, uttering words I could not understand.

"I'm sorry," I said, not even attempting any real explanation. "I got stuck."

Something whirled past my head and hit the wall beside me. I turned to look and saw a little pewter dish lying on the floor.

"You should leave," Mr. Milandrofer said. Behind him rose a great, animal wail.

The next day, I could barely bring myself to look at Mr. Milandrofer during Latin class. I could feel the weight of his avoidance, the note of contrition in his voice when he turned in my direction, not once meeting my gaze, and didn't go to his classroom at lunchtime—not that day, or ever again.

Mr. Milandrofer eventually took another student under his wing: a friendless boy named James Jankowicz who rarely spoke but who turned in flawless work in all his classes. James began studying Greek, I heard. Once, passing through the hallways during the lunch hour, I saw him sitting at a desk with a book open in front of him. Over him, Mr. Milandrofer bent forward, gesticulating.

One afternoon I found Jenny at our old spot in the woods after school. She was sitting on a stump at the base of the embankment, smoking a cigarette inexpertly.

"Watch this," she said, attempting to blow a ring of smoke and coughing.

"Cool," I said, crouching on the damp leaves next to her.

She took another drag and turned to me, her eyes narrow and adult.

"I didn't really go into their house the other day," she said.

"I know," I said. "I went there to look for you."

I told her about Mrs. Milandrofer and the attic and all the dolls, the long hours I'd spent trapped among them.

Her eyes widened. After I finished talking, she stood up.

"Come here," she said. "There's something you should see."

I followed her again along the stones that lay in the trickle of dirty water there at the bottom of the gully. We picked our way a long while, following the stream until we finally reached a point where I could hear the rumble of an overpass above us, just ahead. We were farther out than we'd ever walked, long past Jenny's neighborhood or Nottingham Bend.

A large forked tree leaned from one bank over the other, like a suspended drawbridge. Jenny helped me across it.

"Look."

All along the gully were the dismembered bodies of baby dolls. It looked like a toy store massacre. Blond or brunette or bald, the heads lay toppled among the leaves. Some were wide-eyed; some appeared to be peacefully sleeping. Elsewhere the bodies lay splayed, chunky arms extended in feeble protest, tiny fists or tiny hands reaching into empty air.

I swallowed.

Jenny picked up a decapitated baby doll head and studied it for a long moment. Then, turning to me, she tossed the doll head like a baseball so that it arced into the brush ahead of us.

"None of this was here before," she said.

"People," I said, exhaling like I was about to say something profound.

Jenny nodded like she was agreeing with me. "People are fucking frauds," she said.

"That's not what I meant."

She rolled her eyes and tipped her head back. "Oh, Margaret. You're so oblivious."

"No, I'm not."

"You know why your mom is always over at our house?" she said. "I mean, half the time, my mom's not even there." She looked at me, hard, as if she were inspecting me for something.

I had no answer. The babies in the forest gazed skyward, each lost in its private contemplations. I thought of my mother, her slash of bright lipstick and her books, the way she moved through the world, proud, queenly. I could imagine her standing above the blaze of funeral pyres, like Dido, deified by her people. Or perhaps just a fool, leaping pointlessly into a fire. Love made you foolish. This was a thing my mother often said—she'd learned. She knew better.

"I've heard them," Jenny said. She was no longer looking at me now, and her voice sounded tired. "It's why I try to stay away." She sighed, kicking the chubby foot of a baby to the side. "You know, Margaret, you're so stupid. Like a little kid."

I didn't answer her, but I felt very old then, almost ancient, older than the rocks or the soil or the largest trees that hung over us.

We stood in silence, gazing at the babies for what felt like a long time.

Before the school year ended, new rumors started about Mr. Milandrofer, that he'd been spotted roaming the half-finished houses of Nottingham Bend at odd hours. It was a meetup spot, people said—you know, for *that* type.

People said other things, too. For instance, that Magdalena Milandrofer had lodged a domestic assault charge against her husband, although many people claimed it was actually she who had assaulted him. There was something fierce about Magdalena Milandrofer, everyone said. She seemed like a person you wouldn't want to cross. Just before the final weeks of school, Mr. Milandrofer resigned from his job. We heard the Milandrofers would be moving out before the month ended.

Jenny and I stood a few paces back from their house, watching as movers hauled the ottoman and grandfather clock and box after box of Mrs. Milandrofer's belongings into a large moving truck. I thought of Robert, sucking at the fat slug of his fist, and of Mrs. Milandrofer, lost in her caretaking of all those baby dolls, and of Mr. Milandrofer, his eager greetings and the palpable edges of his loneliness. I could almost imagine him picking his way through the scraggly branches and stray dildos and broken babies to the graffitied, half-built walls of Nottingham Bend, where he'd be met by shadowy faces, shadowy hands, and a certain type of solace.

Once my mother had told me of a time not long after I was born when she was alone and uncertain, a disgraced teenager with an infant, kicked out of her parents' house, driving away from the only place she'd ever known. Banished. "You wouldn't stop crying," she told me, "but the more you cried, the lonelier I felt."

I asked her what she did then, thinking she might say she pulled over to comfort me and was, in turn, comforted. I could picture it, the two of us a single, fused shape. Then a moment of revelation: my mother would be moved from her desolation by a sign—a hawk streaking across the sky, a liquid orange-pink sunrise, or a kindly old woman appearing like an angel to offer her a cup of truck-stop coffee—something that suggested that we are all being watched and cared for in our worst moments, that an omnipotent hand might on occasion reach down from the storm-tossed sky.

My mother did not answer me at first. "I kept driving," she said. "I kept driving, and eventually you calmed yourself and stopped."

ACKNOWLEDGMENTS

I AM ENDLESSLY STUNNED AND GRATEFUL TO EDWARD P. JONES, one of my fiction-writing heroes, for choosing this manuscript for the Drue Heinz Literature Prize. Thank you, sir, for your beautiful body of work, and for the vote of confidence. What a gift.

Thank you to the wonderful folks at University of Pittsburgh Press for all their care and attention in ushering this book into the world: Peter Kracht, Eileen O'Malley, Chloe Wertz, Alex Wolfe, Amy Sherman, Christine Ma, and everyone else who worked on the book.

I'm grateful to the editors of the literary magazines in which some of these stories previously appeared in a slightly different form: *Arts & Letters, Cincinnati Review, Colorado Review, Crab Orchard Review, Crazyhorse, Salamander, Sewanee Review*, and *Subtropics*. Thanks also to the editors of *Best American Mystery and Suspense 2021*. Thank you for believing in my work.

I remain ever appreciative of the wonderful Creative Writing Program and English Department at UNC-Chapel Hill (especially Michael McFee and Thomas Stumpf) and the Writing Seminars at Johns Hopkins University (especially Dave Smith and Mary Jo Salter). Although I've since jumped ship from the practice of poetry, I'm still very grateful to the fine poets who taught me how to read and write in the first place and who have remained so generously encouraging.

Thank you to my brilliant local writing buddies (hello, #writing-church!!!) for being awesome and stoking the flames of literary enthusiasm. Thanks also to Jonathan Farmer and Belle Boggs for helpful feedback on earlier drafts of a couple of these stories.

In-law family, you are the very best (Mary Ashburn, Walser-Smiths, Buckley-Leslies, Smiths, and Backers!). I am lucky to have you. And Pearson family, you are my rock. Mom and Dad, you've been my champions from the beginning—thank you for everything. Lane, Alex, and Adrienne: my Gusto teammates and lifelong best friends, what good fortune that you also happen to be my siblings! (Lane, I'm going to email you a dozen rough drafts now!) Shout-out to my little loves, Josie and Ellie: you make me laugh every single day (even when, for example, I find you in the bathroom dumping all the pump soap directly onto your head while I try to type these very words . . .). And Matthew, my greatest reader, my support, my encourager, my best love: I couldn't do any of this without you.

Last but not least, I love you, Grandaddy! Pour out a little prosecco tonight and whisper to Nana for me that this one's going out to her. . . .